War Stories
3 CRIMSON WORLDS PREQUELS

Jay Allan

Crimson Worlds Series

Marines (Crimson Worlds I)

The Cost of Victory (Crimson Worlds II)

A Little Rebellion (Crimson Worlds III)

The First Imperium (Crimson Worlds IV)

The Line Must Hold (Crimson Worlds V)

To Hell's Heart (Crimson Worlds VI)

The Shadow Legions(Crimson Worlds VII)

Even Legends Die (Crimson Worlds VIII)
(April 2014)

Also By Jay Allan

The Dragon's Banner

Gehenna Dawn (Portal Worlds I)

The Ten Thousand (Portal Worlds II)
(June 2014)

www.crimsonworlds.com

War Stories

Tombstone

Bitter Glory

The Gates of Hell

ISBN: 9780692022542

Tombstone

While I thought that I was learning how to live, I have been learning how to die. - Leonardo da Vinci

Chapter 1

2252 AD
Kelven Ridge
Delta Trianguli I

We were pinned down, bracketed by fire from two directions. Somebody screwed up; somebody really screwed the hell up. Now we had to clean up the mess. Now we had to get out of here alive.

I had no idea how we were going to manage that, though. I was crouched behind a slight ridge, and I'd swear I could feel the hyper-velocity rounds streaming by a centimeter over my back. That's nonsense, of course. My armor was sealed tight, and I couldn't feel anything but the cool metal on my slick, sweat-soaked skin. The first thing I felt from outside would tell me my suit was breached, and that would mean I had a few seconds left to live.

Tombstone was one of the most miserable hells where men have ever tried to live, and you could pass the time trying to count all the ways the planet could kill you. Heat, radiation, poisonous atmosphere – take your pick. Tombstone wasn't its real name, of course, but that's what the locals have been calling it since 85% of the first colonization party died in less than a month. The place was a nightmare, but the elements in the planet's crust were worth a king's ransom, so men were here to exploit that wealth. And we were here to defend it.

I'd drawn a hell of a mission for my first battle. We came in as reinforcements for depleted units already fighting here. Neither side really controlled the space around the planet, so we'd come in hot in fast assault ships and made a quick landing. The ride down had been a rough one; I was grateful the only thing I'd eaten for 36 hours had come intravenously…an empty stomach was a big plus.

The planet had frequent, unpredictable storms, especially in the upper atmosphere. Not storms like on Earth, but intense, violent, magnetic vortices, with 1,000 kph winds and radioactive metallic hale. Our landing AIs did their best to avoid the worst spots, but the disturbances were unpredictable, and some of our ships dropped right through one of the smaller storms, taking 15% losses before we even hit ground.

This wasn't a normal battle or a smash and grab raid; the situation on Tombstone was unique. We'd had troops fighting here for ten years, almost since the initial colonization. In a few years the Third Frontier War would begin, and before it was over I would fight in massive battles I couldn't have imagined, on worlds all across occupied space. But the engagement on Tombstone was one of those small, unofficial battles the Superpowers so often fought between declared wars.

The planet had been explored by multiple colonization groups more or less simultaneously. Both the Caliphate settlers and ours claimed they were first, and each regarded the other as an invader. The governments, greedy for the planet's rare and valuable resources, backed their colonists' claims, and so soldiers ended up here, fighting a seemingly endless struggle on one of the deadliest battlefields where men have ever tried to kill each other.

The diplomats and government types would say that the "situation" on Tombstone was not officially a war, but that was a bureaucrat's distinction, meaningless to those sent here to fight. I doubt a bleeding Marine gasping a dying breath of toxic air drew any comfort from the limited status of the engagement. It did, however, starve us of the strength and supplies we needed to win. Neither the Alliance nor the Caliphate were quite ready for full-scale war, so both governments sent enough troops to keep the fight going, but too few to risk serious escalation. It made perfect sense to the politicians, if not to those sent here to fight and die to maintain a perverse status quo.

To a sane mind there were two choices: Fight to win, whatever the consequences, or negotiate and take the best deal you can make. But to those in government there was a third option - maintain a bloody stalemate, sending in just enough force to hold out and not enough to expand the conflict.

But the politics that led to my being here really didn't matter. Not now. What mattered was getting out of this ravine – actually more of a gully – and doing it without getting blown to bits. We'd been out on a seemingly routine scouting mission. One of the mining operations had reported enemy activity in the area, and the captain sent out a patrol. My platoon was next up in the rotation, so we pulled the duty.

I'd been on planet for about a week, but I hadn't seen any action yet...this was my baptism of fire. I've always thought it would have been easier to draw an assault for a first mission, hitting the ground somewhere and going right into combat without too much time to think about it instead of waiting around for the orders to suit up and go into battle. The idle time was tough, really tough. I had a long and amazing road ahead of me, full of achievement, struggle, and sacrifice. I'd live to wear a general's stars one day and fight alongside friends and against enemies I couldn't have even imagined then. But that was still years in the future - on Tombstone I was a raw private, and I was scared shitless.

When the word came down, I stripped and climbed into my armor, just as the rest of the platoon was doing. It takes long enough to suit up even when your hands aren't shaking like mine were. The armor weighs a couple tons, and until the reactor is powered up it's almost totally immobile in the rack. Once you've done the prep work and setup, you back into the thing and hold yourself in place while the front closes. It's hard to keep yourself suspended in the open suit, but you only need to do it for a few seconds. I felt a little relief once my armor was sealed. At least it wasn't so obvious how scared I was.

The thing that surprised me when I first put my armor on in training was how much it hurts. No one had ever mentioned that before. We're Marines, and we're supposed to be tough, I guess. So no one wants to admit they notice the pain when they get into their armor. Well, I'll say it; it hurts like hell. The suit recycles your breath, your bodily wastes, your sweat. It monitors every metabolic function and administers nutrition, stimulants, and, if necessary, medications. There are monitors and probes and intravenous links that all attach when you close your armor. And most of them hurt going in.

Tombstone was a long term campaign, and we were billeted in firebases scattered all around the Alliance-controlled sections of the planet. Each one covered a designated sector and was located within supporting range of at least two others. My platoon was stationed with another from our company in base Delta-4, which was dug into the side of a rocky mountain along the edge of a long range of jagged peaks. We'd replaced two platoons that were being rotated out after four months' on the line. They were 100 strong when they got there; 41 of them marched out.

We lined up in single file in the ingress/egress tunnel and marched slowly toward the main hatch. The corridor had been cut into the rock and then coated with a high density polymer that insured the tunnel was airtight, even against the planet's corrosive atmosphere. One whiff of Tombstone's air was enough to kill you. There was a double airlock system, but only one of our sections at a time fit in the outer chamber, so half the platoon had to wait. My squad was part of the rear group, and we stood around in the inner chamber for a few minutes while the other section marched through the outer airlock. The doors back into the base wouldn't open again until both airlocks were closed tight and the cleansing/decontamination procedure was completed. The contaminants on one Marine's untreated armor could endanger the entire installation. Tombstone was no joke. It was death itself, waiting for an instant of carelessness to strike.

When we finally got outside we deployed in two long skirmish lines, one positioned about half a klick behind the other. If there was one thing they taught us in training, it was not to bunch up. It makes it too easy to pick us off in groups, and if the enemy decided to go nuclear, they could take out a densely-packed force with one or two warheads.

I was a newb, so the lieutenant palmed me off on the most seasoned squad leader. The sergeant positioned me between one of the team leaders and an experienced private. There were only three raw recruits in the whole platoon, so it was pretty easy for the lieutenant to make sure we were looked after. Years later, when I got my own lieutenant's bars, we were in the middle of the Third Frontier War and getting our asses handed to us. My first platoon command had 36 new recruits out of 50 total strength, and there's no doubt in my mind we suffered heavier losses because of that. I'm grateful that on Tombstone I was surrounded by veterans...experienced men and women who pulled me through the nightmare of combat on that hell world.

The terrain was surreal, jagged exposed rock as far as the eye could see. Nothing could live on Tombstone, at least not beyond some exotic and highly dangerous bacteria. As far as the eye could see there was nothing but sulfur-crusted rock and bub-bling pools of fluorosulfuric acid, heated to the boiling point by subterranean lava flows. The atmosphere was hazy, with dense green clouds of corrosive gas floating close to the ground.

We were moving up toward a long ridge where we could get a good look at the low, rocky plain below. Normally, we'd be able to detect any enemy within 50 klicks, but between the radia-tion, the unstable atmosphere, and the almost constant magnetic storms, our scanners were unreliable. The two sides had been fighting here a long time, and both had figured how to calibrate their ECM to maximize the cover the planet's unique character-istics offered. But fancy electronics were only part of our arse-nal, and the captain wanted us to scout the old fashioned way. We were heading for the high ground with the best visibility to get a better look.

You could say we were scouting, but it was really a search and destroy mission. We were out there to find any enemy troops who had come into our sector and wipe them out. That was the reality of the fighting on Tombstone, lots of scattered actions aimed at taking out as many of the enemy as possible. The war – excuse me, "situation" – was almost purely attritional. Neither

side had enough strength to win conventionally nor the willingness to risk massive escalation, so the idea was to break down
the other side's will to fight, primarily by inflicting losses. Only
an idiot could have embraced that kind of strategy...precisely
the kind of idiot that ran the governments of both powers.

I didn't think too much about why we were there, at least not
back then. I'd gotten my blood up for the landing, and I was
scared to death on the way down, but once we'd made it to the
ground the tension subsided. We marched right to the firebase
and we'd spent the last week sealed in, my biggest concern the
inadequate number of showers and the consequent effect on
the livability of the place. We were bored stiff, and we played
cards or hung out in the media center to pass the time.

Now I was out in the shit, armored up and tramping through
the alien landscape looking for enemies. Enemies I was supposed to kill. Enemies who would try to kill me. That adrenalin
that had faded after the landing was back. I was edgy and tense,
imagining someone hiding behind every rock we passed, just
waiting to take a shot. I had to force myself to focus on my
training and what I was supposed to do. I knew my best chance
to stay alive – and help my comrades do the same – was to do
as I had been taught. But that was easier said than done...espe-
cially in a place like Tombstone.

Tension can be good in a combat situation; it keeps you
focused and attentive. But it can also be dangerous. If you step
too aggressively in powered armor you may find yourself jumping three or four meters in the air, offering some enemy sniper
a juicy target. Move forward too quickly and you end up out of
position and ahead of your team...alone and exposed. The suit
does so much of the work, it you aren't paying attention you can
lose track of how far or fast you've been walking.

We were moving forward slowly, carefully. The lieutenant
was a pro. He'd been a private who came up in the Second
Frontier War, and he'd fought in the Battle of Persis, which was
a bloody mess and also the climactic event of that war. His
unit ended up cut off during the final days of the campaign,
and all the officers and non-coms were killed or wounded. He

was the senior private, and he took command of the remnants of the company, maybe 30 Marines in all. They'd been given up for lost, but when the Alliance forces finally broke through days later they were stunned to find 13 survivors, starving and exhausted, but still holding out – and tying down enemy forces ten times their strength. That got him his sergeant's stripes and, later, an invitation to the Academy.

My suit's AI controlled my internal climate perfectly, but I was still sweating. I could feel the slickness of my arms sliding against the cool metal sleeves of my armor. I was a little light-headed – I still wasn't used to the oxygen-rich mix my suit fed me during combat operations. We'd used it a few times in training, but I think I was a little sensitive to it, and it was taking me longer to adapt completely. The suit had given me the standard pre-battle stimulants which, combined with my own adrenalin – and a healthy dose of fear - really had me on edge.

We'd just reached the ridgeline, and my com started beeping. It wasn't any kind of communication; it was something else my AI picked up. I was just about to report it to Corporal Clark when his voice came through. "Everybody down." He was in control, as always, but his tone was excited, urgent. "Now!"

My body responded to his command before my conscious mind had processed it. I'll never know for sure, but I'd wager the stimulants they give us before battle saved my life that day, because an instant later the spot where I was standing was raked with fire. I was behind a spiny rock outcropping, maybe two-thirds of a meter high…just enough to hide me if I lay very flat.

I was the lowest rung on the chain of command, so I didn't have a data feed on the rest of the platoon or squad, but I could tell from the chatter on the com that we had some people hit. Getting shot on Tombstone was especially bad, because if the breach was more than your suit's auto-repair system could handle you were as good as dead. A scratch on the arm could be fatal if your suit couldn't fix the hole in a few seconds.

The armor does have a significant self-repair capacity. The AI will respond to any suit breach in a hostile environment by immediately increasing the air pressure to keep toxic atmosphere from leaking into the suit. The climate control adjusts, attempting to minimize the effects of any excess heat or cold. While these systems are keeping the Marine alive, at least for a few seconds, the suit deploys a wave of nano-bots to attempt to patch the breach with self-expanding adhesive polymer. It is an extremely workable system, and fast too. As long as the hole isn't too big.

They'd laid a trap for us. The beeping was coming from a series of transponders they'd set along the ridge, powerful enough to send a signal through the dense atmosphere, giving them a precise firing solution. Now we were caught in interlocking fields of fire – they had heavy auto-cannons hidden in multiple locations. It was bait and destroy instead of search and destroy, and we were the targets.

The heavy auto-cannon rounds tore into the rock wall that was shielding me, sending shards scattering in all directions. My body was pressed down against the front of my armor, an instinctive but pointless effort to get farther away from the deadly stream of fire just over my back. My mind raced…what should I do? I looked for a spot where I could get a view out over the ground in front of the outcropping, but I couldn't find anything. I couldn't move up and fire over the ridge; I'd get cut to pieces before I got a shot off.

I just lay there, thinking, I'm going to die here. Six years of training so I can come here and get killed in my first skirmish? I was scared for sure, but even more, I was angry at the waste of it all. But I couldn't think of any way out. I was starting to panic, to forget all the training. Then I heard the lieutenant's voice on the com.

Chapter 2

2243 AD
Abandoned suburbs
North of the Ruins of Old Houston
Texas, USA, Western Alliance

The Corps got most of its recruits in unorthodox ways, and it had a tremendous track record of turning cutthroats and gutter rats into top notch soldiers. But I'd wager they found me in the strangest way of all. I was stealing from them.

I was a thief, a damned good one. I'm two meters tall and then some, and I look like a big clumsy oaf. But looks can be deceiving. I can sneak around without anybody hearing me, and I can strip everything valuable out of a warehouse in the time it takes a guard to finish his rounds.

I was only sixteen, but I already had my own crew. We had our base in an old suburb outside Houston. The fringe areas of the city had been mostly abandoned by the government, and when the police and other services went, so did the residents… or at least most of them. Anyone who tried to stick it out gave up after Houston was nuked during the Unification Wars; they built New Houston about 50 klicks west of the old city, and the fallout-contaminated exurbs surrounding the radioactive ruins of the old metropolis sat almost totally empty for a century.

The radiation hadn't been a major hazard for years, at least this far out, and the place made a great base of operations. None of the monitors and detection devices that were so thick in the inhabited areas. No regular patrols, not even any nosy, pain in the ass residents. We practically had the place to ourselves.

We hijacked freight shipments moving through the area,

and we raided the Cogs living around New Houston. Since the original city had been destroyed, New Houston didn't have the ancient factories and decaying slums most of the other metro areas did. The Cogs lived in cheap prefab housing units and tent cites set up around the big plasti-crete and chemical plants the megacorps built there. They had it a little better than the lower classes in some other cities. There was crime, certainly, but there wasn't as much of an organized gang presence as in other places. It was more a series of company towns, and while the inhabitants lived just above sustenance levels, they were a little more prosperous than Cogs elsewhere. They had a bit more material wealth, a few modest luxuries...and we tried to steal it all.

We snuck into the city sometimes and stole there too. We always targeted the middle classes, never the rich. Going after the upper classes was a fool's game. The wealthy have power and influence; become too much of a problem for them and your days are numbered. But what is some engineer going to do?

I was prosperous, at least my own version of it. I set myself up in a big old abandoned house. It must have been a politician or executive who built the place, because it was huge. There was a big double staircase right inside the entry and a high ceiling – at least six meters. It looked like the floors had been marble at one time and the walls covered with paneling, but there were only a few bits and pieces left; the rest had been stripped long ago by some scavenger who got there a few generations before I did.

I'd traveled a long way to get where I was. My father's name was Gregory Jax, and I have no idea what possessed him to name me Darius. He was a Cropper, a Cog recruited by a megacorp to work on one of the big agricultural preserves. The labor was difficult and dangerous, but no worse than working in one of the factories, and the farming campuses were a little safer than the outer ghettoes of the cities. I think he took the job because he thought it would be better for me. At least I'd grow up away from the gangs, which were really bad in the Louisville slums where I was born. He'd convinced himself it was the right thing to do, and it was only after we got there he realized he'd just gone from one trap to another.

My mother was gone. I never really knew her. She died when I was young; I'm not really sure how. My father couldn't even talk about her without getting upset, even years later. I know her name was Risa, but that's about all. I always meant to ask him to tell me more about her, but the days went by and I never did. Then, one day, he was gone too, and I had no one to ask. I was alone, and my questions about the past would go unanswered.

He died in an accident on the farm. They never told me exactly how it happened, but the machinery was mostly old and poorly maintained, and mishaps were common. It was easier and cheaper to replace workers than it was to inspect and maintain the equipment. The Megacorp was owned by the government, and they established a production quota and a budget. The Corporate Magnates who ran the thing got to keep whatever was left unspent, and they weren't going to lose sleep over a few dead or crippled Croppers. Not as long as profits were rolling in and their skim kept coming.

I was only twelve, but I was already taller and bigger than most of the adults, so they assigned me to take over my father's workload. Technically, he still owed the corporation for transport and housing, so I had to work off the debt. It was all bullshit; the whole system was a scam run by the megacorp. No one ever got out of debt, they just passed it on to the next generation, who became as trapped as their parents before them. They just kept working on the farm until they were too weak or hurt to continue, and then they were discharged, which meant they lost their housing and probably starved to death.

I did the work for a while, but I had no intention of spending the rest of my life in those forsaken fields. One of the supervisors rode me constantly – I think he had been in some sort of quarrel with my father, and now he took it out on me. He was a miserable bastard, and he was relentless. I tried my best to put up with it, but I blamed him for my father's death and one day I'd had enough. He was giving me a hard time about nothing, and I just grabbed him and twisted his head. His

neck snapped like a dry twig. I can still remember the feeling of
his body jerking around, then going limp while I still held him...
and the hideous stench as his bowels released in death. It was
the first time I'd ever stood up for myself, the first time I'd ever
killed anyone.

After the initial adrenalin rush, I panicked. The other supervisors backed away, but they were all calling frantically for security. I knew I'd be lucky if they gave me the formality of a trial
before gassing me...most likely they just shoot me down on
sight. So I ran. I ran, and somehow I got away, past the check-
points and over the perimeter fence.

I was alone, hiding in the rugged ground east of the farm
complex, terrified, frantically trying to think of what to do. I
knew I had to get my implant out or it would lead them right to
me. I sat for what seemed like a long time, working up my courage. Finally, reaching behind me, I sliced into my back, digging
for the implant. I didn't have a knife, but I'd found a jagged
shard of metal when I was running – probably part of a broken
farm tool. I had no idea what I was doing, but I knew the chips
were implanted somewhere in the lower back. I couldn't see; I
couldn't even get a good grip on the makeshift blade as I dug it
into my flesh. I gritted my teeth against the agony, and I could
feel my hands getting slick with my own blood. I got nauseous
and almost threw up, but I managed to stay focused. I knew
I was as good as dead with the damned implant still inside me
broadcasting. I can't remember how long it took – it seemed
like hours, though it could only have been minutes – but I finally
found the thing and got it out.

I lay there a long time, tears streaming down my face. I'd
never been in so much pain. The bottom of my shirt was
soaked with blood. I'm going to die here, I thought. But I
finally managed to get control of myself and think clearly for a
few seconds. I smashed the implant with a rock; it wouldn't be
tracking me anymore. But it would lead them there, to the last
known position it had transmitted. I had to move on, and I had
to do it immediately.

I tried to get up, but I was dizzy and it took me a while to steady myself. I took off my shirt and tore it into long strips, wrapping it around me the best I could to bind the wound. I thought about just lying there until it was all over, but again, something inside me drove me to live. I staggered my way over the rocky hills in the fading light until I couldn't take another step...then I collapsed and passed out.

I couldn't have gotten more than a couple klicks at most. I don't know how they didn't find me, but they didn't. I woke up – it must have been hours later because the sun was high in the sky. My back hurt like fire, but I managed to drag myself to my feet and start heading south. I had no idea where I was going; south was an arbitrary decision. I just kept stumbling on my way, putting more kilometers between me and that damned megafarm.

I knew most water that didn't come from one of the filtration plants was polluted, sometimes dangerously so, but I didn't have much choice, so I drank from the streams I passed. Most of them seemed OK, except for one that smelled so badly of chemicals I passed it by. I did my best to wash the wound every time I reached a body of water, but it got infected anyway. I had a few feverish days when I was too weak to do anything, but finally it broke, and I started to feel better. The wound itself abscessed, and I felt the warm puss oozing down my back. It was an upsetting feeling at first, but almost immediately the pain subsided, and I felt much better.

I'd been eating what I could scavenge, but that wasn't much. The lack of food was making me weaker, but I hadn't had much desire to eat anyway. The fear first, and then the fever had blunted my appetite. But now my fever was past and I was ravenous.

I started looking around, paying attention to my surroundings and trying, for the first time since I ran, to figure out where I was. I found a mag-rail line, and I decided to follow it, figuring it had to lead somewhere. The mag lines were huge plasti-crete structures, suspended about five meters above the ground. As it turned out, I had stumbled onto the freight line serving the megafarms all over the area. It wasn't long before the rail line led into the next agri-complex. I managed to sneak in after dark, and for the first time in my life I stole something. That first theft wasn't anything of great value, just three loaves of bread. But to me, alone, terrified, and hungry, they were priceless.

I made my way south from there, following the rail line, sometimes even sneaking onto a train and riding it to the next stop. The line terminated in New Houston, and by the time I got to southern Texas I was getting pretty good at stealing. I had found a way to survive.

Over time I got better at it, and I moved past just surviving. I put together a small team so we could hit bigger targets. We did pretty well for a long time by limiting our ambitions. We stole enough to get by comfortably, but not enough to make it worthwhile for the authorities to get too interested. Once in a while a few of the other guys wanted to get more aggressive and go for more lucrative jobs, but I always managed to keep control.

The Marine Corps' main training facility was just a few klicks west of our basecamp, and it was a huge complex. There were transports moving in and out of there constantly carrying all sorts of supplies. For a long time we avoided targets that made us a problem for powerful people, but that wisdom finally failed me. I think I just gave in to the desire of the crew to ramp up our efforts. Caution gave way to greed, and we started intercepting the Marine supply convoys, laying in wait for them a few kilometers outside the camp gates. We'd hit three of them and gotten away with it – it was almost too easy. But the night we hit the fourth they were waiting for us. That was the first time I'd ever seen a Marine in powered armor. They came out of the brush and surrounded us. Despite the fact that they were fully armored, they came streaming out of the forest quickly and quietly. I was amazed that soldiers in such heavy gear could move so gracefully. They worked flawlessly as a unit, each seeming to almost predict the actions of the others. I turned and tried to run, hoping to make it into the heavy brush and somehow sneak away. But the first step I took was the last. All I remember was the blinding flash and then the darkness.

Chapter 3

2252 AD
Kelven Ridge
Delta Trianguli I

"OK, everybody keep grabbing some dirt. We're going to maneuver to the right flank by fire teams, so nobody move a centimeter until your team leader orders it." The lieutenant sounded rock solid, like he was sitting in base calmly assigning us a duty roster. I was amazed, and that voice, so firm, so assured, reached out to me and drew me back from the fear and despair. It was like a beacon in the darkness, and I clung to it, forcing myself to focus, to remember my training, to live up to the responsibility I had to my fellow Marines. That was my first lesson in command, the way the lieutenant held us together that day with nothing more than his voice. I don't think I completely understood it until years later, when I was in his shoes and there were troops on the line waiting for my steady voice, needing it as much as I had that day on Tombstone.

The gully behind the ridge was slightly deeper to the right. We'd have enough cover there to deploy and return the fire. We didn't have a lot of time; it was pretty certain the enemy would hit us as soon as they'd picked off everyone they could with their auto-cannons. They had clearly planned their fields of fire, and they knew exactly what they covered. Their infantry would advance in the dead zones between their shooting lanes while the SAWs kept firing, forcing us to keep our heads down until they were almost on us.

The lieutenant's voice had been a lifeline. Now that I was focused again, the training started flowing back. While I was waiting I doubled-checked my weapons, just like they told us to do. It kept me focused and busy while I waited. It wasn't more than a few minutes before Corporal Clark was on the line.

"Alright, fire team A, we're going to turn 90 degrees and work our way east behind this outcropping." He was definitive and in command, not quite like the lieutenant, but still solid. He spoke slowly and clearly so there was no chance any of us would misunderstand. "We're going to go slow, and I want you all to pay attention and stay low. No one gets picked off on this move, you get it?" He paused for a few seconds. "That's an order."

My first thought was, you don't have to remind me to stay low! But then I considered how easy it is to lose focus for a second, a passing instant…and that was enough to get you killed. They pound that into your head in training, over and over again. You can be meticulous for hours, days, weeks…but it only takes one careless second to get yourself scragged.

I made damned sure I stayed low, though it was difficult to move that way in armor. It felt like forever, but it was really less than ten minutes before we reached our new position, which was only about 200 meters from the original one. The rocky spur was higher and thicker here…much better cover, and big enough that we could go prone behind it and start returning some of this fire.

Harden and James were already setting up the SAW, positioning it on a small ledge just below the outcropping. They'd found a spot with a small notch in the stone they could shoot through. Their field of fire would be somewhat restricted, but any enemy force coming at us would be right in their sights for at least part of the time. The enemy could also come up through our old position to try and flank us – but they'd have to go right through their own field of fire to get there. So we'd know they were heading that way if the auto-cannon fire stopped.

I slid over a meter or so to a spot where I had my own break in the rock wall. I'd be able to shoot pretty well from there, so I ground my knee into the loose gravel and braced myself. I peered through the crack and looked out. In front of the rock spur the chopped up, broken ground dropped off gradually, reaching a low point almost a klick from our position. The valley was pockmarked with small craters, about half of them filled with bubbling acid and other nasty-looking liquids. The entire landscape was obscured by slowly moving clouds of greenish gas, which an advancing enemy could try use to cover an advance. The gas interfered with our scanners, making it difficult to either detect or see anything hidden within one of the patchy clouds. But anyone moving through the clouds would have a hard time keeping their own bearings too.

"Good position, Jax." Corporal Clark was double checking the deployment of the team. He was a worrier, very dedicated to the wellbeing of the four troopers he commanded. He was relaxed and informal when we weren't on duty, and he'd made me feel at home right away. Oliver Clark wasn't a convict or other problem case like most of the rest of us were; his father had been a career sergeant, and he was a second generation Marine. He'd been raised to love and respect the Corps, unlike the rest of us, who generally joined opportunistically, usually to avoid prosecution or worse. The rest of us were dedicated Marines too, but we developed that loyalty later. Clark had grown up on it. "Stay alert. You're backup on the SAW, so if either Harden or James gets hit I want you to reposition immediately without further orders. Understood?"

"Acknowledged." We would need that SAW running full out if the enemy attacked. The Model 5 auto-cannon was one of the most successful infantry weapon designs ever put into the field. It accepts two gauges of ammo and can fire up 3,600 rounds per minute using the smaller projectiles. I'd rated well on the thing during training, but combat conditions were another thing entirely. The SAW put out a huge chunk of the team's firepower; I wasn't one to shrink from a challenge, but I was just as happy with it in more experienced hands, and I hoped Harden and James kept their heads down.

We actually had a pretty good position to handle whatever was coming at us. The enemy had laid a trap for sure, but if I had to make a guess, someone over there opened up before he was supposed to. If they'd have waited for us to clear the rocky spur we'd have been caught in the open and torn to shreds. As it was, we were probably outnumbered, but we had decent cover and a good chance to hold out until reserves could arrive.

It wasn't more than a few minutes before the attack began. They hit us with grenades – the Caliphate had a first rate grenade launcher that considerably outranged ours. They started hitting all around us. They were taking potshots, hoping to make up for inaccuracy with volume. The grenades were a marginal weapon against armored infantry in cover. Still, they scored some hits, and we had three or four more down from the platoon. Most of the wounds were minor, but on Tombstone, anything that breached your suit was deadly serious. Even if the repair system patched the damage before the planet killed you, the adhesive polymer wasn't up to handling combat conditions. You might keep fighting with a wounded arm, but if you ripped open the patch on your suit you'd go from WIA to KIA damned quickly.

"Here they come!" It was Sergeant Lassa, my squad leader. It was a few seconds before anything started to show on my scanner, and another few before I caught sight of enemy troops advancing through the spotty cloud cover. I took a breath and leveled my mag rifle. I had a pretty good shot on a small cluster of advancing troops, and I started firing short bursts on full auto. My first shots fired in combat were way off. I was a good marksman in training, but you just don't realize what it's like shooting at targets that are firing back until you experience it. It took me a few seconds to settle down, but once I did my fire got a lot more accurate.

It was hard to tell what we hit until they started coming out of the clouds but, when they did, the SAWs ripped into them. They were trying to advance along the lowest spots, crouching to maximize their cover, but they had to cross some open areas too, and they suffered heavily. They'd expected us to be hit harder by the heavy auto-cannons, but they'd fired too soon and ruined their ambush. We had the better cover now, and they had to come at us the hard way.

I was terrified, so scared I could hardly think. I wanted to run, to get away and go somewhere, anywhere that people weren't shooting at me. I could hear my heart pounding in my ears, feel it in my chest. My hands were sweaty, my legs weak. But I stayed focused and kept squeezing off shots, targeting the enemy troopers as they advanced. It was hard to tell if I hit anyone, but it looked like overall we'd taken out at least a dozen.

Our fire blunted their advance, and they stopped and took cover. There were cracks and fissures in the rocky ground, and the enemy troops scattered, occupying any spot that offered some protection. Our cover was heavier, but theirs was enough to offer significant protection, and they outgunned us, which compensated for our stronger position. The combat had turned into a protracted firefight, and both sides expended a lot of ordnance for very little return.

These were the kinds of fights where carelessness gets you killed. When the shooting goes on this long with no break you can lose focus. A Marine raises his head just a touch too far, trying to get a better shot. That's all it takes to get killed, an instant's lapse in judgment.

I was getting exhausted, mentally more than physically, and running low on ammunition. I was taking single shots now, saving the rounds I had left in case the enemy tried to assault our position. The corporal came on the com and told us to cut our ammo expenditures, but I had beaten him to it.

As a private, I wasn't on the higher levels of the com line, so I had no idea what was happening outside my squad. I knew we were stuck here – we didn't have enough strength to assault the enemy, and if we tried to retire we'd give up the cover of the ridgeline, and they would just move up and shoot us to pieces. I figured there were reinforcements heading to support us – I hoped, at least - but all I could do was guess.

It's hard to separate what you thought years ago from your perceptions years later, but looking back, it was clear the enemy had the initiative. Their trap had failed, at least partially, but they still had numbers for a while. It was up to them to force the issue or to withdraw. We didn't have the strength to attack, but we could put up a considerable defense. They could probably beat us, wipe us out...but they'd pay heavily. The enemy commander had to decide if he wanted a major fight there. His ambush had fizzled and he faced a bloody battle. He could have the day...if he was willing to pay the price.

It wasn't long before we had an answer. The enemy troops started withdrawing, pulling back slowly from one piece of cover to the next. The auto-cannons kept up their fire, keeping our heads down so we couldn't harass the retreating infantry. But that was unnecessary, because the lieutenant was on the line a few seconds after they started pulling back. "Cease fire." His voice was as steady as ever, but I'd swear I could detect the slightest bit of relief. Maybe he was human too. "All units, cease fire. Hold positions." We didn't have ammo to waste shooting at retreating enemies, and if it turned out to be a ruse, the lieutenant wanted us to be armed and ready to deal with it.

But it wasn't a ruse. The enemy didn't want a big battle there. That would come later, and when it did we would know it.

Chapter 4

2243 AD
Camp Puller
North of New Houston
Texas, USA, Western Alliance

"Welcome back. Did you have a nice sleep?"

The voice was deep but friendly, and it was the first thing that came to me in the darkness. The light was next, hazy at first then brighter, clearer. My head felt like a mag train had run through it.

"Here, drink this." I started to get an image of the room, small, with bare metal walls and a table with two chairs. I was sprawled out on a cot, and as I pulled myself up I got a first look at my companion. He was tall, dressed in a neatly-pressed gray uniform, and he was holding out a small metal cup. "Those stun guns give you quite a headache." He smiled sympathetically. "This will help."

I straightened myself out. I was still sitting, but at least I was halfway up. I took the cup and downed it in one gulp. If these guys wanted to harm me they'd had plenty of chances while I was out cold. I felt better almost immediately; it was like the fog in my head just cleared away.

"Welcome to Camp Puller." I was about to say something, but he beat me to it. "I'm Captain Sam Jackson." He paused and smiled. "And you are a very resourceful young man who, among other things, has nothing but a nasty scar where his implant was."

I leaned back nervously. My first thought was, they will figure out who I am and send me back to the farm. For that matter, just removing the implant was a serious crime. He must have read my mind, because he laughed softly. "Don't worry; we're really not interested in whatever you've done. You were stealing from us, and we're willing to overlook that. We're certainly not concerned with what you did to anyone else. Or the fact that you removed your implant." After a brief pause: "We're not cops."

I looked up at him, feeling better but still groggy. "You're a Marine?" I took a good look at him. I guessed he was about 35, though I wasn't sure. He could have been younger or, with a rejuv treatment or two, quite a bit older. His hair was light brown, neatly trimmed, and his face was pleasant, relaxed. He certainly didn't match my expectation of a Marine. The Corps had a reputation for producing savage fighters, but this guy looked like someone who spent his day in front of a workstation crunching numbers. I laugh when I look back – now I realize that Captain Jackson could have dropped me in half a second, despite the fact that he was ten centimeters shorter and at least 20 kilos lighter.

"Yes, I'm a Marine." He could tell what I was thinking, and he smiled again. "Surprised I'm not three meters tall with weapons growing out of my arms?" He reached out and dragged one of the chairs closer to the cot. "We have a few things to discuss. Why don't we start with your name?" He sat with the chair turned around, leaning against the back.

"Jax. Darius Jax." I'd been thinking, I'm not going to tell this guy anything, but my mouth opened and my name came out. It's not like they couldn't find out anyway. I got my implant out, but I couldn't change my DNA. I was in the main database just like anybody else. Besides, I had the strangest feeling he was trying to help me.

"Interesting name. I've seen a lot of guys come through here, but you're the first Darius. Persian king, right?"

I had no idea what he was talking about. My education at the time was almost non-existent. The government didn't waste resources educating Cogs and Croppers. I'd had an hour a day of online classes at the farm, but it was nothing but basics. I wasn't entirely illiterate, but ancient history was well beyond my knowledge base. I didn't even know what a Persian was. Years later, at the Academy, I was finally able to answer his question. Two famous Persian kings, actually, the second enjoying the dubious privilege of facing off against Alexander the Great.

When I didn't answer he just continued. "Doesn't matter. Let me get right to the point." He straightened up slightly in the chair. "I'm here to offer you a chance to join the Corps."

"What?" The word just blurted out. I hadn't been sure what he was going to say, but that was certainly not what I was expecting.

"You heard me, Darius." There was a smile on his face – he was enjoying this, the SOB. "I'd like to make a Marine out of you."

"Why would you want me?" About half a dozen responses came to my mind, but that's the one that came out. I couldn't imagine why they'd be after me. The entire thing seemed ridiculous.

He let out a short breath. "Darius, the Corps is unlike any other military organization. We are looking for a certain type of recruit." He stopped for a few seconds as he put together what he wanted to say. "Most of us have pasts like yours…" He looked me right in the eye. "…or worse." He emphasized that last part and let it sink in before he continued. "Some a lot worse. I'm from the LA Metroplex myself. The Valley."

The Valley was one of the most notorious slums in the U.S., a place where they carted away a new crop of bodies every morning. I didn't know much about other places, but I'd heard of the Valley. If this guy grew up there it was no joke. "So you guys need a thief? What, did your budgets get cut and you're looking for new income?"

He smiled and snorted slightly, not quite a laugh. "No, Darius, we need independent thinkers. We need doers. Not easy to find."

I laughed. "And you think that's me? What makes you think I'm what you're looking for?"

"Well, for one, you obviously cut out your own implant,

which suggests that you have the toughness you will need to make it through our program. A sloppy surgeon to be sure, but it takes a certain grit to do what you did."

"Big deal, you want tough you should head up to Louisville and hit up some of the Gangers there."

He held in a small laugh. "I said tough, not crazy. We aren't looking for psychopaths, Darius. Look at you...you are very measured in how you do things. You haven't been terribly forthcoming with me, but you haven't been overtly hostile either. Measured."

"So the fact that I didn't tell you to fuck off makes me Marine material?" The whole thing still seemed crazy to me.

"It's more than what you say or don't say. Look at how you ran your little gang. You robbed us three times – we were watching you after the first, by the way – but you didn't kill or seriously injure anyone. You did what you needed to do to survive, but you didn't escalate the situation past what was required. It is very clear you are deliberative, brave but cautious. Just what we want."

Still on my mind: "You were watching us?" I hadn't had a clue. "Why didn't you stop us sooner?"

"Why do you think? He had an annoying smirk on his face. He clearly enjoyed these head games.

"My God, you're fucking kidding me." This was getting more and more bizarre. "You were watching to see if you wanted to recruit us?"

"Very good." He leaned forward over the back of the chair. "You are starting to understand. It was pretty clear from your first robbery that you knew what you were doing. You even watched the convoys, and you hit the specific cargo that was easiest for you to move." He paused slightly. "Unless that was a coincidence."

"It was no coincidence." I felt a little naked; they had us completely figured out. "I wasn't looking for the kind of attention stealing weapons or high tech stuff would bring."

"Look, Darius, trust me." His voice changed slightly, less casual, more serious. "You are the kind of recruit you're looking

for. You're clearly intelligent, despite your lack of education."
He smiled again. "And your robberies displayed some first rate
small unit tactics."

He let me think for a minute. Why would I want to be a
Marine anyway? Just because they invited me? "Look, I appreciate the offer, but why would I want to join up anyway? So I
can go get my ass shot off...what? In space?" He nodded. "You
figure I'll join up so you don't turn me in. Because it's better to
take your deal than end up getting sent to the lunar mines for
stealing?"

"Or sentenced to gas by the megafarm magistrate back
home?" He had a self-satisfied smile on his face. "Of course
we know who you are, Darius. We're not imbeciles." He paused,
clearly enjoying my dumbstruck silence. "But to answer your
question, no, if you say no to us we won't turn you in. Not for
your robberies and certainly not to the megacorp that runs that
farm."

"You'll just let me go?" I looked at him quizzically. "Just
walk out the door?"

"Yes. With a stern warning never to steal from us again."
He looked at me and his eyes were deadly serious. "A very stern
warning."

I was quiet for maybe half a minute, trying to process everything he said. Free to go? I could just walk out? "So if that's
true, why would I ever agree to sign up? If you're not blackmail-
ing me with prosecution why shouldn't I just leave now?"

He let out a deep breath. "Well, Darius, the first part of
that answer is the fact that you're asking the question at all. I
just told you that you could leave any time you want to. Why
are you asking me questions at all?" He paused for an instant,
but continued before I could answer. "It depends on what you
really want, Darius. You're smart enough to get by as a thief for
a while, at least until you step on someone else's toes and you
end up mining meteor fragments on the moon. Or more likely
dead."

He rolled up his sleeve. "You see this arm?" I looked at him,
confused. "I got this blown off as a private. My first battle."

I thought to myself, this guy needs work on his sales pitch if that's his idea of an inducement. But I kept listening anyway. I was curious where he was going with this.

"This is a new one. A perfect regeneration. You'd have to be a member of the Political Class here for that kind of medical priority. But in the Corps all you have to be is a Marine. What was your medical priority rating before you ran? Zero?"

I frowned. "So you're saying if you get my arm shot off you'll grow me a new one? You're a lousy salesman."

"No." He looked at me with the first hint of impatience I'd seen from him. "I'm saying that the Corps is someplace that respects all of its members. We don't prioritize our people and throw most of them away because it's expedient. An injured Marine gets the care he needs, whatever that is. Private, general...it doesn't matter. A Marine in trouble gets the support he needs." He stared right at me, his eyes boring into mine. "Haven't you ever wanted to belong somewhere? To be part of a team where everyone has your back?"

"So it's that simple? I say yes, and you make me part of this team you're talking about?" I had to admit to myself, the prospect of not feeling totally on my own every second was appealing. I also thought it had to be bullshit.

He laughed. "Far from. If you say yes, I will give you a chance to make it. If you sign on you will do six years of training." He paused, smiling wickedly at the blank expression on my face. "Yes, that's right. Six years. You'll get the education you never got before, and you'll learn how to really use that reasonably effective brain I think you have. You'll also work like a dog; like nothing you have ever experienced. You think they worked people hard on that farm?" The wicked grin widened, becoming downright maniacal. "You'll end up face down in the mud puking your guts out from physical training you can't imagine now. Our program is serious." He paused, and the grin slowly vanished. "It's dangerous too. People die in training. You may die in training."

"So you sell the Corps hard and then try to scare me away?" My head was spinning. I didn't know what to think. "So if I make it through your training, then what happens?"

"Then you'll graduate as a private." His voice was serious now. All the earlier informality was gone. "And when you make your first drop you're one of us." Long pause. "For the rest of your life."

"After my first drop?"

"Graduating from training gives you the right to drop with a Marine unit. Completing the drop makes you a Marine. We're combat veterans, every one of us. You may end up being a mechanic or a computer tech in the Corps, but the first time out you're a private and a combat soldier. Even our medical staff starts out fighting."

"Everybody starts as a private?" I was intrigued. This was very different from the society I'd seen my whole life, where birth and connections were everything. It amused me to think of a Senator starting out as a field hand on the farm.

"Everybody. You may be a general someday, but until then you'll always know that whoever ordered you into battle has been there himself." He was exaggerating to make a point, but it turns out he was right...I would become a general one day, and I would never ever forget what it felt like to climb into that first lander.

"So fine, the Corps takes care of its own. That's all great, but it still sounds like going out there and getting all shot up for the politicians who sit behind desks and tell everyone else what to do. The Marines may have a different attitude, but they still fight for the system that worked my father to death on that farm."

"I knew you were smart." His grin was back. "Most recruits aren't this much of a pain in the ass. But the good ones usually are." He hesitated, as if he was trying to decide how to discuss delicate matters. "Darius, the system is what it is. I'm not here to defend it or even worry about it. But if you become one of us you will see a whole universe you can't imagine now. The colony worlds are nothing like Earth. I'm posted here, but this isn't my home anymore. When I retire it will be to Atlantia or Arcadia or one of the other frontier planets. Earth is dying,

choking to death on corruption and repression, but mankind
has another hope for the future. The future isn't here; it's out
there." He pointed upwards.
    He got up and spun the chair around. "We're not offering
you a job, Darius. We're offering you a home. One you need
to prove yourself worthy for. When you hit the dirt on that
first drop you are reborn; your sins are washed away. It's in the
Marine Charter...a full legal pardon. If you want, you can come
back to Earth when your ten years are done. You can walk right
onto that farm and tell the administrator you killed one of his
supervisors a few years back. You can tell him to eat shit if
you want. They can't arrest you, and if they tried they'd have a
Marine strike force showing up to get you out."
    He sat back in the chair, sitting closer, looking right at me.
"When you muster out, if you want to settle on a colony world,
you'll get a land grant or resource allotment. We take care of
our own, and once you're one of us, you're always one of us."
He slapped me on the knee and got up again. "Think about it,
Darius. I'll have some dinner sent in here. Then sleep on it.
We'll talk in the morning." He turned and walked out without
another word, and the door slid shut behind him.
    I sat for a long while just thinking about everything he had
said. My first reaction was to tell him to forget about it. I was
only sixteen - six years of training seemed like an eternity. And
leave Earth? Fight on other worlds? It was just too much.
    But then a lot of what he said came back to me, and I started
to think about it. I had grown up on the lowest rung of the
system. My parents were penniless Cogs with no prospects to
improve their lives or mine. I got only a rudimentary education,
little or no access to medical care, and barely enough food to
survive. At the time, that just seemed to be the way of things.
A Cog's life is ruled by necessity, by the daily struggle to get by.
There wasn't time to think about anything else or to contem-
plate the inequities of the system or the failings of the government. The utter powerlessness and vulnerability made all that
seem very far away. A Cog worries about getting food today, not
a better life tomorrow.

When I ran from the farm, I started to become someone else, but only to a limited extent. My horizons had expanded, but not all that much. I stole because I didn't have what I needed to survive, and later because I got better at it and could live a more tolerable life, albeit at the expense of my victims. I had my crew, but we were drawn together by necessity and opportunity, not by any great commitment to each other.

I tried to imagine what it would be like to be part of a group like he'd described, but it was just too much to wrap my head around. I put it out of my mind and drifted off to sleep determined to turn Captain Jackson down, to go back to my hideout and lay low and be more careful about picking my targets. For some reason, I believed him when he said they would let us go. But I thrashed around all night, my decision already made consciously, but still conflicted somewhere deeper inside myself. Something he said got to me on a level I couldn't entirely understand or control. When he came back the next morning I tried to say no, but all that came out of my mouth was, "Yes, I'm in." I was on my way.

Chapter 5

2253 AD
Firebase Delta-4
South of the Kelven Ridge
Delta Trianguli I

By the time I got to Tombstone, I was a different person. Marine training is long, longer than anything I've ever heard of for any military organization. Part of that is because our wars are complex. No uneducated conscript can survive on a 23rd century battlefield. The suite of weapons and equipment we utilize is extensive, and it takes considerable effort to master. But the Marine program is as much about evolving the individual as teaching him to shoot and walk around in armor, and that is what really takes time.

I adapted well and really excelled at training. I'd never felt a part of anything meaningful, and when I had the opportunity to join a team that truly worked together, I jumped at it. Some of the others in my trainee class took longer. Many of them had even worse backgrounds, and they'd sunk deeper into depravity than I had. Bitterness and hatred hadn't entirely consumed me as it had with some of them. I was an outlaw, yes, but never a bloodthirsty one. I stole to survive, and later to live comfortably, but my crew didn't murder the people we robbed. I'd killed the supervisor, but he had abused me for some time, and I was sure he had been responsible for my father's death. Some of the others in my class at Camp Puller were real hard cases, broken people who had been driven to do some truly horrible things to survive and to lash back at the world. It took time to repair that kind of psychic damage, and that's part of the reason Marine training is six years.

Now I'd made my first drop, and I'd fought my first action. I was a full-fledged Marine. My crimes were gone, pardoned away in exchange for my service. I could go back to Earth when I mustered out if I wanted to, and I would be free from any consequences from my past. But even then, Earth was already starting to seem like something far away and long ago. I didn't realize it at the time, but the concept of home was changing for me.

We'd been on one mission that particularly made an impression on me. Three of our troopers were out on patrol, and they ended up cut off by superior enemy forces. The lieutenant didn't hesitate - he mustered the whole platoon, and we scrambled out to try to link up and get them back home. The Captain was in on it too, sending a group of snipers and a heavy weapons team from base Delta-3 to assist us. We fought for four hours, the lieutenant pushing us relentlessly the entire time. In the end we broke through, but too late to save them. They were all lost.

The mood was somber when we got back to base. We were in a profession where people got killed - there was no way around that. Yet we mourned every one of them, and every trooper in the platoon wondered how he'd failed, what he could have done differently. I felt the loss too, and the futility of our fruitless, costly fight to save them. But then I realized it wasn't fruitless. Mathematically it was, of course. Had we abandoned them we would have had three casualties instead of the eight we ended up with. But combat isn't decided solely by numbers or equations; it is a test of morale, of the willingness of men and women to fight, sometimes under impossible conditions. Those three Marines died on that plateau, but they were never abandoned by their comrades. They knew to the last that their brothers and sisters were fighting to reach them...and the troops struggling to break through saw how the Corps treats its own. If it was them next time, trapped and cut off, they knew at least that they would not be cut loose, that no officer was going to make a cold blooded decision that they were expendable. The Corps stood by its own...wherever, whenever, whatever the cost.

I'd been on-planet for five months, and I wasn't one of the

new guys anymore. Combat on Tombstone wasn't cheap, and we'd lost eighteen of our fifty since we landed. Half of them were wounded, all thanks to the armor's impressive repair and trauma control mechanisms. Our suits were a hell of a lot better than the Caliphate's in that regard – their nanotech was way behind ours. In a place like this, a serious wound was pretty much a death sentence for one of them.

We evac'd the wounded on the transport that brought us replacements. We had eighteen fresh new faces wandering around the base, and I was in the unfamiliar territory of mentoring the new people. Somewhere in five months of serving in hell I'd become not quite a veteran, but at least seasoned. I knew my way around this miserable planet and how to survive its many hazards, and I was determined that none of these 18 newbs would go out and get themselves killed doing something stupid. Others had done that for me, and some of those people were now dead or shipping out to the hospital on Armstrong. It was my turn, my debt to start repaying.

We'd just celebrated the new year...the new Earth year, of course. A year on Tombstone was only 61 Terran days, and just over 20 of the 73 hour local days. I'd never celebrated the new year before I'd become a Marine, but we had a nice little party in base Delta-4 and welcomed the new additions to the platoon. Six of them were experienced and were transferring from other units or the hospital. The rest were fresh from Camp Puller, the class that was half a year behind mine.

There was a lull in the action as the new Earth year began. Both sides were building up and replacing losses, and while we did frequent patrols there was little action. One interesting thing happened, though. We managed to intercept and decode a Caliphate message that gave the exact arrival date of their next convoy. I'd been with the patrol that caught the transmission, and we were pretty excited for a while. Taking out a couple hundred of their troops while they were still in the launch bays would save us a lot of trouble down here. But in the end nothing came of it. Alliance Gov considered engaging enemy forces in space to be an unacceptable escalation. Neither side had attacked the other's naval forces in the system, and they weren't looking to start now. Everyone knew that full-scale war was coming, but nobody was ready for it yet. It was frustrating fighting a war you weren't allowed to win, but there was nothing we could do about that.

I ended up going out on patrols with most of the new people. The lieutenant was insistent that the fresh arrivals pair up with a more senior private any time they went outside. It was something that stuck with me years later when I was in command of my own units. You want to keep your new people under the command of the most experienced non-coms available, of course. But it really helps to have them paired off with an experienced private, regardless of how good a team or squad leader they have. Human psychology is complex thing, and there are considerable differences in how a person interacts with a command figure and how they function with a peer at their own level. I sometimes wonder how many of my own people the lieutenant had saved over the years by teaching me that lesson.

Chapter 6

2252 AD
McCraw's Ridge
Day One
Delta Trianguli I

This was shaping up to be a significant battle. It started small, just two patrols running into each other. They exchanged some fire, and that would have been the end of it, but neither side backed down. The Caliphate sent in reinforcements and pushed back our forces, taking the main ridge.

It looked like worthless ground to us, but the captain wasn't going to give it up without a fight, and we got the orders to suit up. We were the farthest away, and when we got there the entire company was formed up, covering a front stretching over five kilometers. They had already counter-attacked and retaken the ridge when we arrived, and we were fed into the line, allowing the units that had taken losses to condense their frontages.

The ridge was named after the megacorp that claimed the resource rights in the area. McCraw Resources was a huge mining concern that had a number of places named after it, including an entire planet on the Rim. It was one of several Alliance companies operating on Tombstone, though the only difference between them was which Corporate Magnate managers got the richest. A McCraw may have started the company centuries ago, but now it was essentially owned by the government, just like all the megacorps. The Magnates who ran it stole what they could, but in the end they answered to Alliance Gov.

We dug into our new positions, and the lieutenant directed the placement of our SAWs and SHWs. He was very careful about arranging them to maximize their fields of fire and also to provide mutual support. Any enemy attack against one of our heavy weapons would come under fire from at least two others. It made an impression on me how he obsessed over the placements himself rather than just ordering the teams to deploy. That stuck with me years later when I was in his position. I've always believed that low-level heavy weapons are a huge key to victory, and that belief started that day.

The enemy had fallen back but not withdrawn entirely. They'd fortified another ridge about five klicks north, and it didn't look like they were planning to leave. Their position didn't look quite as good as ours, but it was strong enough to discourage an attack, at least until we were heavily reinforced. We exchanged sporadic long-ranged fire, but it was mostly quiet for about six hours, with occasional excitement when someone got careless and was picked off by long-ranged fire.

It's hard to stay alert for hour after hour, especially when nothing much is happening. The suit can keep you pumped up on stimulants, but you have to be careful and save that for when you really need it. Otherwise you end up strung out, and you lose as much effectiveness as you gain. But you still have to stay sharp. Snipers can pick off a target at five klicks, no problem, and we'd lost two people already because they let their guard down. Newbs were particularly vulnerable, but I've seen veterans lose their focus for a few seconds too, and that's long enough to get scragged.

Finally, we got intermittent scanning reports on approaching enemy forces. Normally, we'd have a complete breakdown of anything so close, but on Tombstone you generally had less information than you wanted, and even that was unreliable.

Fresh troops meant they were planning another attack, and the lieutenant made his way all along the line, checking and adjusting our positions. Physical proximity really wasn't necessary for communication, but still, it was a morale boost to have him crouching next to you while he spoke.

"How's everything, Jax?" He put his hand on my back, a seemingly pointless gesture among armored troops, but one that was nevertheless somehow reassuring.

"I'm good, sir." I turned to face him, another bit of instinctive body language that had dubious utility when suited up. In non-combat situations I would have saluted him, but the Corps dispensed with the clunky salutes among armored troops in battle. You could barely manage it in a fighting suit in normal conditions. No one wanted a casualty because a Marine was struggling to salute in armor and got his head blown off. And there was no point in advertising where the officers were.

"You've come along well, Darius." His voice was gentle, sincere. "You were nervous as a cat when you first got here, but you are calm and cool now. You've been great with the new guys, too. You're a valued member of this platoon. And you ended up with quite a first assignment. My first was a cakewalk, a quick raid that was over in six hours." He paused for a second. "You've taken all Tombstone could throw at you. I'm proud of you."

I got a little choked up. This was the first time anyone had really told me I was worth anything. Except my father, of course, but that doesn't count. I already felt at home in the platoon, but this sealed it. "Thank you, sir." I hesitated, trying, not terribly successfully, to keep the emotion out of my voice. "That means a lot." I'd have followed that man anywhere. I'd drawn the short straw getting posted to Tombstone, but I swear there wasn't a better commanding officer in the Corps than the one I got.

"Carry on." He crouched down and started over toward Private Samms, about 100 meters to my right. He stopped for a second and turned back toward me. "And stay low." His head snapped back forward and he was on his way. I had a minute or two to think about what he had said and then all hell broke loose.

My AI warned me about three seconds before the first explosions...grenade and mortar fire. I instinctively crouched lower just before I was pelted with dirt and shattered chunks of rock. The grenades weren't too bad; we had good cover, and they had to drop one right next to you to cause serious damage.

The mortars were another matter. The rounds coming in were heavier than the usual ones; if one of them hit within twenty meters, you'd better have good cover between you and it.

Fortunately for me, they were concentrating the mortar fire to my right, and the worst thing I had to deal with was a grenade landing behind me. It covered me with debris and caused some minor damage to my external sensors, but all things considered, I got off light.

We returned fire with grenades, but ours were no more effective than theirs against troops in heavy cover. They had the edge on heavier ordnance right now, and it occurred to me that mortars that big were usually battalion level assets. The Caliphate called their battalions tac-forces, and they were about 35% larger than ours. It was odd to see that kind of firepower in a company level fight.

"Ok, platoon…" The lieutenant's voice, calm but urgent. "…we're looking at a major attack incoming at any time. I just spoke with the colonel…" Holy shit, I thought…the colonel! He was the planetary theater commander…the top dog. Something big must be brewing. "…and we've got support inbound. But we might have to hold out for a while against tough odds." He paused. "I told him he could count on us. Now you're not going to make a liar out of me, are you Second Platoon?"

A chorus of "no, sirs" flooded the com, and mine was as loud as anybody's. We were ready. Still, I figured if the colonel was getting involved, we were likely in for a rough ride. I was right.

Tactically, the ridge was of limited value, not worth a major fight to hold. We could have pulled back and actually enhanced our longer term positions. We held most of the surrounding hills, and any enemy penetration here would quickly become an exposed salient. But what we didn't know…what we didn't need to know…was under the ridge ran a rich vein of trans-urianic elements…not the fleeting scraps manufactured in labs that decayed in nano-seconds, but naturally-occurring stable isotopes that were non-existent on Earth and still not fully explained by physicists. These strange substances had been found on a small handful of worlds and, vital for high-yield spaceship drives, they were priceless. The deposits under the ridge were worth more than all of our lives - at least to Alliance Gov - and while the Corps generally had a different set of priorities, it followed orders. Where we were told to fight, we fought. And right now that was on McCraw's Ridge. I was positioned almost dead-center, along a spiny Y-shaped rock outcropping...a spot that would later be known as the Cauldron.

Chapter 7

2252 AD
McCraw's Ridge
Central Sector – "The Cauldron"
Day Two – Morning
Delta Trianguli

They'd hit us five times the day before. Of course, the days were our own construct, existing largely on our suits' chronometers. Tombstone took over sixty Earth hours to complete its rotation, and it was never really dark, not even at night, thanks to the electrical activity and chemical reactions in the upper atmosphere. The eerie glowing clouds didn't give off the light the sun did, but it was enough to see by, especially with your visor set to mag 2 or 3.

Now we were on day two of the battle, though we'd fought more or less continuously. The second day notation had more importance for record-keeping than any real tactical significance. You'd want it to be correctly noted what day of the battle you were killed on, after all.

I was only a private, barely a rung above the lowly position of "new guy," so keeping track of planetwide resources wasn't something I spent much time on. But to my knowledge, our total strength on Tombstone was approximately three battalions. The enemy had more, but only marginally so – about two and a half of their tac-forces – the rough equivalent of four battalions. Now they'd deployed what appeared to be an entire tac-force against us, which was an unprecedented troop concentration on Tombstone. A ten-year struggle between widely-dispersed patrols and platoons was seeing its first pitched battle.

We'd been taken by surprise by the enemy build-up, but the colonel responded quickly, shifting forces from all over to reinforce our position. It's amazing how minutes can drag into eternity when you're outnumbered 5-1 and waiting for reserves that are "almost there."

I hadn't moved more than 50 meters in the last 24 hours. I was behind the rocky crest of the ridge when the attacks started, with a good field of fire across the broad plain in front of us. Just to my right there was a spur of the outcropping that ran perpendicular out from our location. Any attack on our position forced the enemy to either split his forces or concentrate on one side or the other.

The first attack came right at me, with all the strength to the left of the rocky spine. We hit them hard with fire on the way in, but there were a lot of them, and it looked like they might overrun us. They almost did, but they'd made a mistake in ignoring the other side of the rock spine. The lieutenant swung around with one of our squads, firing at the enemy flank from the cover of the perpendicular line of rock. Faced with heavy fire from two directions they withdrew with heavy casualties.

The lieutenant pulled back the advanced squad before they were exposed to the resumption of enemy long-ranged fire. The Caliphate forces had suffered at least 40 casualties; we'd lost 3, and two of those were wounded. We got them both patched up and stabilized before Tombstone finished them off. The enemy casualties were mostly KIA, either from the initial hit or the consequences of their suits being breached.

The second time they didn't make the same mistake; they split their forces evenly on the two sides of the spur, but the lack of force concentration did them in. The two groups, unable to support each other, were both beaten back, again with heavy losses.

There was a brief lull, probably while they brought a fresh unit up to attack. When they had reinforced they charged us again, and the last two assaults came close to taking our position. The enemy commander sent a small group against the left side of the spur, just enough to demonstrate and prevent a repetition of the lieutenant's flanking maneuver, while the main force concentrated against the right. They came at us twice that way, but our lines barely held, reinforced at the last minute by arriving reserves fed in squad by squad.

Things quieted down for a few hours, giving us the "night" respite between our Earth days. We had more troops arriving all the time, and we finally got the orders to pull back. The entire company was being rotated to the reserve to rest, replaced by a fresh unit that had just marched up.

I was positioned between Corporal Vincennes, my team leader, and Harden and Quincy with the SAW. Harden had been the team's lead SAW operator since before I got to Tombstone, and he'd been through four partners since then. It was considered something of a jinx posting, but I escaped this far because of my marksmanship ratings. I hadn't gone through sniper school, but the lieutenant kept me as an informal sharpshooter rather than a body managing Harden's ammo feed. So I stayed in the line on a standing order to try and target enemy officers and non-coms if I could identify them.

"Hey, Sam, how's it going over there?" Harden and I had become pretty good friends. Most commanders probably would have forbidden this type of chatting over the com, but the lieutenant believed the unit was a living organism. As long as it didn't interfere with vital communications, he encouraged limited banter."

"Not too bad. I'd say we held pretty damned well." He paused, and I could hear him taking a deep breath. Not a bad use of a couple million rounds of ammo." Harden was a little bloodthirsty; he'd lost a brother in the service and I don't even know how many partners. I didn't know it then, mostly because I'd had no one really close to me since my dad died, but you get that way if you lose enough people. We're professionals, but that only goes so far…enough pain will make any of us into vengeful sadists howling for blood.

"Yeah, we did ok." I was a little more circumspect. I wasn't all that comfortable with the killing yet, and I found it hard to rejoice as he did in the enemy dead littering the field. After all, most of them were just conscripts with no choice in the matter. The Caliphate was pretty rough with its recruiting; it was a theocracy and a dictatorship that made the Alliance look like a big happy family. Its recruiters could pressgang just about anyone except the clergy and the nobility.

"Just ok? It was a shooting gallery, baby!" Harden was overstating things. We did give the enemy a bloody nose, but it was hardly a walkover. We were pulling back with 31 troops; we'd gotten here at full strength with 50. I couldn't get over the losses, even if we did inflict almost ten times that on the enemy.

"We lost a lot of friends today, Sam." My voice was soft; I was trying hard not to sound like I was scolding him.

"Yes, we did." His spoke more slowly, his tone darker. I think he got the point. "But it could have been a lot worse…a lot worse. If we'd been overrun, the whole unit could have been wiped." He paused, and sighed. "But we did pay the price."

"Yes, we paid the price." The last of our wounded had been evac'd, but we were leaving seven dead on the field. I thought quietly to myself for a few seconds then I shifted my mind to more relevant things, with the soldier's knack for mourning the dead one minute and focusing on duty the next. "You need help packing up that thing?"

"Nah, let the newb handle it." The light auto-cannon really wasn't all that large, just a bit unwieldy. Still, I had a twinge of sympathy for Quincy. It wasn't that long ago I was the newb.

I climbed down carefully from the perch I'd occupied for the last twenty hours. Keep your head down, I thought. Although the fighting was in a lull, the sporadic sniper fire had never stopped. What a stupid way to get killed, losing focus on your way to the rear to rest. I took one last look out over the field, thinking the worst of it was over. I was wrong.

Chapter 8

2252 AD
McCraw's Ridge
Central Sector – "The Cauldron"
Day Two – Afternoon
Delta Trianguli I

We pulled back about five klicks, just behind the next ridge. We were well within range of enemy mortars and other ordnance, and we wanted some cover. On a more hospitable world we might have popped our helmets and actually eaten some solid food, but that wasn't an option on a planet like Tombstone. So I enjoyed the epicurean delight of another shot of high-energy intravenous nutritional formula, kindly served by my suit's AI. It wasn't exactly a stick-to-your-ribs meal, but you could definitely feel the increased energy level.

Sleep was another issue. We'd been going for about 40 hours, the last 24 under combat conditions. I was tired. You could go for several days on stims injected through the armor's medical maintenance system, but there was no substitute for actual rest. Plus, the less you relied on the stims, the longer you could go on them before getting really strung out. The armor is more tolerable than anyone who hasn't worn it would think, but it wasn't built for taking a nap. The most comfortable position was sitting on the ground leaning against something. I staked out a fairly choice spot against a good-sized rock outcropping and closed my eyes. I fell asleep in a few minutes.

When I'd first gotten to Tombstone, a well-trained but completely untried Marine, I found it very difficult to relax at all.

Even in base when we sat around, waiting days, even weeks before getting the orders to suit up, I was nervous as a cat, expecting the alarm to sound any minute and scared to death about going outside, going into battle. There are certain clichés about soldiers, and I have found that many of them are true. One of these is the fact that we can sleep anywhere, and it wasn't long before I'd joined that club. I was still scared to death whenever we fought; I still am to this day, though I have since learned to more or less ignore it. But even back then, if the shooting stopped for a few minutes, I could take a nap.

We're good scroungers too, another military stereotype that turns out to be true. Despite living in the most hostile environment imaginable, cut off from virtually everything except official supply routes, there was a fairly active black market in the firebase. I never understood how the most active participants got some of the items that did. Later I came to realize that the officer didn't just look the other way – they actually helped things along a little behind the scenes. All of our officers start as privates, and they knew very well that a posting on a place like Tombstone was a cheerless enough existence. As long as nothing degraded combat readiness, it was helpful to boost morale any way possible.

I'd gotten maybe 45 minutes' sleep when I woke up to a jarring on my leg. My visor automatically went transparent and I could see Harden standing above me, kicking my leg. It was a gesture best performed by veterans; a little too much power behind the kick and the force amplification system in his suit could have damaged my armor. It was best done to a seasoned Marine too...startle a sleeping newb and you may end up getting shot to pieces or sliced in half with a molecular blade.

I was seasoned enough not to over-react. "I was sleeping, asshole." Not normal chatter for the comlink, but I was mildly annoyed, and my tone conveyed it.

"What are you gonna do, sleep your life away?" He was always cheerful, which was surprisingly irritating at times. Now, though, it seemed like a facade. Something was bothering him.

"Wouldn't want to waste a minute of the Tombstone experience, would we?" I wanted to be pissed, but he was a good guy; he just never shut up. "I think it will be a big vacation spot once we're done fighting for it."

He sat down next to me, leaning back against the rock wall. "I wonder how long we'll be posted here." His upbeat tone was gradually fading, becoming a little more somber. Tombstone wore everyone down. "The unit we replaced had been here six months. We're almost there, but I haven't heard squat about us getting rotated out."

Of course, I'd considered it too, but I wasn't sure I should tell him what I really thought. It looked to me like both sides were increasing the strength deployed here, and they were probably going to do it by extending the tours. "I think we'll be here awhile." What the hell, I thought. Tell him what you think. "It's obvious the expeditionary force here is being increased. If they bump the postings to a year they can bring in the unit that was going to replace us as an incremental force."

"Fuuuuck." He stretched the word out impressively. "I hadn't thought about it that way, but you're right." He paused for five or ten seconds, both of us silent as we thought about that unpleasant prospect. "Man, I hate this shithole." He slapped his hand lightly against the ground as he spoke.

I nodded, though it wasn't all that obvious a gesture in armor. "We made it this far; we'll make it a year if we have to." I said it, but I wasn't sure I believed it. A lot of us hadn't made it this far, and it was anyone's guess how many would get through another seven months on this hellhole.

I expected him to say something - he always had something to say, but not this time. What was there to say? We were here, and we had a job to do. That was all there was to it. Whether we liked it or not wasn't part of the equation.

"I'm getting the shakes." He'd switched to direct laser com. "The last month, maybe more." His voice was serious, more so than I'd ever heard it.

I let out a short breath, thinking about what to say, wishing he'd gone to one of the real veterans who might have something wise to tell him. But he'd come to me, and we were Marines...

we were there for each other. Always. "It can't be too bad, Sam. I lost count of how many you dropped this morning. It's not affecting your shooting any."

"I've managed to control it when we're fighting. I guess it's the adrenalin or something. Focuses me." He paused. "But it's bad before, and it's starting to get that way after too. It took me the whole walk back here to settle down." His voice was edgy; he was really worried.

Sam Harden was a decorated Marine who'd been in half a dozen engagements. He was sure to be bumped to corporal and given his own team after this posting. But none of us were immune to the nerves, the fear. It gnawed at you, even as you pushed it aside, and it could come out at any time. We all controlled it in our own ways. Over the years I've known guys who had lucky charms, some who prayed before battle, still others who played different mind games with themselves. Some of them focused anger and rage; others relied on a sense of discipline.

When you start to lose your control, even a little, it becomes harder to get it back. Doubts prey on your confidence, and eventually the fear that you won't be able to regain control adds its own pressure. Marines, especially veterans like Harden, didn't like to talk about this kind of thing, so if he was coming to me it was probably really bad.

"Sam, you're one of the guys who pulled me through when I got here. You've done it for other guys too...I've seen it." I was trying to sound upbeat and supportive, but I really had no idea what to say. I was so green I barely knew how I kept myself together. "This place gets to everybody sooner or later. Don't let it eat away at you. When it's important, you'll be ready. There's no one here I'd rather have backing me up."

He sat quietly for a minute then he turned and looked at me. "Four partners. Four partners I've lost here." He looked down at his feet.

"Sam, that has nothing to do with you. We're in a dangerous business." I frowned, though of course he couldn't see that in armor. The next time I heard that jinx bullshit being joked about I was going to have a talk with whoever started it. "Not one of them got hit because of anything you did."

"I know you're right." His voice was really unsteady. "But still, I should have been able to do something, kept them safer somehow."

He really sounded like shit. I was in way over my head. My first thought was, he shouldn't be in battle right now. But what could I do? I wanted to run to the lieutenant and tell him about this, or at least the squad leader. It was the hardest situation I'd run into since I'd been in the Corps. Harden had come to me in confidence. He'd be furious if I ratted him out. It felt wrong. But letting him go back to the line in his current condition didn't seem any better. I talked to him a while longer, trying to make him feel better, all the while trying to decide what to do.

In the end, I got up and walked away and kept my mouth shut. It was a mistake I have regretted ever since. I didn't know it then, but we were about to get called back to the lines, and Harden would be dead in two hours, him and Quincy both. I was never sure exactly what happened; I think he got rattled and decided to move the SAW, and they ended up exposed and were chopped up by enemy fire. By the time I got over there they were both dead, riddled by half a dozen rounds each. They'd had a good position; if they'd stayed put they probably would have been fine.

Things were hot on the line when they got hit, so I didn't have time for grief or guilt. But a few hours later, when the situation calmed down for a while, I just sat on the ground in shock. My stomach clenched, and I wretched, though there wasn't much in my digestive tract to come up but a little foam. My suit's systems tried to clean up inside my helmet, doing a fairly reasonable job.

It was my fault; I knew it was my fault. I didn't want to betray Harden's confidence…I wanted to be a good friend. So I didn't tell anybody he was too unnerved to go back into the line. I didn't do anything.

Harden died thinking of me as a friend, but I failed him when he needed me. We were more than friends; we were comrades in arms. I owed him more than he got from me. He was my brother, and I didn't have his back. He thought I did, and I thought so too, but that was superficial. I could have saved his life, but I didn't. A live Harden who hated me the rest of his life would have been a thousand times better than a dead friend whose confidence I'd kept.

I never forgot the lesson I learned that day.

Chapter 9

2252 AD
McCraw's Ridge
Central Sector – "The Cauldron"
Day Three
Delta Trianguli I

We were in the middle of the third day of the biggest battle ever fought on Tombstone. Our estimates of enemy strength on the planet turned out to be wildly inaccurate. My distrust of intelligence services, which would continue to increase at an exponential rate over the years, started that day. It wasn't the last time I'd see bad intel, but it was the last time I'd believe it.

Not only were we facing more enemy troops than should have been possible, but we were also up against a tac-force of Janissaries. We'd been outnumbered all along on Tombstone - we knew that - but we'd had the qualitative edge. My battalion was an elite assault unit, one of the best in the Corps. Most of the enemy troops were colonial troops, well-equipped, but definitely second line. One on one they had never been a match for us.

But the Janissaries were front line troops, every bit as elite as we were. They were the only fighting force with even more training than we had, since they were essentially bred as soldiers and raised from childhood in the barracks. Worse, they were fresh, and we'd been fighting for two and a half days, beating back every conscript and colonial regular they could throw at us. We had half our total strength on the whole planet deployed, but I still wasn't sure we'd be able to stop them.

But stopping them wasn't an option; it was a necessity. If we'd fallen back before the battle we could have fortified the surrounding hills and maintained a strong defensive line. But if we pulled out now, broken and beaten, we'd compromise our control over the entire sector...and lose the most productive mines on the planet. A defeat here could be enough to shatter the stalemate on Tombstone. I wasn't up in the chain of command, but I didn't have to be to know our orders. Hold at all costs.

I was back almost exactly where I'd been for most of the last three days...nearly dead center in our line. The fighting here had been fierce on the first day, and it looked like it had been just as intense while we were in reserve. The dead and wounded had been pulled back, but from the shattered pieces of armor and equipment I had a pretty good idea the fighting had been brutal.

We weren't back long before we were attacked, but we beat it back without too much trouble. That's when we lost Harden and Quincy. When they went down I shifted over, covering a larger frontage. Corporal Vincennes and I were the only ones left in the fire team. We tried to get Harden's auto-cannon set up, but it had also been hit. It might have been repairable, but not in the field, so it was useless to us. The corporal set me up just left of where the cannon had been, and he headed 200 meters to the right.

We were a laughable defense. Any serious attack would have cut right through us, but fortunately the enemy didn't hit us before we were reinforced. The corporal and I had held that forlorn hope for about ninety minutes before the lieutenant came jogging over with reinforcements. The captain had sent up the last of the company reserve, and he cut the frontage our platoon had to cover. The lieutenant took advantage to pull some strength from other sectors to strengthen our weakened center.

He brought the platoon weapons team with him, though only one of the original crew of three remained. Langon, the platoon's technician, was backing up Private Glenn, and they were handling the thing a man short. The medium auto-cannon was a double-barreled hyper-velocity weapon that put out three times the firepower of Harden's lighter version. They set it up right where we'd had the SAW, though they had to clear some of the rock out to make enough room. Fortunately, Langon had the plasma torch with him, so it only took a few minutes to dig in. When they were done, it was in a great spot, with good cover and able to direct fire on either side of the rocky spur.

The lieutenant also brought Graves, the sniper, and he placed him in a big rock outcropping just behind our line. He had the marksman's weapon of choice, the M-00, AI-assisted sniper's rifle. It was longer than our infantry weapons and fired a single shot at even higher velocity and greater accuracy. The AI interface helped compensate for weather, visual irregularities, even projected movement of the target. An expert sniper could score a hit as far away as ten klicks.

I'd trained on the weapon at Camp Puller, and I'd been fast-tracked for sniper school based on my performance. Snipers were all veterans though, so I couldn't go right into the training program from Puller, and I'd been stuck on Tombstone since then. I expected to go after this campaign, though things would turn out differently, and I'd never end up being a sniper. But I always respected the effectiveness of well-utilized sharpshooters.

After he'd deployed everyone, picking out their exact positions himself, the lieutenant settled in directly on my left. He gave us a few short instructions and a little pep talk, but mostly he left us alone. We knew what we were doing, and we knew what was coming. The Janissaries would be here soon, and we'd be waiting for them.

This was the first time I'd faced veteran, elite troops, and it was a lot different that the colonial regulars we'd been fighting. They started out with a heavy bombardment, blasting our entire ridge with rockets and frag shells. We had good cover, and I doubt they expected to inflict a lot of casualties. But they knew we were tired, and they wanted to rattle us as much as possible. They also directed some of the bombardment behind our line, creating a complication for any troops redeploying or reinforcements moving up.

We returned fire, but we had a lot less ordnance then they did, and I doubt we accomplished anything but a superficial show of defiance. Still, I cheered like everyone else when the captain ordered the company's mortars to open fire. I was still enraged about Harden and Quincy...the guilt would come, and when it did it would be severe, but right there on that battle line I wanted blood. I wanted vengeance.

They didn't fire for long, and about half an hour after they'd opened up they stopped. Their lines were silent for a few minutes and then shells started impacting the plain in front of our position. The Janissary mortars were firing smoke shells. It wasn't real smoke of course, though that's the name we gave it. It was a dense radioactive steam used to shield an attack. Opaque, it blocked visibility, and the radiation and chemical makeup interfered with scanners. The heat of the steam clouds made infrared and temperature-based scanning useless as well, so the stuff was very effective at screening an advance. It was a powerful tool, and I never understood why we didn't use it too.

This was it. We knew they'd be coming up behind those clouds, and that this would be the climactic attack. Either we'd hold here or they would win.

"OK, Third Company." Captain Riklis was addressing the entire unit. His voice was steady, and in it I could detect barely controlled anger. His blood was up. This was the first time I'd faced Janissaries, and I wasn't aware yet just how much of a rivalry we had with them. When Marines faced Caliphate Janissaries there was no quarter even thought of...it was a fight to the death. "I know you're all tired, and we've suffered heavy losses already. And these bastards are fresh. This is going to be one hell of a brawl." I really liked that he was being straight with us, not sugar coating things. He was rallying us, but with respect. We were professionals; we knew the obstacles to victory, and we were ready to face the challenges and win in spite of them. "But there is no unit – none! – in the whole damned Corps I'd rather have under me today. I know...know with every fiber of my being that whatever comes through that smoke, Third Company is going to be ready...and we're going to wreck it!"

Before I joined the Corps, before I ended up on a battle line waiting for an enemy to come and try to kill me, I never thought about how words could affect me. They were just words, after all. But when he was done I was so worked up I'd have faced the entire enemy force alone if I had to. I've never figured out whether it's real confidence a leader like that inspires or just mind games that provoke a response, but I never forgot how it made me feel, just when I needed that extra bit of courage. I would be giving a version of that speech many times myself in the years to come, and I would fight with other officers whose ability to rally troops would astonish me. But that day I was on the line with the captain and the lieutenant, and as far as I was concerned, no Caliphate force ever made was going to make me fail them.

I crouched down, digging my foot into the grayish gravelly dirt and pushed up against the rocky spine, bracing myself and aiming my mag-rifle out at the hazy, faintly glowing clouds. My AI would take whatever bits of data my scanning devices could glean and combine it with the info gathered by the rest of the platoon, giving me the best guess at where enemy troops were approaching. The smoke was very effective, but it wasn't perfect cover. Troops moving through would disturb the clouds, at least somewhat, and if the AIs could factor out the wind and weather-caused effects, they could actually do a decent job of finding concentrations of troops coming forward.

"Ok, platoon." The lieutenant's voice was calm, even more so than the captain's. "You men and women are the best warriors in the field, anywhere. Janissaries are good troops, but they aren't that tough. They can't be that tough, because they're not Marines!" His style was a little different than the captain's. His voice was relaxed, almost like a teacher in a classroom, but then all of a sudden he'd amp it up and get us whipped into a frenzy. "We're going to do the work, platoon. I want everybody to focus. I'm going to call out enemy locations as we have them." He paused. "And we're not retreating, no matter what. Anybody who leaves their position won't have to worry about Janissaries; they'll have to worry about me!"

My AI started projecting figures in front of me, the shimmering blue images displaying percentages projecting the location of enemy troops. We didn't have enough data to get any solid leads yet, but there were a couple spots north of 40% probability. I started firing some bursts at these locations, and I could tell that a few others were doing the same. I didn't know if I hit anything – probably not - but it was worth expending a little ammo in the effort.

The auto-cannon didn't open up yet, though. It was an extremely effective weapon on defense, and the lieutenant didn't want to give its position away too soon. With any luck, the enemy would blunder right into the center of the field of fire. Their own scanners were compromised by the smoke too, so they couldn't really attack with any precision.

I'd been scared to death before the attack started, as I always was, but now I wasn't really thinking about that anymore. I was so focused and so pumped up by the captain and the lieutenant, the fear morphed into a nervous energy, an edginess that made it hard to stand still. I could hear my heart beating in my ears like a drum.

"Enemy troop concentrations." The lieutenant, still totally calm. My God, doesn't anything rattle him? "Transmitting coordinates. Open fire."

The enemy troops were off to my left, but I had a clear line of fire, so I switched to full auto and sprayed the area. The mag-rifle had enough kick to knock a man over, and probably break his arm as well, but in armor you just felt a small vibration. I emptied an entire clip into the smoke, and the autoloader slammed another one in place with a loud click.

A few seconds after we started shooting, the enemy opened up. Their position given away, the advancing troops had no reason to continue to hold their fire. They couldn't aim any better out of the clouds than we could into them, but our entire front was saturated with fire. It was clear there were a lot of troops coming at us.

I crouched lower as the rock wall in front of me was blasted. Shards of shattered stone flew all around, but the outcropping was thick enough to provide cover, and other than some rocks bouncing loudly off my armor, I was fine. I could tell from the chatter on the com that 1st Platoon on our left had some casualties...they probably got careless when they were firing and didn't get down quickly enough.

We got locations on two more enemy troop concentrations, and when they all opened up we were well into a serious fire-fight. Even with our cover, we were taking losses. I assumed we were inflicting them too, but it was hard to tell. All of this seemed like an eternity, but only a few minutes had passed since the enemy launched the smoke and started their attack.

Then they started to emerge from the smoke. It was surreal watching them move forward, zigzagging as they jogged toward our trenches. Their armor was similar to ours, a little bulkier, maybe, and the alloy they used was different, giving the suits a darker look. They didn't have the camo system we did, and their suits were dark silhouettes against the glowing clouds as they came forward.

Their formations were scattered, with significant gaps. I could see they'd taken considerable losses from our fire. Their assault doctrine was well thought out, and they executed it flaw-lessly. One group would find the best cover they could – low ground, rocks, gullies – and open up on our position with every-thing they had. A second line would advance, supported by this covering fire, and find their own protected areas. They would then start shooting while the first group advanced. It was a standard leapfrog tactic, but they were so well drilled they could maintain enormously heavy fire while leaving precise lanes open for their advancing troops. I couldn't help but admire the disci-pline and skill, even if they were trying to kill me.

But we knew our stuff too, and we targeted the units moving ahead, ignoring the covering fire. We were taking heavy losses, but it was still the best exchange rate we'd get; if they got to our lines and broke in we'd lose our positional advantage...and there were more of them than us.

There was a crack in the rock wall next to me, and I was able to lie down and shoot through a very small opening. It was great cover, and gave me a wide coverage area. They were getting close, so I switched to semi-automatic and started targeting individual troops with 10-shot bursts. I didn't have a sniper's rifle, but I managed to take down a target just about every time I shot. I must have dropped 7 or 8 when I realized we weren't going to turn them back.

The auto-cannon was firing full bore, but the enemy troops were very good at using any bit of cover as they advanced. We'd taken out a lot of them, probably enough to send lower-quality troops feeling for their lives, but we wouldn't have broken, and the Janissaries weren't going to either. They were weakened and disordered, but we were still going to have a close range fight.

If we'd had a secondary position we could have fallen back, keeping them under heavy fire as they came over the rocky spur and eventually wearing their attack down. But there was nothing but open plateau behind us – we'd be the ones caught in the clear and cut to pieces. No…it was win or die right along this ridge line.

I have always found that my memories of combat are blurry, surreal. It's hard to recall the time passing. I remember this charge of the Janissaries as something that went on forever, but it wasn't more than ten minutes from when they dropped the smoke until they started climbing up over the rock wall.

I saw them coming, at least six of them heading toward my spot. The whole thing happened in slow motion. I took one last shot through the crack on the rock, hitting one of the attackers. At least four or five projectiles from my burst hit his leg, tearing it off completely. He dropped hard to the ground and writhed for a couple seconds before Tombstone finished the job.

I paused an instant watching him fall, and then I realized with a start that there were no more targets…I had waited too long. Something took over, instincts maybe or, more likely, training. I rolled over on my back, whipping my rifle around, and I blasted at full auto, taking out two more as they climbed over the rocks.

The next two seconds lasted a lifetime. I'd emptied my clip, and I could hear the autoloader moving a new one into position. The entire process had always seemed nearly instantaneous to me, but now it felt as though it was taking forever. I looked up, and I could see the enemy troops coming over, and one of them was turning to me. I could hear each heartbeat pounding in my head as I brought my mag-rifle up to target him. He was doing the same, but his was loaded and mine was empty. I'd have a new clip in place in less than a second, but in that instant I knew it was going to be too late. I stared up into the barrel of his gun, and I knew I was dead.

And then I wasn't. Just before he fired, his body lurched backwards, his arm flying upward, spraying the air with fire. The top half of his body twisted to the right, the bottom to the left. He wasn't cut in half, not quite, but he fell in a gruesome heap, half a meter from where I was laying. Standing there, silhouetted against the reddish light, was the lieutenant, his arm raised, bloodied blade extended. He'd driven its edge, a single molecule thick, into my would-be killer's side, striking with all the enhanced power his suit's nuclear-powered servo-mechanicals could deliver.

I was laying there in shock, thinking I should thank the lieutenant when his voice boomed into my headset. "Get the hell up, Jax!" His voice was still relatively calm, but even his controlled tone was affected by the stress of battle. "This isn't time for a nap."

He jogged past me without another word, leveling his mag-rifle and shooting down half a dozen Janissaries who were coming over the rock wall and taking aim at the auto-cannon. Glenn was working the gun alone now, targeting the second wave of enemy troops still emerging from the smoke and advancing on our position. Langon was down. I didn't know then, but he'd taken a hit early. His suit's auto-repair managed to close the breach, saving his life for all of ten minutes. Then he took a second hit, this time in the neck, and he fell to the ground, dead.

I climbed up to my feet, watching the lieutenant for a second. I glanced over the rock wall – there were no troops approaching my position, so I spun to the left. All along the line there were Janissaries pouring up and over the broken ridge. It was a confused melee, with point blank fire and blade fights everywhere.

The Caliphate troops had their own version of the molecular blade, and it was longer and more effective than ours. They trained with it more than we did too, and they thought they could beat us in a hand to hand fight. But our close range fire drill was very effective, and not many of them got near enough to one of our troops to force a knife fight.

The snipers played a key role too, picking off enemy officers and non-coms, targeting them even when they stood centimeters away from our own troops. Our sniper tactics and training were light-years ahead of theirs, and it showed. This range was child's play to the sharpshooters, and they scored hit after hit. The company's three snipers went a long way toward helping us cope with the enemy numbers.

Still, we were gradually being pushed back from the ridgeline. The enemy's third wave came pouring over the rocks, and we had nothing left to face them. I was standing against the outcropping, with enemy troops climbing over to my right and left. I crouched down and fired as they came over, facing left for a second than switching to the right. I heard the autoloader slamming my last clip into place, and I knew things would be over soon. We were being overrun at every point, and enemy troops were racing to the rear. The snipers' positions were compromised, and one by one they were taken out.

I was determined to go down fighting and not panic, but it's hard to stay cool when you know you're likely to die at any instant. I just kept firing, using small bursts now to conserve my last ammo, and somehow I didn't get hit. My heart was pounding and I could feel the sweat trickling down my back. I just kept fighting, waiting for the inevitable end. My resolve was strong, but my mind wandered. I wondered if it would hurt. Would I die in an instant, never knowing what hit me? Or in agony, bleeding into my armor, choking on the Tombstone's toxic atmosphere?

I was so focused I wasn't even watching the scanner. If I had been I would have seen them. Reinforcements, a whole company, running forward with blades out, into the melee. The enemy, weakened by the staggering losses they had already taken, turned to face the new threat. But now they were on the defensive, their momentum lost. They fought bitterly, but in the end our fresh reserves were too much for them. The troops who'd made it over the ridge were almost entirely wiped out and their reserve waves, seeing that the attack had failed, retreated.

It was the first significant battle I'd been in, and we'd won. I was glad, but I didn't feel the elation I'd expected, just crushing fatigue, and the somber realization of the losses we'd suffered. As the adrenalin and anger subsided, pain and sadness took its place. It had been a hard several days, but we'd proven our worth. And we'd met the Janissaries head on and bested them.

It had been a difficult and costly day, but it wasn't over yet. The enemy had spent their strength on that last attack and, while we were just as battered, we'd managed to stabilize our greatly thinned line. A counterattack was out of the question, but we were in good shape to repel anything they had left to throw at us. But both sides remained on their respective ridges, trading sporadic long-range fire.

The lieutenant walked over to me, crouched low behind the ridge. He was working his way down the reduced frontage of the vastly shrunken platoon, checking on each of us. There were only fifteen of us left in the line, though of the 35 casualties, about 20 were wounded or suffering from suit malfunctions. Maybe ten were wounded lightly enough that they'd be treated right here on Tombstone and return to duty fairly quickly. The rest would be shipped off to one of the Marine hospitals, probably Armstrong, and likely be reassigned elsewhere when they recovered.

A unit is an odd thing; it has a life of its own. The traditions, history, and achievements create a culture that survives, even as the soldiers themselves come and go. The men and women die or get reassigned, but the unit goes on, remaining much the same as it was…as long as it doesn't lose too many people too quickly. With about half of the personnel still standing or likely to return soon, I was confident the platoon would remain the place I'd come to think of as home. Especially with the lieutenant. I knew he'd make sure it stayed the same.

He was about ten meters from me when it happened. He was facing in my direction, walking right toward me. He was very hands on, and he wanted to see firsthand that each of us was ok. He was just passing a section of the rocky wall that dipped low, forcing him to crouch further down to stay in cover. I saw it all, and to this day I remember it as it were in slow motion.

He turned suddenly. I don't know if someone from behind commed him, and he instinctively turned or he saw something on his scanner, but he spun around, and when he did he came up out of his crouch. It was careless, a small slip made by the most careful and consistent man I'd ever met. That one time he lost his focus, let his guard slip. One small mistake that 99 times out of 100 would have been harmless. But that day it was tragic.

I saw his head snap back hard. His body seemed suspended in the air, though I know that is just my memory of it. He crumpled and fell, sliding down the slight embankment and landing on his back.

I rushed over, screaming into the com for a medic as I did. I can't remember if I kept my own head down in my panic, but if I was careless, my fortune was stronger that day than the lieutenant's. He was lying with his head on the low side of the slope. I reached over and cradled his upper body, lifting his head as I did.

The sniper's shot had struck him in the neck, tearing a huge gash in his armor. The suit's repair circuits had managed to patch the breach with self-expanding polymer, and while it didn't look too secure, it was keeping out Tombstone's heat and toxins for the moment.

But the wound itself was mortal. In a hospital he could have been easily saved. If I could have opened his armor, a medic could probably have kept him alive until he was evac'd…even I might have managed it. But opening the suit would kill him on the spot, and the wound was just too much for the suit's trauma control system, which was damaged by the shot and only partially functional.

He turned his head slightly to look up at me. "Darius…" His voice was throaty, labored. His lungs were filling with his own blood.

"Yes, sir? I'm here." My heart was pounding, and I was in shock, but I was determined to be strong for him, as I knew we would be for me. "What can I do for you, sir?"

"Tell the men and women." He was rasping, coughing up blood, trying to get the words out. "Tell them I am proud…" - he coughed again, trying to continue speaking through the gurgling sounds - "…proud of them. Tell them I was honored to lead them, and…" - more coughing - "…and tell them I know they will always make me proud."

"Yes, sir." I was fighting back a sea of tears, but there was nothing more important to me than to be there for this man in that place.

"Darius?" He turned his head. "Darius?" He was slipping away, not sure where he was.

"I'm here, sir. It's Darius."

His voice was weak, almost inaudible. My AI automatically cranked up the volume so I could hear. "Tell them I'm proud to die here with so many of our brothers and sisters." He went into another coughing spasm and he started speaking incomprehensibly, hallucinating about something, though I couldn't tell what. I had lots of chatter on my com, from others in the platoon, from the medic I could see trotting over…but I shut it all down except for the lieutenant's line.

Finally, he stopped the random talking and his coughing subsided. He turned his head slightly, further in my direction, and he said, "The Corps forever." He was silent after that, and I knew he was gone. The medic knelt down, but I told him it was too late. A great Marine was dead.

His last thoughts, dying painfully on a hellish world far from home, were for us, for the platoon he'd loved and protected and led with such dedication. People speak of duty and devotion, but the lieutenant had lived it to his last breath. He was a good man sent to an impossible place, and I can't even count how many of his soldiers he pulled through that nightmarish campaign. We lived, many of us, to leave Tombstone, but we left him behind, having given his last full measure to the Corps.

Chapter 10

2253 AD
Armstrong Medical Center
Armstrong Colony
Gamma Pavonis III

I'd like to say I left Tombstone triumphantly, amid victory parades and celebrations, but that's not how it happened. I didn't march out at all; I left as a casualty, unconscious and kept alive by machines. I'd come through the battle of McCraw's Ridge, fighting non-stop for three days without a scratch, but it was a tiny skirmish three weeks later that took me down. My squad was on a routine sweep of the perimeter when my luck ran out. We encountered an enemy patrol and exchanged a few shots before both sides broke off. Nobody had a stomach for a serious fight, not so soon after the Cauldron.

But those few shots were enough. One of the rounds caught me in the shoulder, and as far as I know, I was the only one hit. It wasn't a bad wound, but it impacted at a strange angle, tearing a large chunk off my armor. On a more hospitable world it would have been minor, but we were on Tombstone. The repair system in my suit tried to restore atmospheric integrity, but the hole was just too big. The corporal managed to get a manual patch over it, but not before I'd breathed a half a lungful of Tombstone's noxious atmosphere. It was as if I'd inhaled fire; the pain was unbearable. I felt like I was suffocating and burning to death both. I could feel the blood pouring out of my nose and welling up in my throat. It was only a second or two before the suit's trauma control kicked in and flooded my system with painkillers and tranqs, but that instant stretched out like an eternity, and it was nothing but relief when the darkness finally took me.

As I faded away I was sure I was done, but they got me out of there and into a med unit back at base. My lungs were a total loss; the unit would be doing my breathing until I was evac'd to a facility with regeneration capability. My suit's trauma control had put me out on the field, and the medical AI kept me in an induced coma, so my last view of Tombstone was the one I had just after I was shot. When I finally came to it was weeks later and in a much more hospitable environment - the Marine hospital on Armstrong, surrounded by doctors and med techs. I woke up and took a painless deep breath, and it was a minute before I'd regained enough presence of mind to be surprised by that fact.

My chest was a little sore from the transplantation surgery, but my brand new lungs, exact copies of the ones I had before, worked perfectly, and my shoulder and other injuries had long since healed. I had a few weeks of observation and physical therapy ahead of me, but then I was on my way to a month's leave and a new posting.

The Corps tried to return wounded soldiers to their original units, but with the time and distances involved it just wasn't always feasible. Although I wouldn't miss Tombstone, I was sorry I wasn't going back to my old platoon. They were my brothers and sisters; I'd shared the danger and death of the front lines with them, and they had carried me back when I got hit, when even I had given myself up as lost. They saved my life; they were there for me when I needed them. Just like Captain Jackson had told me more than six years before.

I hated leaving for another reason. A unit is like a living organism; it can wither and die without the support it needs. When I left, the platoon was still reeling from the loss of the lieutenant. The wound was still raw, the grief palpable. They'd get a new CO - they probably had one already - but it would be a long time before anyone filled the void left behind.

The platoon is a dynamic entity. It's pride, its battle history, its traditions - they remain. But the men and women come and go. Marines die, they get wounded, they get promoted or transferred. Slowly but steadily, the living memory of the lieutenant would fade. He would become less the source of raw pain and loss and more an honored entry in the unit's history.

For me, though, the memory would always be there, and it would never fade. Up to that point, no one had impacted my life as strongly as the lieutenant had, and I can't begin to list the things he taught me. I only knew him for the six months I'd served under him, but he was the first person who truly won my unreserved respect. I can't think of anything more meaningful to say than this - Lieutenant Brett Reynolds was a truly good man in a universe that had very few of those. I resolved that my career would be a tribute to him. I would live up to his expectations; I would become the type of Marine he had been, the kind he wanted me to be.

I wish I could say that the years long struggle on Tombstone ended in glorious victory, but I can't. When the war became official, the Caliphate hit the planet with thousands of new troops, backed up with a naval task force. Cut off from resupply or reinforcement, our units on the ground held out the best they could. One by one the enemy captured our firebases and mining settlements, pushing our people into an ever-shrinking perimeter. As far as I know, none of the troops posted on Tombstone when war was declared ever made it out. My old unit had rotated off-planet long before then, so I didn't know any of the men and women who were sacrificed there. But they all hurt. They were all my brothers and sisters...all Marines.

The soldiers that had been lost there over a decade were expended wastefully, sent by a government that was too greedy to share the wealth of the planet and too cowardly to fight hard enough to win. The politicians had viewed the monthly loss rates on Tombstone as a cost of doing business. That sort of calculus repulsed me, and for the first time I thought – really thought – about how the Alliance was governed. The ultimate futility of if all only made the suffering and waste that much more bitter.

Chapter 11

2257 AD
AS Guadalcanal
En route to Tau Ceti III

The wardroom of the Guadalcanal was sparse, just a few bare metal tables and about a dozen chairs. She was an older ship, a fast assault vessel of the Peleliu class, and she showed her age. My last posting had been on the Gallipoli, one of the first ships of the new Ypres class, slated to replace the old Pelelius. The newer ships were no more spacious - real estate on a spaceship was always at a premium - but the common areas were definitely nicer.

I'd bounced around to several units over the last few years, the result of my unfortunate streak of getting wounded in each of my first three assignments. After my third wound I got another transfer and my promotion to corporal. I made two drops as the junior two-striper in the squad and then I was transferred here to take over my own fire team. Just about half my military career had been spent in the hospital, and each time I got the best care possible, just as Captain Jackson said I would.

The war that everyone had been anticipating while I was on Tombstone finally became official. The Third Frontier War had begun, and we were fighting both the Caliphate and the Central Asian Combine. We had our hands full, outnumbered and facing more threats that we could effectively counter.

I was waiting in the wardroom to meet the platoon's senior corporal, who was going to help me get acclimated and introduce me to the four other members of my fire team. I needed to get them comfortable with me quickly, because we were on the way to an assault, and it was a big one. Tau Ceti III was the Caliphate's largest and most important colony world, and a major strategic hub. We'd been pushed back in the first two years of widespread fighting, but now we were taking the offensive; we were taking the war to the enemy. Operation Achilles would be the biggest assault in the history of warfare in space, and every reserve, every logistical asset that could be scraped up had been committed. I was anxious and hopeful, determined that my fire team would be among the best in the entire operation.

My thoughts were interrupted when the hatch slid open and a man in a slightly rumpled set of duty fatigues walked in. He was around my age, maybe a year or two younger. His brown hair was closely cut but still somehow just slightly messy. I'd become very "by the book" military, and I was always meticulous with my uniform and my appearance, a trait I obviously didn't share with my new acquaintance.

"Corporal Jax?" I got up as he walked over. "I'm Erik Cain." He extended his hand. "I'd like to welcome you to the platoon."

I clasped his hand and we shook. He was fairly tall, but when I stood up I towered over him. "The pleasure is mine Corporal Cain."

"Please, sit." He motioned toward the chair where I'd been seated, and he dropped into the one next to it. "You are taking over a good team, one of the best. I know, because they were mine." He was friendly, but I could also tell he was taking his measure of me. As I was doing with him.

"I can promise you I will do my best to look after them, Corporal Cain."

He smiled and leaned back in his chair. "I appreciate that. And it's Erik, please."

"I'm Darius." I relaxed a bit in my chair, though my posture was still better than his. "I want to thank you for taking the time to welcome me into the unit. I know how close-knit a group a good platoon can be. The troops can be a little apprehensive when they get a commander from outside rather than one promoted from within."

He nodded approvingly; it was clear he had similar thoughts.

"I completely agree." He was looking right at me, his eyes boring into mine. "I've read your file, Darius. I'm sure you'll be a great addition. But if I can help get you off on the right foot with the troops, it's the least I can do." There was a soft buzzing sound - he was getting a message on his earpiece. "Excuse me, Darius, I just have to attend to something quickly." He was getting up as he spoke. "I shouldn't be more than ten minutes, and then we'll go meet your team."

"No rush. I'll be here when you get back."

He looked back over his shoulder. "Help yourself." He pointed toward the dispensers on the far wall. "Believe it or not, the coffee's actually pretty good." The hatch slid open. "I'll be right back." He walked out into the corridor, and the door closed behind him.

I didn't know it then, of course, but I had just met someone who would be very important to me, a trusted colleague and my closest friend. I had respected the lieutenant and some of the other troops I'd fought with, but Erik was the first real friend I ever had. We would fight side by side for years, and climb the ranks together. He would save my life more than once, and I would save his, and the two of us would face challenges neither of us could have imagined sitting in that wardroom.

But looming ahead of us before any of that was Operation Achilles. Morale was good; we were anxious to get at the enemy, to end the war in one bold stroke. Of course, that wasn't to be. Achilles turned out to be a bloody mess, a disaster that almost lost us the war then and there. We had some dark and difficult days ahead of us.

My first few years in the Corps hadn't been easy and, though I didn't know it yet, the next few to come would be even more difficult. But as I sat there and took stock, I came to realize that I had indeed found a home. Yes, we fought and struggled, and some of us died, but there were things on the frontier worth fighting for. When I was discharged from the hospital on Armstrong I spent my month's leave on the planet. I had the time to just look around, and what I saw amazed me. The people were busy, industrious...and free.

They were having local elections when I was there, and half a dozen candidates were running. I stood one day and watched a live debate in the main square. I was mesmerized - they were actually arguing issues and hurling pointed questions at each other. It was nothing like Earth, where the elections were a farce and the government controlled every aspect of its citizens' lives. These people were building a future, for themselves and for mankind, and we were here to protect them.

It made me think about Earth and wonder why the people accepted the system that oppressed them so badly. It was a nightmare, a grotesque, a hideous perversion of the human condition. But it worked, after a fashion. The Cogs were ruled by deprivation, by the need to focus solely on the basics of survival. The middle classes were governed by the fear of losing what they had. They could see how the Cogs lived, and to them, not born to such deprivation, it was a terrifying prospect. Part of me resented that they, mostly educated and vital to the functioning of society, meekly accepted the system when they could have agitated for change. I wanted to despise them as cowards and blame them for the plight of the Cogs, for the reality that my parents were forced to live.

But it is easy to make such judgments, and far more difficult to be honest with yourself. If my father had been offered a middle class life, if we'd been able to live in an apartment in the Louisville Downtown or the Washbalt Core instead of some miserable leaky hut on the farm...I'm not so sure I wouldn't have been ruled by the same fear of losing it. I like to think I would have fought for change, but I'm not so sure. I would now, of course, but then, never having seen what was possible? I just don't know.

But none of that mattered anymore. By a bizarre road I had found my path. For the first time I felt my life had purpose and I knew the sacrifices were worthwhile. I was finally home.

Bitter Glory

To the wise, life is a problem; to the fool, a solution.
                                        - Marcus Aurelius.

Chapter 1

Control Center
AS Wasp
In Earth Orbit

The command chair was surprisingly hard and immobile. Garret would have sworn the small ridge along the back was designed specifically to poke him in the spine. He'd ached to sit there for so long, but always in his imagination the captain's seat was comfortable, inviting. Now that he was there, shifting his weight awkwardly, he had a new thought…maybe the captain shouldn't be too comfortable. Perhaps it was the fate of the commander to be constantly on edge.

Whatever the truth, he would soon find out. The privilege of command was now his, and the burden as well. He'd longed for this day since the first time he donned his midshipman's whites, and his service since then had been an uninterrupted road to the captain's chair. Garret was a brilliant officer; all of his commanders agreed on that. But he was cocky too, an arrogance based on enormous ability, but one still uncontrolled by wisdom. His evaluation reports all said the same thing - he was a tactical genius with an uncanny capacity to anticipate enemy maneuvers. They also said he was audacious, even reckless… that he lacked caution.

Many young officers were overly ambitious, thinking themselves immortal, going into battle boldly, fearlessly. Most of them gained caution with age and learned to understand the realities of war. Those who didn't usually died. But Augustus Garret was too skilled, too capable. His enormous abilities saved him multiple times when his daring seemed likely to get him killed. His ego grew, and he came to believe he could handle any situation, that no crisis could overwhelm him.

He'd talked many times with one of the professors at the Academy about the heavy responsibility of being in that seat, of the sometimes terrible consequences of decisions that were the captain's alone to make. Captain Horn had been a decorated officer with a spotless record and an unimpeded trajectory to the admiralty. Instead, he ended up, years later, still a captain, but now behind a desk teaching midshipmen. One of those decisions years before had gone horribly awry, but Garret never knew just what it was that had so affected Horn he could no longer face the command chair. He was very fond of Captain Horn, but he was also young and arrogant enough to be sure nothing like that could ever keep him from his own destiny. Horn had sent Garret a message after his promotion, congratulating his old student. He ended with a reference to an ancient passage, saying to Garret that it was now time to put away childish things. He doubted the heroic young captain would take his council to heart, or even grasp his meaning, but he tried nevertheless.

Garret smiled as he glanced around the small control center, each of its five workstations gleaming white and silver. Wasp was so new they were still peeling protective polymer wrapping off the equipment. She was the second ship of the class to enter service, and she was all his. He had already decided she was perfect...other than the hideous chair.

His crew hadn't boarded yet. Technically they were all still on leave like him, scheduled to report the next day....today, actually, as it was well past midnight, station time. But Garret couldn't stay away. He'd wandered down to the bay, intending only to take a quick look at the ship sitting in her docking cradle. It was quiet on the station, almost eerily so, with no one around except the skeleton crew working late night maintenance.

She was the most beautiful thing Garret had ever seen. Aerodynamics wasn't an issue in spacecraft design, but Wasp had a sleek, streamlined hull anyway, largely the result of the need to wrap the ship around its dual torpedo tubes. The heavy plasma torpedoes were something new, and they made Wasp a very dangerous vessel, one with a punch that could hurt even a capital ship. Nothing was free, of course, and that offensive power came at a high cost in sacrificed armor and defense. The fast attack ships were known as "suicide boats" for a reason, though the crews tended to take the name as a badge of honor.

Garret admired his ship's form, 102 meters of dark grey heavy metal alloy, held in place by two large brackets and connected to the station by half a dozen snaking umbilicals. They were almost done fueling the reactor; the food, equipment, and other supplies had already been loaded. In another hour she'd be ready to go, waiting for her new captain and crew to board and take her out.

He had promised himself he wasn't going to go aboard again tonight, but after standing in the docking bay for a while he couldn't resist. His captain's credentials gave him 24 hour access, even though the ship was technically closed to all but maintenance personnel. He climbed through the access portal and made his way methodically down the tube. The umbilical was a zero gravity environment, and it was slow going, grabbing the handholds and sliding himself along.

The attack ships didn't have the same level of artificial gravity as larger vessels. When the ship was underway, the core would rotate, providing the feel of partial gravity to much of the vessel, but that would be half Earth-normal at best. In the docking cradle she rotated along with the station, and once Garret climbed out of the tube he experienced a reasonable facsimile of the station's 0.85 Earth-normal gravity. It wasn't actual gravity, of course, but it felt real enough.

He lost track of how long he'd wandered around the ship, prowling its empty compartments, before he ended up on the bridge, back in his uncomfortable but prized chair. A capital ship had many levels, and mazes of corridors, but Wasp was a vastly simpler vessel, with three decks, two above the spinal-mounted torpedo tubes and one below. Each deck was traversed by a single primary corridor with several small lateral access-ways. Serving aboard Wasp would be a cozy affair.

He leaned back in the command chair and breathed in deeply. There was an odd collection of smells in the air, the scent of plastic packing materials mixed with faint burning odors from new systems activated for the first time. Later today he would sit in this very spot and give the orders for Wasp to break free of the station's embrace and begin her voyage to whatever destiny awaited her. The Alliance was at war, so that future would no doubt include a considerable amount of combat. Garret had no idea whether Wasp would be assigned to a battlegroup or a detached hunter squadron but, wherever she went, he was certain his crew would do their duty. He would see to that.

He knew he should go back to his quarters on the station and get some sleep; the day ahead promised to be a momentous one. But he couldn't bring himself to leave the ship...his ship, and every time he shifted his body to go, he just ended up sliding around in the chair. Eventually he closed his eyes, not sure if he was asleep, awake, or somewhere just on the cusp between the two. His mind drifted back, dreamlike, over the years that led to this day, to his service as a junior officer, and deeper into the past...to a younger Augustus Garret, what seemed like a lifetime ago.

Chapter 2

Bluestone Manor
Alliance Sector
Terra Nova – Alpha Centauri A III

The Garrets had lived on Terra Nova for almost a century. Indeed, for as long as there had been a Terra Nova, there had been Garrets living there, and for the last 70 years Bluestone Manor had been their home. The first Augustus Garret on Terra Nova had arrived as a penniless adventurer, one of 40 brave souls sent to claim the first habitable world man had discovered outside his native solar system. The family documented its history well, especially the early days on Terra Nova, but no one could ever seem to recall why the oldest son in each generation was saddled with the name Augustus. Reasons had long become immaterial, however, and the custom was deeply forged in family tradition.

The Manor was really just a large house, ramshackle in design and expanded haphazardly over the generations as the family grew. Despite the grand name, there was nothing extraordinary about Bluestone Manor; it was big, but by no means a mansion. The Garrets got by fairly well, but they were not truly wealthy. Few people on Terra Nova were.

Man's first interstellar colony had never lived up to its early promise. The planet proved to be lacking in many resources, especially compared to other worlds being rapidly discovered, and it was quickly bypassed for more promising destinations. The early settlers also discovered that Terra Nova was home to a massive array of local bacteria and viruses, many of which were highly resistant to treatment. The young colony suffered a num-

ber of devastating plagues before its medical services caught up
with the virulent native pathogens.

Terra Nova had become an aging world, a place from which
young people with options emigrated, leaving behind older generations and those lacking the resources or motivation to start
over someplace else. With the Alliance's massive expansion into
space, there were always opportunities for adventurous colonists
willing to leave all they knew behind and step into a new life, and
many young Terra Novans did just that, draining the colony of
its most promising and dynamic inhabitants.

There was another route off Terra Nova...military service. The Alliance Marines and navy had expanded rapidly as
the number of occupied worlds increased, and the Superpowers battled for control of the choicest real estate. The Marines
were somewhat of an odd organization, recruiting most of their
strength from the slums of Earth. It was an unorthodox strategy, but one that seemed to work well. The Alliance Marines
were considered one of the finest military formations in space,
and their record was largely one of victory.

But Terra Nova was a naval community through and through,
and most of those who sought adventure or opportunity in the
military signed up for service with the fleet. Though the divided
world was itself demilitarized by the Treaty of Paris, the inhabitants of the Alliance Sector provided the navy with its single
largest source of new recruits.

The Marines started everyone at the bottom...even the
Commandant of the Corps had made his first assault as a private. But the navy was different, and the divide between officers
and crew was more pronounced than that in the Marine Corps,
the stratification more rigid.

Most Terra Novans, uneducated and living in the planet's
ramshackle ghettoes, joined the enlisted ranks of the navy and
served out their careers in that capacity, usually becoming spe-
cialists in one area or another. Few enlisted crew advanced to
the officer ranks, and there was a practical and social divide
between the commissioned and non-commissioned personnel.
While most Marines came from Earth, the vast majority of the

navy's recruits were colonists, pulled from all the worlds the Alliance had settled.

That divide between the classes was a reality within the active service navy, but entry into the coveted officer corps was entirely egalitarian. Every year the fleet recruitment office offered the Test, which was open to any applicant. The Test was infamous, not only for its great difficulty, but because it was highly unorthodox. It annually confounded the majority of those who took it, including many of the most intelligent and educated applicants. But each year a small number, substantially below 1% of those who took the Test, received the coveted invitation to take the formal entrance examinations to the Naval Academy. To anyone who had passed the Test, those exams were a formality.

Augustus Garret, at least the eighth of the family to bear the name, had wanted to go to the Academy as far back as he had memories. As a child, his room was filled with models of the navy's most famous ships and, as long as he could remember, his only goal in life was to take the Test...and to leave Terra Nova to become a naval officer and win glory and fame.

Garret was a poor student, though everyone who knew him agreed he was extremely intelligent. He was rebellious, unhappy at being stuck on Terra Nova. He argued with teachers and was prone to skip classes and get into all sorts of petty trouble. There was nothing on Terra Nova he liked, not school, not friends, not the Garret family businesses...nothing but Charlotte Evers. Charlotte was a tall, thin girl, with a striking mane of red hair. He'd known her as long as he could remember. He had no memories that didn't include Charlotte, at least no pleasant ones. They'd grown up together, and they'd been inseparable.

No one in the family thought the surly and rebellious Augustus would ever pass the Test, and they all assumed he'd marry Charlotte and settle in to take his place managing the moderately successful Garret businesses along with his cousins. Time, age, and responsibility would mature him, they thought, and he would settle in and find his place. But Augustus had other ideas.

The day of the Test finally came, and the 18-year old Augustus reported to the naval testing center. He was told to arrive two hours early to clear the DNA testing, but he made sure to be there four hours ahead of time. The Test was serious business, and the navy made it virtually impossible for anyone to cheat. After his identity was confirmed he was led down a long, narrow corridor by a Marine in spotless gray fatigues. The floor was a utilitarian composite tile, and the walls were bright white. There were small doors, hatches really, on both sides of the corridor every four meters or so, though there didn't seem to be handles or controls on any of them. They passed at least ten of the doorways before his escort stopped and pulled a small controller from his pocket. He pressed a button, and the hatch on the right slid open.

"When I seal this cubicle, you will be locked in for the duration of the Test. You may activate the Test whenever you wish by verbally advising the AI that you are ready. From that point you will have six hours to complete all sections." The Marine sounded bored, monotone. Garret imagined he'd been through the speech more than a few times.

"The cubicle contains a relief facility and a station that dispenses water and nutrition bars." He motioned for Garret to step inside. "The red lever is your distress control. If you suffer a medical emergency or need to leave for any reason, activate this lever, and assistance will be dispatched. In this event, your test results will be invalidated." The Marine paused, allowing Garret to consider what he had said. "Do you understand everything I have explained to you?"

Garret looked back over his shoulder. "Yes." He was trying to hide his excitement, but it was difficult. All his life he'd been dreaming of this moment, and now it was here. He was scared too, though he wouldn't let himself admit it. In the back of his mind the uncertainty played on him...what if I don't pass?

"As I explained, when I close this door you will be locked in until the Test is complete." He stepped out into the hallway, leaving Garret inside, standing in front of the workstation. "Are you ready?"

Garret sat down in the seat. It was some type of imitation leather, and it was surprisingly comfortable. He leaned back and let a small smile creep onto his lips. "Yes, I'm ready." The door slid shut behind him, leaving him alone, sitting silently staring at the workstation.

He could feel his heart beating, pounding loudly in his ears. Garret was prone to bravado, and he'd expressed nothing but cool confidence about the Test. But now it was just him, and it was time. His tension was building. His mouth was dry, his stomach tight. His life's dream…and it all depended on the next six hours.

He took a deep breath, and he pushed the fear aside and stared at the workstation's screen with a focused intensity. "I am ready to begin."

Chapter 3

Naval Admin Building
Alliance Sector
Terra Nova – Alpha Centauri A III

Garret sat quietly, trying not to look nervous. It wasn't easy, because he was scared as hell. He was a cocky kid, but this was a lot for him to bluster his way through. A transport had arrived at Bluestone Manor that morning to take him to see Admiral Halperin. The four Marines who arrived at the door offered no explanation; they simply instructed him to come with them. Halperin was another Terra Novan, and the highest ranking officer ever to come from the planet. Garret couldn't understand why the admiral would want to see him, and his mind raced with possibilities, good and bad. It must have something to do with the test, he thought, but he couldn't imagine what would warrant attention from so lofty an officer.

The conference room was starkly decorated, attractive but utilitarian. He was shown in and a steward in a crisp naval uniform offered him a refreshment. Garret politely refused, and he sat quietly, trying not to look scared. He tried to keep his mind busy, but there was nothing to do, and he kept drifting back to the question of why he was there. He looked around the room, absentmindedly kicking the leg of his chair, counting the ceiling tiles to estimate the size of the room. Anything to pass the time. Finally, the door slid open with a whoosh.

"Mr. Garret, please excuse me for being late." A tall man in a perfectly-tailored blue naval uniform walked through the open door. "As a rule I am very punctual, but I'm afraid I don't get home to Terra Nova very often. Well…you know how family obligations can be."

Garret certainly understood not coming back to Terra Nova often…if he ever got out, he doubted he'd want to return. "Of course, admiral." Garret would have waited all day if he had to, not that he had the impression he had any choice. An insistent Marine escort wasn't easily sidestepped. "I am at your convenience." He wanted to ask why he was there, but he decided to play it cool and wait and see what Halperin had to say.

The admiral didn't make him wait long. "I'm sure you are curious why we brought you here." Halperin looked a bit apologetic. "I am sorry if your escort was a bit brusque. I ordered them to bring you to HQ, and I'm afraid they follow my orders quite literally around here." He paused, looking down just for a second. "I should have been more specific. My intention was for them to provide you an escort, not descend on your home like stormtroopers."

"It's quite all right, sir." Garret let a little of his relief out in the form of a tiny smile. "I am always available to you, sir."

"That's good to hear, Mr…may I call you Augustus?"

"Of course, admiral."

"Well, Augustus, I will waste no more of your time." Halperin had an amused little smile on his face. "I had you brought here because of your results on the Test."

Garret could feel the rush of excitement building, but he tried, unsuccessfully, to suppress it. The Naval Academy! Was it really possible? He was going to be a midshipman? A naval officer? "Are you saying that I passed the Test, sir?"

Halperin let his grin expand into a full blown smile. "Passed it? Over 185,000 people took the Test this year, Augustus…and you finished first."

*   *   *   *   *

It had been a crazy two weeks. That's all Garret had…two weeks. Half a month to settle his affairs and say goodbye to everything he'd known all his short life. He'd longed to leave

Terra Nova as far back as he could remember, but he found it more complex and difficult a thing to do now that it was real. It's one thing to chafe at the relentless monotony of a place like Terra Nova, quite another to leave it all behind, especially when it's the only home you've ever known.

Garret's dreamy, childhood visions of leaving had never focused on the images he now lived, things like saying goodbye to his mother and father...possibly forever. Looking at familiar places and things acquired a painful twinge as he now wondered if he'd ever see them again. When leaving had been an unreal dream he'd been cavalier about it, but now his former certainty that he'd never return seemed cocky and arrogant.

Then there was Charlotte. She'd taken the Test too, but she didn't pass - there would be no Academy for her. Pursuing his dream, his destiny, meant leaving her behind. There'd never been a time in his life he could remember when she hadn't been a part of it, not a meaningful thing he didn't share with her before anyone else. For as long as he could remember, he and Charlotte had been just that...he and Charlotte.

He knew he loved her. There was nothing he wouldn't do for her, no sacrifice he wouldn't make. Save this one. He could feel his destiny, it coursed through his being. Turning his back on the navy, on the fast track to the command ranks his test results opened to him...it was unthinkable.

He sat long one day at the edge of a stream that ran through a small valley down the hill from Bluestone Manor, a place where he'd spent countless hours with Charlotte. He couldn't imagine life without her...or how he could leave her behind, stuck on Terra Nova alone. But turning down the navy, walking away from his dream, from the glory he knew in his heart he'd achieve? That was inconceivable. All his life he'd imagined this, and now everything he'd ever wanted was there, right in front of him. Everything but Charlotte Evers.

In many ways, Charlotte understood him better than he did himself. She was truly happy for him; she knew better than any-one how desperately he wanted – needed – this. Everyone had humored him over the years, indulging his declarations about a naval career, but Charlotte had truly believed. She knew in her heart that Augustus would achieve whatever he set his mind too.

She threw her arms around him joyfully when he told her, but inside she felt an emptiness, a cold despair. She knew he would go, that almost nothing could stop him from pursuing his dream of glory. She could, perhaps. If she begged him not to go, he might stay. But she wouldn't…couldn't…do that to him. The Augustus who remained on Terra Nova would be dead inside, his spirit broken. He would always regret the chance he'd let pass, and she would blame herself…and one day he would blame her too. She loved him too much to be the reason he lost his dream. And if she begged him to stay and he went anyway, it would destroy her.

In the end he swore her empty promises, and she believed them…they both believed them. He would return after he graduated; they could be together even with his naval career. It might not be ideal, and they would probably be apart frequently, but they could do it. They were 18 and they loved each other, and that made it easy to believe.

The First Frontier War had been over for fifteen years, and the Alliance was more or less at peace. The interregnums between declared wars were hardly without fighting, but incidents were scattered, and most of the navy's ships split their time between patrol duty and port. He would probably do most of his service in dock anyway, on some base or colony world. So why, he thought, couldn't they be together?

It was raining the day he left. She stood on the platform watching as he boarded the shuttle. They said their goodbyes, talking long and quietly. She managed to hold back her tears… mostly. They repeated their promises to each other, but inside she felt dead, empty. She held on to him tightly, dreading he moment she had to let go, to watch him walk away in the cold drizzle. It took all the strength she had to do it, to loosen her arms and let him pull away…to give him to his destiny.

He turned one last time and looked back at her. She was grateful for the rain that hid her tears. He smiled and waved… the same Augustus she'd loved for so long. She forced a smile to her own lips, and watched him climb up the ladder and disappear into the shuttle. It was only then the last shreds of solace from the hopeless promises they had sworn dissipated, and Charlotte knew she had lost him forever.

She stood there, unmoving, tears streaming down her cheeks like rivers, as the shuttle fired its thrusters and blasted up into the dark gray sky.

Chapter 4

Control Center
AS Wasp
Tau Ceti System
Inbound from Gliese 15 Warp Gate

Third Squadron was deep in enemy territory. Wasp and her two sister-ships were inbound at 0.03c, engines shut down and reactors on minimal power. They were three small ships approaching a heavily defended Caliphate sector capital. They would be massively outgunned in any conventional fight... everything relied on stealth. This was a raid, one with a very specific objective.

Tau Ceti III was a staging ground for a planned Caliphate invasion of the newly settled Alliance world of Armstrong. Third Squadron was here to take out the troopships. The Caliphate was stretched thin, attacking on multiple fronts. Alliance Intelligence believed if the three heavy transports at Tau Ceti were taken out of action, the enemy would be compelled to postpone the invasion. It was a desperate, high-risk mission, but the payoff was huge. The Alliance was losing the war and didn't have the forces available to defend Armstrong. Third Squadron's daring raid was likely the only chance to hold on to a promising new colony.

Garret had commanded Wasp for almost nine months, the first six as part of the Amiens battlegroup. It was boring duty for an aggressive, young captain. Amiens and her support ships were stationed at Columbia, positioned to defend that colony against an expected attack...an invasion that never came. Battlegroup duty was frequently boring and uneventful, not at all what Garret had imagined when he got his captain's stars.

Finally, the high command issued new orders. The threat to Columbia had proven to be false intel, and Amiens was heading to the recently-opened shipyards at Wolf 359 to be refitted with the new external missile rack system. Once complete, the ship would be able to carry 40% more missiles, dramatically increasing its firepower. Best of all, by Garret's reckoning, it put his ship, and the entire 3rd Squadron, out of a job. Out of a boring job far back from the front lines, at least.

The Tau Ceti raid was just the sort of thing Garret had dreamed about, a chance to win true glory. They were going in silent, right until the moment they fired. The plan gave Garret a lot of autonomy, even though Squadron Captain Simmons was in overall command. Alliance Intelligence had managed to sabotage the scanning grid on the Gliese 15 warp gate, allowing 3rd Squadron to transit undetected. It had been a considerable operation, run by a young agent named Gavin Stark. Garret didn't know how Stark had infiltrated the Tau Ceti defense network, and he didn't care. That was a job for spies. His part was blasting one of those transports into atoms.

Wasp's vector had been carefully calculated, courtesy of more data provided by the intelligence types. As long as the transports were still in the same position, Garret's ship – and the rest of the squadron – had come through the warp gate on a heading straight toward the targets.

"Lieutenant Forsten, do we have a reading on the transports yet?" Garret leaned back in his seat and wiggled around, trying to get comfortable. He'd commanded Wasp for eight and a half months, but he still hadn't gotten used to the chair. And it was even worse wearing the bulky combat gear. The suit was cumbersome and annoying, but it would also save his life if Wasp was hit and lost pressurization.

"No, sir." Forsten was another Terra Novan who had taken the test and scored well. Garret hadn't known him personally before taking command of Wasp, but he vaguely recalled the family. "Scanning continuously, captain."

I hope the bastards haven't repositioned those damned ships,

Garret thought – I really don't want to do a burn before we fire. As soon as Wasp – or either of her squadron-mates - fired their thrusters they would become much easier to detect. They might pull off a small burn and stay hidden, but their chances dropped enormously.

"Very well. Notify me as soon as you have any readings." He turned to glance behind him. The bridge of the fast attack ship was cramped, with low ceilings and exposed structural members and conduits. Garret hit his head at least once a day, and that was after eight months getting used to it. "Ensign Vickers, please advise Engineer Carson that I'm going to want the reactor at 110% power on sixty seconds' notice."

"Yes, captain." Vickers was from Sandoval, an idyllic world that had initially been colonized primarily by refugees from London. He had a heavy British accent, something that had become an increasing rarity on Earth. In the almost-century since the formation of the Alliance had combined most of the English-speaking nations into a single Superpower, there had been a trend toward consolidation of speech patterns into a single "Alliance" accent…at least among the middle class and colonists. The massive Cog communities that inhabited the Alliance's slums still spoke mostly with the historical regional accents typical for their predecessor socio-economic classes.

Garret's plan was daring. And dangerous. His orders were simple…attack the transports. It would have been pointless for Captain Simmons to issue more specific commands. The squadron had entered the system with a pre-plotted vector and velocity, and the ships had maintained a communications blackout since transiting. Simmons had to rely on the judgment of his ship captains in how they would make their attack runs. For Augustus Garret, this was an invitation to throw caution to the wind. He was going right down the throat of his target ship. If Wasp remained undetected, he'd be able to drop two plasma torpedoes right into the guts of the target.

"Captain, I have a scan on the transport group, sir." Garret knew immediately from the excitement in Forsten's voice. "All ships are located precisely as expected."

Garret's expression morphed into a feral smile, the look of a predator on the hunt. "All personnel, the mission is a go." His stomach clenched, and he could feel the excitement, the tingling in his arms. Wasp hadn't seen any action during the time she was posted to the Amiens battlegroup...this would be Garret's first combat as a ship captain.

"Ensign Carson, prep the tombs." The five acceleration shells on Wasp's bridge were mounted to the port side wall in a single row. The shells looked a bit like upright coffins, which explained how "tombs" had become the nearly universal slang used to identify them.

"Tombs ready, captain." Carson's response was almost immediate. He had run a diagnostic on his own just before Garret's command. Without the tombs, the crew would probably be crushed to death or suffocated by the massive acceleration Wasp's engines would put out after the ship fired at its target. Tau Ceti was a major Caliphate choke point system...there were enough warships orbiting the planet to blast Third Squadron's three tiny craft to plasma a dozen times over. Running like hell was the only viable tactic, and Wasp would be blasting with all the thrust she could generate.

There was a lot of talk about new expandable systems designed to be built into the chairs and workstations themselves, eliminating the need for separate shells. Garret was skeptical, but he was all for it if it was real. Getting rid of the tombs would be a huge space saver. And extra room on a warship meant additional weapons, bigger reactors, and more powerful engines. More combat power.

"Lieutenant Forsten, run a diagnostic on the weapons control system. I don't want any slipups." Garret knew weapons control was functioning perfectly, but he thought it would do his crew some good to have something to do. Other than sit and wait to see if they were detected before they got to the firing point. If they were picked up before they fired they had very little chance of getting out of the system. Garret knew that, and so did his crew. There was no point giving his people time to sit and think about that.

"Yes, sir. Commencing test now."

"Very well, lieutenant." Garret turned toward the communications workstation. "Ensign Randall, put me on shipwide com."

"Yes, sir." A brief pause. "Captain, you are online."

"Attention all personnel." Garrett's voice was steely, firm. He was exhilarated at the prospect of commanding his people in combat, and all he wanted them to hear was the resolute voice of their captain. "We will be entering firing range within the next twenty minutes. We have served together for some time, but this will be our first combat operation." He paused, but just for a few seconds.

"We are here to forestall a Caliphate invasion of one of our worlds. We can save hundreds of Marines from death in combat. We can spare thousands of civilians from the nightmare of an occupation that could last for years." He could feel his excitement growing. How many times had he imagined addressing his crew before battle? His mind flashed back for an instant, over the years, thinking about his own commanders and the things they had said as their ships went into combat. Now it was his turn.

"There is no crew I would rather have right now, and no ship in the fleet I would trade for our own Wasp. I know each of you will do his or her duty." He took a breath. "We have reviewed this operation multiple times. At the first alarm, all personnel not directly engaged in weapons control are to report to the tombs." The first alarm would be sounded three minutes before they reached the firing point. "The second alarm is the firing point. When that klaxon sounds, I'm counting on fire control to pump two plasma torpedoes into the belly of the beast. You'll have three minutes to enter your final targeting solutions."

He took a quick glance around the bridge before continuing. "Weapons teams, I want you in your shells within one minute after firing. We'll have to leave it to the ship's computer to run the damage assessment." The computer would have done most of the work anyway. Much of what the crew did on a warship was redundant, supervising and confirming data crunched by the ship's AI. But Garret wanted that redundancy; he wanted to know that both man and machine were at work.

"Exactly 90 seconds after we fire, the ship's computer will execute a full strength burn of the engines. We will be accelerating at 21g, so anyone caught outside their shell is going to be in rough shape. It is vital that we begin thrusting as soon as possible...any delay will only decrease the probability of our escape. So the scheduled burn will not be delayed." He paused. "Not for any reason. Make sure you are in your shells on time." Another pause, longer this time, the seriousness of his last point hanging in the air. "Now let's go and get these bastards!"

Garret couldn't see the faces of the crew, not most of them, at least. But from the expressions of the bridge officers, he decided his little speech had done its job. He flipped the com, switching to the direct line to Engineer Carson. "Lieutenant, I want you monitoring the reactor constantly while we're in the tombs." The chief engineer had a special shell with internally-accessible readouts and a special AI interface. Garret planned to run the reactor well over its specified capacity, and he wanted it watched carefully.

"Yes, sir." Carson seemed tentative. There were a few seconds of silence before the engineer added, "Sir, I still advise against running the reactor at 120%...especially as a massive power spike."

"Understood, engineer." Garret's voice was calm and even, not at all unpleasant. It was Carson's job to warn him of the risks, and he wasn't going to slam the engineer for speaking his mind. But Garret knew what he was going to do. "Continue according to plan." The chance of a critical reactor accident was a lot less than that of getting blown to bits by the enemy fleet if they didn't haul ass out of the system. At least that's what Garret believed...and his was the only vote that mattered. It was on his shoulders. If his people escaped successfully - or if they were blown to atoms by a reactor explosion – it would be his responsibility...the result of his decisions.

"Five minutes to firing point, captain." Forsten's eyes were glued to his display as he spoke. He was manning the tactical station, but he was also Garret's XO.

"Very well, lieutenant." Garret glanced around the room. He was pleased with his people. This would be the first time into battle for many of them, but they were all focused and in control. He took a breath himself. He'd seen plenty of combat during his years as a junior officer, but this was the first time he was in command, and he felt a tension, a tightness in his gut. It was different – worse – than what he'd always experienced before. Garret was cocky and aggressive, but that didn't mean he was immune to fear. He'd been afraid every time he'd gone into battle. But this was new.

The klaxon sounded the first alarm. Three minutes to launch. "Bridge crew to the shells." Garret didn't need the crew for the next three minutes, not just to relay him reports he could get directly from the computer. In truth, there was no reason he couldn't button up too, but there was no way Garret was leaving his command chair. Not until the last second.

The second alarm sounded. The lighting on the bridge brightened as the reactor surged to full power. "Reactor at 120%, sir, and functioning within acceptable parameters." The relief in the engineer's voice was obvious. Massively spiking the reactor power was dangerous, and he was glad it was over with.

"Very well, engineer." Garret could feel his face flush. The excitement coursed through his body, driving away fear and doubt. "Weapons control, fire!" Garret's command was superfluous. "His crew already had their orders, and before he'd even finished speaking Wasp lurched hard as her dual tubes launched two over-powered plasma torpedoes toward the enemy transport.

Garret got up from his chair and walked to his shell. He pressed the button and stepped back as the front opened. He hated the tombs. He paused and took a deep breath before he stepped backwards into the enclosure. The front closed with a loud click, and Garret felt the injection delivering the drug cocktail that would aid his body in enduring the forces of acceleration.

He couldn't move in the shell, but he still had access to the comlink. He waited quietly, counting off the seconds, then he winced as Wasp's engines fired on full power and the pressure hit him. Even in the tomb, 20g was a lot to take. The shell increased atmospheric pressure, helping to force the air into his straining lungs. He could speak, at least enough to give commands, but it took considerable effort.

"Enemy transport A identified as a Sahara-class heavy troopship." Garret had been waiting for ship's AI to complete the damage assessment. He could feel the tension in his body, waiting. "Both torpedoes impacted the target amidships. Preliminary data indicates massive structural damage, internal fires, and loss of atmosphere."

Garret's felt the urge to jump with excitement, but the shell held him firmly in place. Bullseye, he thought, a huge smile creeping over his face...that ship is gone!

Chapter 5

Control Center
AS Wasp
Struve 2398 System
Approaching Lacaille 8760 Warp Gate

Garret took a deep, unassisted breath. The crushing pressure was gone. For most of the past three months, Wasp and Scorpion had executed an almost constant series of acceleration and deceleration burns, putting three systems between them and Tau Ceti. They'd been deep in enemy territory when they began their flight, and they'd transited through Caliphate and CAC systems since. But the next jump would bring them closer to home.

Lacaille 8760 wasn't a very important system, but at least it was Alliance space. They'd been out of touch for three months, with no communication at all except direct ship-to-ship laser transmissions. At least they'd be able to connect with the Commnet system in Lacaille and get caught up on the status of the war.

The two vessels were all that remained of Third Squadron. Badger took a chance hit from the orbital fortress during its attack run and lost an engine. With half its thrust capacity gone, the ship had no chance to escape. Squadron Captain Simmons' last orders were to forbid Wasp and Scorpion from trying a hopeless rescue. Garret almost ordered his ship to come about anyway, but he realized Simmons was right. Wasp had a full crew, and his responsibility was to them now. The Alliance was at war and couldn't afford to throw away ships and trained crews on hopeless acts of heroism. Especially when they didn't have a chance to make a difference. There was no way to decelerate and return to help Badger, not in the time she had left.

Garret listened silently to the incoming transmissions, grimly following the battle and the ultimate destruction of the squadron flagship. He ordered the AI to restrict the com to his shell only – he didn't want his crew listening when they couldn't do anything to help. It wouldn't help Captain Simmons and his people, and it would just sap the morale of Wasp's crew.

He could feel the elation from the successful attack run draining away, flushed excitement replaced by frustration and grief. That wasn't just a ship under attack – it was Garret's commanding officer, his comrades in arms. He was following Simmons' orders, and he knew there was nothing he could do to alter the outcome...but he still felt disloyal. He hated himself for running for the warp gate while his brothers and sisters were being hunted down and destroyed.

His thoughts drifted, as if his mind was trying to force itself away from the tragedy unfolding on the comlink. He thought of Captain Horn at the Academy and, for the first time, he truly understood the immense pressure on the captain's shoulders... and the kinds of decisions it was hard to live with.

The drama dragged on, Badger thrusting as strongly as her sole surviving engine could manage, trying vainly to outrun her pursuers. Simmons pushed his ship to the breaking point but, with only one engine, she simply could not produce the thrust she needed to outrun the Caliphate hunter-killers. The HKs were the enemy's answer to the fast attack ships, and they relentlessly pursued their wounded prey, finally closing to firing range two light minutes from the warp gate.

Simmons and his crew didn't go down without a fight, and their fire inflicted heavy damage on two of the attacking ships. But Badger was damaged and outnumbered 4-1. The mathematics of war asserted themselves, and she erupted into a massive fireball as two plasma torpedoes hit in rapid succession.

Garret felt the breath sucked from his lungs as he realized what had happened. The end came so quickly, Badger wasn't even able to send out the Delta-Z signal of a doomed ship. One second she was there, firing at the enemy with all she had and the next she was just gone.

It had been almost three months now, and it was still surreal to Garret. Part of him kept waiting, half-expecting to hear Simmons on the com, giving orders to the squadron. But there was nothing. Wasp and Scorpion were on their own.

"Nelson, calculate time to warp gate insertion at present course and speed." The command AIs were something new, installed just before Third Squadron embarked on its current mission. The quasi-sentient artificial intelligences were custom designed to interact seamlessly with each captain. Garret, always a student of military history, had named his Nelson. It would be a few years before he realized the stunning unoriginality of his choice. By then, there would be dozens of Nelsons serving the command officers of the fleet.

"Yes, admiral." The AI spoke normally, in a voice that could easily have belonged to one of the crew. "Insertion in one hour, eleven minutes, 47 seconds." The AI paused for an instant. The hesitation was for effect, not because Nelson needed time to calculate. It was all part of the overall programming to make the computer seem more human. "Scorpion will transit 37 seconds later."

"Very well, Nelson." Garret still wasn't sure what he thought about the AI. He felt a little silly conversing with it as if it were a member of the crew. But there was an efficiency to it he couldn't dispute.

"Ensign Randall, get me Captain Compton." Garret wasn't ready to let the AI do everything.

"Yes, sir." Randall worked his board for a few seconds then turned toward Garret. "I have Captain Compton, sir." Terrance Compton commanded Scorpion. He was a good friend of Garret's, his constant companion through five years at the Academy. The two had graduated from the same class, and they'd served together much of the time since then. Garret's commission was three weeks older than Compton's, so that made him Third Squadron's new CO.

"Very well, ensign." Garret nodded as he flipped on his ship to ship com. "Are you as sore as me, Terrance?" Garret didn't have Compton on visual, but he'd have bet his friend was smiling, trying not to laugh in the middle of his bridge.

"I'm pretty worn out, but I imagine not as much as an old man like you." Garret was three months older than Compton, a fact the younger man had begun to enjoy more and more as the two progressed from brash new officers to ship captains. "That was quite a run. I've never spent so much time in the tombs. At least we're almost home." Then, with a grimmer tone. "But we didn't get back without a price, did we?" Compton hadn't found it any easier to run away while listening to the enemy hunt down and destroy Badger.

"No." Garret's voice was equally somber. "We didn't."

The two men were silent for a moment. Finally, Compton spoke up. "So, squadron commander…what's up? Any orders?"

"Let's just stay on course and transit back to friendly territory." Garret fidgeted around in his chair trying to get comfortable. The bruises all over his body didn't make the rigid seat any more restful. "I think the crews have had enough of the shells for now." Garret took a quick breath and continued, "Besides, the reactors and the engines need a break. We've been working them hard without a stop."

"No joke there. I have the engineer doing a full diagnostic on both. He should be done before we transit."

Garret frowned. He should have ordered that too. Careless, he thought, annoyed with himself. Compton had gotten one up on him, but Garret would be damned if he was going to admit it.

"Ok, Terrance, just stay on course and tidy things up on Scorpion. Check in with a status report before we transit."

"Will do." Compton was technically insubordinate with his overly casual demeanor, but ship captains were an elite fraternity, and it wasn't uncommon to dispense with the formalities. They both had their helmets on, and no one else was listening… and these two were as close as brothers.

"Garret out." He flipped the comlink and double-checked to confirm the line was closed before he spoke. "Nelson, have the engineer conduct a full diagnostic of the reactor and engines before we transit."

Chapter 6

Control Center
AS Wasp
Lacaille 8760 System
Inbound from the Struve 2398 Warp Gate

"Something's wrong here." Garret was whispering to himself, but Nelson heard him.

"Are you addressing me, captain?" The AI's smooth voice was loud in Garret's earpiece.

"No, Nelson, just talking to my…" Garret paused for a few seconds then snapped his head to the tactical station. "Lieutenant Forsten, I want silent running immediately. Scorpion too. Inform them by direct laser com." Garret was looking straight ahead, staring at the main viewscreen, but he was seeing nothing but his thoughts. Something was wrong…he didn't know what it was, but he could feel it…

"Wasp and Scorpion on silent running, captain." Forsten tried to hide his confusion at Garret's order, though not entirely successfully. The term was archaic, a reference to old wet-navy submersibles. It was originally literal, a method of operation designed to avoid detection by sonar devices that picked up sound. The term was more symbolic in the space navy, though the purpose was the same. In modern usage it meant a minimum expenditure of energy in order to maintain a small scanner profile.

"Nelson, connect to the Struve 2398 warp gate scanners. I want a complete report on any ships that have passed through." It was a border gate, and with the CAC and Alliance at war there shouldn't be any traffic at all. But something was off.

"Warp gate scanners non-responsive, admiral." Nelson's tone changed slightly, suggesting a state of heightened concern on the part of the AI. It was purely for Garret's benefit, part of the algorithm that controlled Nelson's interface with the admiral. "With your permission I will perform a scan for residual transit signatures, filtering out the imprints of Scorpion and Wasp."

"Yes, proceed immediately." Garret found it a little unsettling when his AI predicted orders before he issued them. He pulled up the database entry on Lacaille 8760 and skimmed through it. A backwater system...two planets, neither of which had been worth a major colonization effort. Just a small outpost and a research station examining storm activity on the first planet.

"Captain Garret, warp gate residual scan inconclusive. Energy traces detected, but not in sufficient quantities to confirm any transits within the last 72 hours."

Garret's head snapped around, a pointless gesture since Nelson wasn't actually on the bridge. To him, inconclusive meant someone had come through that gate. The war's been going on for five years, he thought...that energy signature should be stone cold.

Warp gates emitted pulses of energy whenever matter passed through them. The amount of energy was variable, based on the mass and time between successive transits. The exact calculation was still being hotly debated among Earth's physicists, but the presence of any energy at all meant something had gone through the gate. Readings in the range Nelson detected could conceivably be the result of a meteor transiting recently. Or it could be the remnant of a fleet's passage weeks earlier. There was no way to be sure.

The enemy came through here, he thought. He couldn't prove it, couldn't be sure. But he felt it...and the more he thought about it the more it made sense. Lacaille was a pretty worthless piece of real estate; that much was true. But it was also lightly defended, especially for a border system. And its other connection was Wolf 424...and that led to Ross 614 and its four warp gates. It was a long way around, but an invasion

through Lacaille could ultimately threaten Columbia, Atlantia…
most of the rest of the Alliance core worlds.

Garret was taking a big leap. An invasion by that route
would pose significant logistical problems. But if the enemy
could pull it off, the surprise would be devastating. All he had
to go on was some trace energy readings and his own gut. But
he was convinced.

"Nelson, get me a direct laser com link to Captain Compton."

The AI responded almost immediately. "Captain Compton
is on your line sir."

"Terry, take a look at these warp gate energy scans I'm sending over and tell me what you think."

Garret was about to instruct Nelson to transmit the full
report when Compton responded. "I've already seen it, Augustus." Compton was smiling, though Garret couldn't see it on the
audio-only connection. "I was about to com you about it." He
took a deep breath. "And I know what you're thinking."

Garret could tell Compton was on edge. Stress tended to
bring out his British accent. Compton was from London, the
son of a moderately powerful politician and a strikingly beautiful Cog girl who'd caught his eye. Reginald Compton eventually
tired of his teenaged concubine, and he returned her to the East
End slum where he'd found her. But he couldn't quite bring
himself to banish his son to the life of a penniless Cog, so Terrance grew up in the care of hired nannies in a flat his father
rented expressly for the purpose.

Reginald suggested a naval career for his son. It was a respect-
able option, and one that effectively rid him of his embarrassing
offspring. The navy was not above political influence, and he
was sure he could pull some strings and get his son admitted to
the Academy. But Terrance saved him the trouble, scoring in
the top 1/10 of 1% on the Test and gaining admittance without
political favors. Compton had always been a loner…until he
met his roommate at the Academy, a cocky little shit from Terra
Nova. The two became friends almost immediately, closer than
brothers…though that didn't stop them from competing sav-
agely with each other at every opportunity.

"Are you thinking the same thing?" Garret was always surprised at the extent he and Compton thought alike.

"There's not much evidence to support that kind of conclusion, you know." Compton's voice was unconvincing, as if he were offering a perfunctory note of caution he didn't really believe.

"Yes, but that's not what I asked you." Garret knew his comrade had to play devil's advocate, but he was annoyed anyway.

"Yes, it occurred to me." Compton's admission was grudging. He was aggressive by nature, but he was still more cautious than Garret. He wanted more evidence, while Garret was ready to follow his hunch all the way. "But I'm not convinced."

"Well I am." Garret's conviction was growing as he spoke. But what should he do? How could the remnants of Third Squadron derail a major CAC invasion force? "So, assuming we're right, what do we do?"

Compton sighed. His head didn't like the leap Garret was making, though his own gut agreed with his friend and commander. "Well, first we need to figure out what they're planning." He paused a few seconds, thinking. "They would need to set up some kind of logistics pipeline running through this system." Another pause. "If you want to risk the energy output, I'll launch a probe. We can confirm if the warp gate scanners were knocked out...or it it's just a com failure. Then we'll know."

Garret hesitated. A probe could reach the warp gate with minimal thrust, but it would still increase their own chance of detection, especially if the enemy had seeded the area with their own scanner buoys. Whatever Garret and Compton were going to do, they would have to remain undetected as long as possible.

When Garret didn't respond, Compton added, "I know it's a risk, but I think it's worthwhile. It's doubtful they'd picked up a low-power probe at long range, and if they have buoys deployed, they've probably picked us up already anyway."

Garret was still silent, but he realized Compton was right. If there was any kind of enemy detection grid here, it would probably have found Scorpion and Wasp when they passed through.

He couldn't be sure, but it was time to take a gamble. "Alright, Terrance. Do it." A slight pause, then: "As little power as possible."

"Will do." Garret could hear Compton speaking to someone on his own bridge. "We'll launch in two minutes, Augustus. Computing minimal thrust required to offset out current velocity and complete a level two scanning run."

"Very well." Garret was nodding, though Compton couldn't see.

"Computations complete. In six hours we'll know for sure." Compton's voice was slightly distracted – he was managing the probe preparations on his end.

"Good luck, Terrance. Talk to you in six hours."

Chapter 7

Control Center
AS Wasp
Lacaille 8760 System
Approaching Asteroid Belt

Garret was watching his screen closely. The probe had left no doubt – the enemy had been there. The warp gate detection grid had been completely obliterated. There was no sign of enemy scanner buoys, however, and Garret had refused Compton's request to have the probe execute another burn to revector for a closer inspection. He was betting the enemy didn't bother with seeding a temporary net around their entry warp gate. From their perspective, it only led to friendly territory, and the last thing they could have expected was for two Alliance ships to transit from there. Garret could be wrong, but he felt comfortable enough with his guess that he didn't want to increase the risk of detection. Every time they fired thrusters – on the ships or a probe – they increased the chance that anyone else in the system could pick them up on a scan.

Wasp and Scorpion were coming in slowly, heading toward the densest section of the system's asteroid belt. The shattered remains of the system's third planet, the belt was an ideal place to hide…or to find anyone who was trying to stay hidden. They'd had to exert significant thrust to change their own vectors, but Garret had kept it to an absolute minimum…which meant no additional burns to build velocity. They had no idea what was going on in Lacaille, or in any of the systems down the line, but stealth was the one thing they had working for them. Garret was going to hang on to it as long as possible.

"Captain, I have Captain Compton on direct laser com." Forsten turned to face Garret as he spoke.

"Connect to my com." Garret knew Compton wouldn't be calling without a good reason. "Yes, Terrance. What is it?"

"We've had two intermittent scanner contacts." Compton paused. "They may be nothing. With the density and makeup of this asteroid belt, it very well could be a phantom reading."

"But you don't think it is." Garret knew Compton well enough to understand that Scorpion's captain was convinced he'd found an enemy ship hiding among the asteroids.

"No." Compton paused and sighed softly. "But it's mostly a hunch I'm going on. That's not a lot to justify abandoning silent running to go chasing what is probably a figment of my imagination."

"I'm willing to go with your gut." Garret trusted Compton's intuition, and besides, it made sense. If the enemy had come through this system and moved on to the next, the asteroid belt is precisely where they would have hidden a scout. "Transmit the coordinates over here, and I'll take a look and get back to you."

"On the way. Compton out."

Garret looked down at his display. The coordinates of Compton's scanner contact were already there. He stared down at the figures. Intercepting the projected vessel wouldn't require a huge vector change. If Garret buttoned his people in the shells and executed a full burn, it would take about 30 minutes to put Wasp and Scorpion on a direct trajectory for the suspected scanner sighting. It would make his tiny squadron easier to detect… blasting at full thrust was like lighting a signal flare. But if the target was sitting stationary, the rapid thrust was the likeliest way to catch them before they could accelerate and flee. Besides, if it was a scout sitting there, Garret's ships would pass by pretty closely on their current heading – they might be detected even in silent running.

"Nelson, calculate an optimum thrust angle and duration to intercept the projected target." Garret was still considering what to do, but in his gut he'd already decided. "Lieutenant Forsten, I want a full diagnostic on all weapons systems." He paused then added, "And instruct Scorpion to execute the same." He smiled. He knew Compton would think of that himself, but he couldn't resist giving Scorpion's CO a little jab by reminding him.

"Thrust plan ready, captain." Nelson waited until Garret had finished speaking. "Shall I enter into the nav computer?"

"Yes…and transmit to Scorpion as well." Garret looked around the bridge. His people had performed well, not just in the attack on the troop transports, but also in the extended flight afterwards. He was proud of them. Now maybe they'd score another kill in this campaign. "We will execute in 15 minutes."

"Weapons diagnostic complete, captain." Forsten had run the test quickly; Garret was impressed. He'd trained his crew hard since taking command, and now he could see the payoff. "All systems 100% operational and ready."

Garret flipped on the shipwide com. "All personnel, I want everybody in the shells in five minutes. We will be executing a 30-minute full thrust burn. The ship's AI will make an announcement one minute before we cut thrust. I want everyone out of the shells and back at their posts in two minutes. All personnel will take a grade two dose of stims as soon as we cut thrust. The shells have been programmed for automatic injections." Garret paused and took a breath. "When we emerge from the shells we will be under combat conditions, approaching our target. I know I can count on each and every one of you to be at your 100% best. You have my complete confidence and my unreserved pride."

Good, he thought…that should pump them up. He stood up and stretched slowly. Thirty minutes wasn't a long time in the shells, but after the flight from Tau Ceti there wasn't a spot on him that wasn't sore already. "Ok, people, let's go. Into the tombs."

Chapter 8

Control Center
AS Wasp
Lacaille 8760 System
Entering Asteroid Belt

Garret could feel the excitement building inside him, the same electric feeling he'd had at Tau Ceti when Wasp was bearing down on the troop transport. We really caught them with their pants down there, he thought...time to do it again. Wasp and Scorpion had burst into the asteroid belt and confirmed Compton's scanner contact was real. There they were, two CAC freighters tucked in neatly behind one of the larger asteroids, sitting at a dead stop.

"Battlestations." Garret spoke softly, his voice betraying none of the excitement he felt. Wasp's klaxon sounded, calling her crew to their positions. Garret sounded the red alert early. He couldn't see it on the bridge, but he knew his people were rushing to their stations, and he wanted to give them extra time to get in position. Wasp was back on silent running, and with no acceleration and no unnecessary energy use, the ship was a zero gravity environment. His people were well-trained, but zero gee still slowed response times, no matter how much practice the crew had.

"You were right, Terry." Garret was speaking privately with Compton – both ships were at battlestations, and the captains' helmets were on and sealed. Suicide boat crews took survival suit protocols seriously. A battleship was a lot of dense heavy metal alloy wrapped around you, but it didn't take much of a hit to tear open the thin hull of a fast attack ship. You didn't want to die in agony because you were too careless to button up your suit.

"Looks like." Compton was trying to hide his self-satisfaction. He and Garret had been trying to one-up each other since their first year at the Academy, and spotting these ships first was a definite point for him. "What do you think? Supply for an invasion force?"

"Probably." Garret had been thinking the same thing. "We're too far out for positive ship-class IDs, but it looks like these are a couple of big tubs." He took a deep breath. "They could carry reloads for a serious task force. We could be sneaking up behind a major op…"

Nelson interrupted. "Captain Garret, we are detecting energy output from the enemy vessels." There was a pause while additional readings came in. "Energy profile consistent with impending engine burn."

"Looks like they're going to run for it." Garret was still listening to Nelson while he was talking to Compton.

"Yep…we're getting that too." Compton sounded slightly distracted…he was also getting reports while he spoke with Garret. "Should we kick things up?"

Garret was silent, thinking. Most freighters had low maximum thrust capacities, but the CAC had a few combat transports that could accelerate fairly quickly. They still weren't close enough for positive IDs, and he wasn't about to let these guys escape. "Prepare for 3g thrust in three minutes. That should be enough to close before they can get out of our attack arc, and at 3g we won't need to button up in the shells." Three gees of thrust wasn't pleasant to sit through, but the crew could take it without any special protection.

"Got it. Three gee burn to commence in three minutes." Compton repeated the order to his own tactical officer. Then to Garret: "Happy hunting, Augustus."

"And to you. Let's take these bastards down. Garret out."

"Torpedo solution locked into firing computer, captain." Forsten's voice was firm and confident. Garret had really come to appreciate the skill and poise of his tactical officer. "Ready to fire on your command."

"Very well, lieutenant." Garret flipped his com to his AIs circuit. "Nelson, I want a 3g burn, commencing in two minutes. Synchronize with Scorpion. Thrust vector directly toward enemy vessels. Adjust to match any movement by the target." Wasp was going after one of the freighters and Scorpion the other.

"Yes, Captain Garret. Thrust solution calculated and ready to execute."

Garret leaned back in his chair, counting down roughly in his head. His hands tightly gripped the end of the armrest, and his legs tingled with nervous excitement. Back into battle, he thought...his second attack as commander. He'd imagined this all his life, and now he was there, leading his ship, about to attack the enemy. It was just like he'd always expected...and nothing like it too. He was tense, but he felt strangely at home, as if this was where he'd always been meant to be. He was energized by thrill of command, the exhilaration of battle, but the pressure was there too, worse than he'd imagined it. He was keenly aware that the lives of his crew hung on every decision, every word that came out of his mouth, and it bore down heavily on him.

"Prepare for engine burn in six zero seconds." Wasp's central AI made the announcement, acting on Nelson's instructions.

Garret shuffled in his chair, trying vainly to position himself comfortably before the engines fired. The rest of the bridge crew was doing the same. Three gees wasn't really dangerous, but no one was going to enjoy it either.

"Three zero seconds to burn." The main AI's voice was generic, not exactly mechanical, but not as natural as the individual units either.

"Captain, the enemy vessels are firing their engines. Preliminary estimates indicate thrust of 4g." Nelson's voice this time, in Garret's headset. "Compensating thrust angle to match."

Four gees...that's about right for a freighter, Garret thought. If that's the best they can do, we've got them.

"Executing thrust in 5 seconds...4, 3, 2, 1."

The ship lurched as the engines fired, and the near-zero grav of the bridge was replaced with the crushing feeling of 3 Earth gravities. Garret breathed deeply, struggling slightly to manage it.

The enemy ships were thrusting at an angle roughly perpendicular to Wasp's approach vector, trying to maneuver their way out of the vessel's firing arc. Nelson had recalculated the thrust angle to compensate, but Wasp's initial velocity was considerable and, at 3g, it would take much longer to significantly alter the ship's composite vector. Still, unless the freighters could do better than 4g, they weren't going to get away...at least not before Wasp and Scorpion got off a shot.

"Approaching maximum firing range, captain." Forsten had a variety of duties, but this was his primary one. The ship's tactical officer, he was the captain's direct conduit to Ensign Jinks and his crew manning the weapons systems.

"Hold fire, lieutenant." Garret's eyes were focused like lasers on his screen. The display projected a 3-D image, showing the relative positions in space of Third Squadron and the fleeing enemy transports. "I want to get a good shot. We can get a lot closer in than this." He glanced up, over at Forsten. "Advise Captain Compton to wait until optimum firing range as well." Garret knew he didn't need to tell Scorpion's CO to hold for his best shot. If anything, Compton was cooler and more patient than he was. But there was no reason to be careless. Garret the junior officer wouldn't have considered that; as a captain, he was steadily becoming aware that everything that happened under his command was his responsibility. If one of his people screwed up, it was their fault – and his for letting it happen.

"Nelson, confirm optimum firing range based on current acceleration and vectors." Garret had done his own calculation; now he wanted to see how close he'd come.

"Recommended firing range is 2,435,000 kilometers." Nelson's response was immediate. Garret smiled – it had taken him several minutes to do his own rough estimate. "We will reach firing position in 4 minutes, 35 seconds."

"Very well, Nelson, transfer firing instructions to Lieutenant Forsten's station. Nelson could have handled the entire firing process, but Garret wanted to keep his tactical officer involved. He relied on Forsten for insight and input into strategy, and he felt bypassing him could only lessen his focus and attention.

"Lieutenant Forsten, Nelson is sending the firing plan to your display." Garret looked over at the tactical station. "It's your shot, lieutenant. Give Ensign Jinks the go-ahead when you are ready."

"Yes, sir." Garret could hear the enthusiasm in Forsten's voice. Helping his junior officers develop was important to Garret, and he took it seriously. When he'd served as tactical officer on the cruiser Chicago, Captain Lissen, the CO, had been very hands on. He'd micromanaged his officers and constantly second-guessed them. He was a capable officer, but toxic to his staff's confidence and growth. Garret promised himself he would be different when he rose to command rank, and he'd never forgotten his pledge…though now he realized how difficult it could be to sit back and trust someone else with important operations.

"Approaching optimum firing point." Forsten was calling off the attack sequence. "Tubes one and two, loaded and ready. Firing system fully charged." The plasma torpedoes were enormously powerful weapons for a vessel as small as a fast attack ship, and firing them took almost all the power Wasp could generate.

"Ensign Jinks confirms targeting solution." Forsten was staring down at his screen. Nelson and the attack computer had both plotted and verified the solution, but the tactical officer and chief gunner checked it anyway. Missing with a plasma torpedo was a huge waste of ordnance. Wasp carried only 8 of the weapons, and she'd expended two of those attacking the troop transport in Tau Ceti. Once all 8 were gone, the ship would have very little striking power. She had secondary weapons - two dual laser turrets and a spread of light cruise missiles, but nothing with much chance of hurting a larger ship.

"Firing solution confirmed. Torpedo launch in 20 seconds…" Wasp would have to repower its systems after firing the torpedoes. She'd be virtually non-functional for almost a minute after launch.

"Ten seconds…" And if she missed, it would be at least fifteen minutes before she could recharge the plasma system for another shot. A quarter of an hour was an eternity at close fire range; any ship moving at substantial velocity would likely pass out of fire arc and range before the system was ready to go again.

"Five, four, three." Garret braced himself as Forsten counted down. It was reflexive – the ship would lurch hard when the mag-cannon fired the torpedoes.

"Two, one…firing!" Wasp bucked once, then again a couple seconds later. The tubes didn't fire simultaneously; the system needed to stagger the energy drain, so there was a 2.4 second delay between launches.

"Torpedoes away, captain." Forsten's voice was firm, but a little tense. In a minute they'd know if they scored a hit.

Garret was watching the tactical officer, observing his body language. He was impressed with the young lieutenant. He was aggressive, and he kept his cool, even in battle.

"Torpedo detonation in ten seconds…five…four…three…two…one." Forsten started down at his screen, silent for a few seconds. "Sir, scanner reports two direct hits!" His voice rose in pitch – he was excited, and it showed.

He's young, Garret thought, listening to the tactical officer's outburst…but he's good too. And Ensign Jinks as well. Forsten and Jinks had fired four torpedoes on this cruise, and they'd hit with all of them.

"It's gone, sir!" Forsten turned to face Garret, a wide smile on his face. "The enemy freighter…it's just gone!" The scanners confirmed it. Wasp's torpedoes had obliterated the enemy vessel.

Garret tried to hide his smile. "Good work, lieutenant, but let's maintain our composure." Forsten had a great future, but he needed to control his excitement better. There's nothing wrong with him but youth, Garret thought with amusement… and he'll grow out of that.

Forsten turned back to his screen. Garret would want a

report on Scorpion's shot as well, and he didn't want to wait until he was ordered to check. "Scorpion scored a direct hit as well, sir. Their second torpedo detonated approximately 30,000 kilometers from the target." He was silent for a few seconds as he read the data. "Enemy ship is critically damaged, sir. Secondary explosions…she's streaming air. No detectable power generation." Forsten turned again to face Garret. "My preliminary analysis is she's dead in space, sir."

Garret was monitoring the damage assessment reports as well, though he'd remained silent and allowed Forsten to report. He sat silently, savoring the moment. He felt as much excitement as Forsten…probably more. He could feel the thrill, the intense satisfaction. But he hid it better.

"A good showing all around." He turned to his left. "Ensign Randall, prepare to bring us about for deceleration."

"Yes, captain." Randall turned to his workstation and spoke softly into his com. An instant later: "Coming about now, sir."

It was hard to sense the effects of the positioning thrusters, but Garret had been in space for more than a decade, and he could feel the subtle force. Wasp was equipped with six of the small jets, which were used to change the orientation of the ship itself. Wasp had changed to a facing opposite the vector of its current velocity. To an onlooker with a perspective to see the ship's movement, she would appear to be flying backwards. When Garret ordered a new engine burn, the thrust would begin to decelerate the ship.

"We are in position and ready to begin deceleration on your command." Randall paused, looking down to check his display. "Scorpion reports ready as well."

"Both vessels are to decelerate at 1.5g, commencing in two minutes." Garret leaned back in his chair. There was no point in subjecting the crew to any higher gee forces until he decided where they were going next. But first it was time to land a small jab. Scorpion had sighted the enemy ships first; he conceded that. But Wasp had landed both her torpedoes and Scorpion just one. He knew his self-satisfied smugness was immature and beneath the dignity of command. But that didn't stop him.

"Ensign, get me Captain Compton on my com."

Chapter 9

Control Center
AS Wasp
Wolf 424 System

"Oh my God. There she is." Garret was speaking quietly to himself. He stared into his display, mesmerized. He was feeling a mix of sensations…excitement, tension, fear. They'd just transited into the Wolf 424 system, and they were running silent again. He was still elated from taking out the two transports. Until the first scanning report in Wolf 424 came in.

The initial data confirmed it was big, more massive even than the large supply ships. At first Garret thought it might be another, even larger, freighter. Then it fired a laser blast no transport could have managed. Wasp was still far out, and the scanning data was rough. It took the AIs longer to identify the contact, but now they'd confirmed it. A Shang-class capital ship.

Garret swallowed hard. This was no unarmed freighter… it was a battleship with twenty times the tonnage of Wasp and bristling with weaponry. And it was chasing something, a much smaller vessel.

"Ensign Randall, get me a laser com link to Captain Compton." Garret was staring at his screen, waiting for an ID on the second ship.

"Yes, sir." Randall was silent for a moment. It took a little time to set up the direct laser link. Finally, he turned and looked over at Garret. "I have Captain Compton on your line, sir."

"Terrance, are you picking up what we are?"

"I think so." Compton's voice sounded tense, distracted. "What the hell is a CAC battleship doing here all alone?" A short pause. "And who are they pursuing?"

"No idea. I've been trying to figure who might be..." Garret stopped abruptly. Ensign Randall interjected, something he'd only do if he had critical information.

"Sir, we're getting a distress signal from the smaller ship. Alliance protocols." Randall was edgy. He didn't like interrupting Garret's communication, but he knew the captain needed to know.

Garret's head snapped around. "Any ship ID?"

"Working on it, sir." Randall was focused on his workstation. "The signal is really broken up."

"Did you get that, Terry?" Garret was looking over at Randall as he spoke, as if staring at the back of the ensign's head would make him work faster.

"Yes. We're picking it up too." Compton sighed. "No ID yet here."

"Captain, it's the Burke." Randall looked up from his display and met Garret's gaze. "It's a research vessel. We don't have any information on its mission or manifest yet."

"Very well, ensign. Let's..." Garret hesitated, thinking. Burke? Why was that familiar? He couldn't place it, but he knew the name.

"Sir?" Randall was looking intently.

Garret waved the ensign off. Why, he thought...why do I know that name? Then it hit him. Charlotte. He hadn't heard from her for a couple years, but the last letter she sent had mentioned her new posting. It was a research ship, and he was pretty sure it was the Burke.

"Captain?" It was Randall. His voice was halting, tentative. Garret had just silenced him, but he knew the captain would want to hear what he had to say. "Sir, we're getting more info from the Burke."

Garret snapped out of his dreamy trance and looked over at Randall. "Report, ensign."

"Sir, the Burke has heavy damage. Her engines are out, and she's moving at better than 0.03c. It looks like she got caught behind this enemy offensive, and was trying to escape. Just before she got out of range she took a hit and lost her reactor." Randall glanced down at his board and back to Garret. "The enemy battleship is ceasing pursuit. Its thrust appears to be well below capacity." He paused, unsure how much he wanted to speculate. "Sir, it looks like she's damaged as well." Another pause. "It's hard to be sure at this range, but my guess is she's in rough shape."

Garret's mind snapped away from Burke, from Charlotte. He felt a stirring in his gut, the feeling of a predator stalking wounded prey. "Terry, you still there?" He thought he'd left the line open.

"Yes, I'm here."

"What do you think of that? Garret was pulling up the incoming data on the enemy ship as he spoke. "She looks pretty badly hurt."

"She's still a capital ship, Augustus." Compton's voice was measured. He was considered one of the most aggressive commanders in the navy, but in his partnership with Garret he tended to be the restraining influence. "If you're thinking of taking her on we better be damned sure she's hurt and hurt badly."

"I know, but if we can take out an enemy capital ship…" Garret let his thought trail off into a long pause. "I'm going to launch a probe to get a closer look. I know it may give away our location, but I think it's worth the risk." He paused again then added, "It doesn't look like she could catch us anyway."

"I hope you're right." Compton knew Garret was dead set on going after the battleship. He felt it was his place to offer at least a passing note of caution. Not that Garret would listen anyway. But Compton's caution was half-hearted; he wanted to go after the enemy ship as much as Garret did. "But I agree. I say do it."

"Ensign Randall, I want a probe launched toward the enemy battleship."

Randall turned and looked at Garret for a few seconds. He opened his mouth, but he closed it again without a word. He was going to warn that the probe would significantly increase the odds of them being detected, but Garret knew that, of course. "Yes, sir." He worked at his board for a few seconds. "Probe ready, sir."

Garret leaned back in his chair and took a deep breath. "Launch."

Wasp shook as her magnetic catapult fired the probe. The reactor on the small drone fired up and it blasted toward the enemy ship at 40g.

"You there?" Garret's line to Compton was still open.

"Yes. Still here. And you're going to tell me to get ready to restart my reactor because we're likely to be detected now anyway." Compton let a little amusement slip into his voice. He knew Garret well, better than anyone. The two of them thought alike most of the time.

"Yes…" Garret suppressed a small laugh. "…that's what I was going to tell you." He was glad his connection with Compton was audio-only. He didn't want to give the smug SOB the satisfaction of seeing the amused look on his face. "And run a weapons diagnostic. If we go in, we've got to be perfect."

"Yes, sir." Compton's tone was an odd cross between respectful and mocking, especially on the "sir."

"Just do it." Garret had to clamp down on another laugh. "Garret out." He turned to Lieutenant Forsten. "Lieutenant, have the engineer prepare for high-speed reactor activation."

"Yes, sir." Forsten was already reaching for his board, and a few seconds later he was passing Garret's order to engineering.

Garret swung around toward Randall's station. "Ensign, run a full diagnostic on the plasma torpedoes and point defense systems. I want everything ready to go on short notice."

"Yes, sir." Randall snapped his reply quickly and hunched over the workstation, punching in the parameters for the test. He could feel the tension, in his shoulder, his stomach. He knew his commanding officer well enough to realize Wasp was going into battle. But this time it wasn't going to be a troop transport. Battleships were dangerous adversaries, even when they were all banged up already. If Garret went after this wounded prey with just Wasp and Scorpion, he was going to have one hell of a fight on his hands, and everybody on Wasp and Hornet would be in there with him.

Garret had become almost totally absorbed by the idea of taking on the enemy battleship. But he had the Burke to deal with too. And possibly Charlotte. If she was on board he had to rescue her. He knew it was his duty to help the Burke no matter what, but the thought of his childhood love stranded forever on a ghost ship was too much to imagine. Could he take on the enemy ship and save Charlotte? Was she even on the Burke?

"Ensign Randall, send a communication to the Burke." So much for running silent. He didn't have a direct laser link set up to the research vessel, so Wasp would be broadcasting in the clear, advertising her presence. "Request a complete status update." He took in a deep breath and held it for a long while before exhaling. "And ask if they have a Charlotte Evers on their crew."

Randall nodded, but the look on his face was one of confusion. "Yes, sir." He paused for a few more puzzled seconds before turning to his panel and setting up the communication.

"Lieutenant Forsten, prepare an attack plan to take out the enemy battleship. I want a course that keeps us as close to the Burke's projected location as possible."

"Yes, captain."

Garret leaned back, his face a mask of determination, with only the slightest shadow of doubt in the background. I'm coming Charlotte, he thought, though he wasn't even sure she was on the Burke. I can take out this battleship and loop back to get you in time. He paused for a few seconds before muttering under his breath. "I know I can."

Chapter 10

Control Center
AS Wasp
Wolf 424 System

"He knows we're here now." Lieutenant Forsten verbalized his thought. The enemy battleship had just increased its thrust to 5g. It was attempting to vector away from the two incoming attack ships, but its thrust capacity appeared to be well below normal.

The probe had transmitted back a much more detailed analysis of the CAC battleship. She was, in fact, heavily damaged. Her exterior missile racks had been ejected, and her hull was pockmarked with damage from nuclear detonations. She'd taken a number of laser hits as well, and it appeared that many of her systems were running at substandard levels.

"Yes, lieutenant, it would appear so." Garret's tone was firm, a mild admonition to Forsten. Blurting out his thought wasn't a major transgression, but Garret didn't want to let discipline erode, especially not now. Not when he was going after a ship twenty times the size of Wasp. He stared at the incoming data on his screen. The enemy ship was a Shang-class capital ship, which made her one of the CAC's largest battleships. She was a powerhouse, bristling with weapons, but Garret was focused on one thing.

"Lieutenant Forsten, get me Captain Compton."

"Yes, sir." A short pause. "I have Captain Compton, sir."

"Terry, you've seen the data, right?" Garret's voice was soft, distracted. He was still deep in his own thoughts as he spoke.

"Reviewing it now."

"I need your gut." Garret pulled out of his introspection, focusing completely on Compton. "You think her bays are knocked out?"

The Ming class battleships carried 18 heavy fighter-bombers, usually C-111 Monsoons. If the Ming could launch five or six of those, it wouldn't matter what shape the rest of her weapons were in...Scorpion and Wasp wouldn't get close to her.

"My gut is her bombers are long gone." Compton sounded fairly confident, though perhaps not entirely convinced. "Considering the amount of damage, I can't believe she managed to recover any of her squadrons." He paused, staring at the steadily growing list of data on his screen. "I don't see any way those bays could be operational." I hope, he thought silently.

"I agree." Garret's voice was strong. He'd made his decision. "I just wanted to confirm with you." He took a deep breath. "Get your folks ready for battle. Garret out."

He turned toward Randall's workstation. "Ensign Randall, plot an intercept course." Garret was staring intently at his screen. "Compute minimum thrust necessary to close to firing range." He looked up from his workstation. "We still have to rescue the Burke."

"Yes, sir. Calculating now." Randall's voice was distracted; he was already working on the plot.

"Coordinate with Scorpion. I want a synchronized attack run." Garret could feel the excitement building. The chance to take out a CAC battleship was more than he could have hoped for, and he could hardly sit still in his chair.

"Yes, sir. Almost done with the plot."

"Augustus?" It was Compton on the command line.

"Yes, Terry? You should be receiving our projected intercept course in a few seconds. I want you to synchronize. We're going in together, and we're going to plant four plasma torpedoes right in her gut."

"Augustus..." Compton's voice sounded troubled. "I want to take this battleship on too, but shouldn't we link up with the Burke first? Those are Alliance civilians on there." He paused. "And we don't know what their condition is. Aren't they our first priority?"

Garret hesitated. On some level he knew Compton was right. He thought about Charlotte again, possibly trapped on that damaged ship. He couldn't imagine not saving her...if she was there at all. But the lure of the battleship was too strong. It took hold of him and pushed other thoughts aside. Two suicide boats trapped behind enemy lines taking out a battleship? It was the most glorious thing he could imagine; it was everything he'd dreamed of his entire life. His mind raced, justifying what he wanted to do. He didn't have to choose - he could take out the battleship and still save the Burke. He was sure he could.

"We sent a communication to the Burke, Terry. We should have a response in about an hour." Garret knew he was rationalizing, but he was ready to believe his own justifications. "We'll get right back to the Burke after we take down this battleship." By then we'll have an update, and we'll know exactly what we're dealing with.

Compton started to respond, but he cut himself short. He knew Garret too well to think he could change his mind. The lust for glory was too strong. Compton felt it too...he wanted the battleship as much as Garret did. But the civilians needed them too, and there was no guarantee they'd get back to save them. They had no concrete information on the battleship's specific damage. It was possible, likely even, that Scorpion or Wasp...or both...would be destroyed in the fight. A capital ship, even a wounded one, was nothing to take lightly.

"Alright, Augustus." Compton sighed softly. He'd given in. "Send me the attack plan and I'll get it locked in over here."

"You should have that any minute. Garret out." He leaned back in his chair, staring at the information scrolling across his screen. His mind drifted, images of a young Charlotte, smiling...she always smiled for him. He'd loved her then...and in his moments of self-honesty he knew he still did. But he'd left her behind, discarded her to pursue his dreams. He could sugarcoat it any way he wanted, deep down he knew he'd chosen glory over her. He'd done it twice...once when he left for the Academy, and again after graduation. He could have arranged a posting that would have allowed them to be together. But Augustus Garret wanted a trajectory to captain's rank and beyond. And officers on the command track didn't have spouses; they didn't have girlfriends and boyfriends. They were married to the navy, and they sacrificed all they had to the service.

Was he doing it again? Was he deserting her when she needed him? No, he told himself. He would rescue Charlotte right after he destroyed the enemy battleship. There wasn't a doubt in his mind about it...at least not one he'd let himself consider.

Chapter 11

Control Center
AS Scorpion
Wolf 424 System

"Activate all point defense batteries." Terrance Compton sat in his command chair, looking straight ahead as he snapped out orders. Like everyone else on the bridge – everyone on Scorpion – he was wearing his survival suit, and his helmet was on and sealed. His ship was heading into battle.

"Point defense lasers ready, sir." Lieutenant Kiernan shot back the reply almost immediately. "Projected time to firing range, 45 seconds."

"Very well, lieutenant." Compton's voice was calm. They'd known the enemy capital ship had at least one functioning laser cannon…they'd seen it firing at the fleeing Burke. Now they knew the battleship had a missile launcher operating too. The incoming volley was small, only 11 missiles, but Compton wasn't going to let his people get sloppy. If they screwed up, if one of those 75 megaton warheads got through, it could vaporize Scorpion with a near miss. "I want the shotgun crews on standby, ready to fire on anything that gets through."

"Yes, sir." The shotguns were something new, a series of multi-barrel coilguns blasting heavy metal projectiles into the path of oncoming missiles at hyper-velocity speeds. At the velocities involved, it didn't take a very large chunk of osmium-iridium alloy to take out a missile. Compton had never used the shotguns before, but he had high hopes for the innovative system. Squadron Captain Simmons had run some training exercises with the new weapons before 3rd Squadron left the Amiens battlegroup, but none of Scorpion's crew had ever fired them under combat conditions.

"Laser batteries engaging enemy missiles, captain." Kiernan's voice was mostly calm, perhaps just a touch of edginess. Odds were, Scorpion and Wasp could intercept 11 missiles, and it looked like that was all the enemy battleship had to throw at them. Still, there were no guarantees...it was very possible that one or more of the warheads would penetrate the point defense zone and detonate close enough to cause serious damage.

Compton nodded slightly, but he didn't respond. He knew it was hard for the crew to sit there, waiting to see if they survived or not. There were six, maybe eight members of the crew – less than 10% - directly involved in the anti-missile effort. Everyone else had to sit tight...and see if their comrades saved their lives.

"Three missiles destroyed." Kiernan was counting the hits out loud. Compton hadn't ordered her to do it, but it was arguably within her sphere of duties. He didn't see what harm it would do, so he let her keep it up, though he was as focused on the tactical display as she was. "Five down."

It's the lasers, Compton thought...the lasers are the big threat. He was still a bit distracted by the missiles, but he was thinking mostly about the Shang's laser batteries. They'd fired one at the Burke...and it was a heavy laser cannon, part of the battleship's main armament. It had been a bad shot, nowhere close to the target, but the probe reported it was at full power. A heavy laser cannon was a weapon designed to fight other capital ships – it could destroy Scorpion with one direct hit...or blast it to rubble with two or three glancing shots.

"Nine missiles intercepted, sir. Coming into shotgun range."

That caught Compton's attention. He wanted to see his newest weapons in action. The point defense lasers were very effective, but they had to score a direct hit on an enemy missile hundreds of thousands of kilometers away. The shotguns were an area effect weapon...any missile caught within a 2 klick radius had at least a 30% chance of destruction. Thirty percent didn't sound very effective, but successful point defense was based on a layered approach, and the shotguns promised to add another tier of defensive protection to the mix.

"Both remaining missiles destroyed by shotgun batteries, sir." Kiernan was turned around, facing Compton.

That was quick, Compton thought. Destroying two missiles wasn't a very conclusive test, but he was impressed anyway. He wasn't looking forward to the next missile barrage that would head his way, but he'd be curious to see how the shotguns fared against a heavier attack.

"Projected entry into laser range in 12-14 minutes." Kiernan again, following the book on making announcements. "Laser interdiction systems report fully operational."

The LIS, commonly referred to as angeldust, fired bursts of reflective material to interdict and dissipate incoming laser fire. They were highly effective when well-targeted, but it was notoriously difficult to place them properly. Lasers attacks traveled at lightspeed, so gunners had to anticipate the lines of fire in advance. Success tended to be a seamless cooperation between man and machine, the computers calculating possible angles of attack and the gunners adding their own gut instincts.

"Very well." Compton hated this part…the waiting. He knew his ship could damage the enemy vessel, even destroy it. But the plasma torpedoes were a short-ranged weapon, and Scorpion would have to endure the enemy laser fire long before it could launch its own attack. "Prepare for random zigzag pattern, 1-3g bursts, 4-20 second intervals."

"Yes, sir." Kiernan bent over her workstation, furiously entering data for a few seconds. "Evasive maneuver instructions locked into navcom, sir. Ready to activate at your command." Once the program was activated, Scorpion's navigation computer would execute a series of semi-random engine burns designed to confound the enemy's targeting systems. The randomization wasn't total, however; the navcom would keep the ship within preset parameters of its initial course.

Compton sat quietly, waiting just as everyone else to see what weapons the wounded battleship had left. He was focused on the enemy, as he always was in battle. But he couldn't get the

Burke out of his mind. He was nagged by the thought that their first duty was to rescue those civilians. He glanced at the chronometer...in about fifteen minutes a response from the research vessel should reach Wasp and Scorpion.

"Entering projected laser range in one minute, captain." Kiernan's crisp voice pulled Compton from his thoughts about the Burke.

"Very well, lieutenant." Compton cleared his head, forcing himself to concentrate on the enemy battleship. "Execute navcom program."

"Yes, captain." Kiernan moved her fingers over the workstation and, almost immediately, Scorpion lurched hard as the AI executed nearly 3g of thrust.

"Angeldust crews authorized to fire at will." Good anti-laser crews needed freedom to use their own instincts as well as the numbers crunched by the AIs...and Scorpion had a very good crew. Compton trusted his people, and he wasn't going to second guess their shots.

"Yes, sir."

The ship lurched hard again, thrusting now at 1.8g. The engines were firing along a radically different vector, but that change wasn't perceptible inside Scorpion. The vector change moved the ship slightly from its previous line, making it more difficult for a laser battery to score a hit.

""Laser fire, sir." Kiernan drew out the words slightly, eyes on the display waiting to continue the report. "Clean miss. It appears to have been aimed at Wasp." A short pause then: "Definitely a heavy laser cannon."

Damn, Compton thought. They'd detected the shot against Burke from far out, and there was no way to measure accurately its power. Now they knew for sure. It was one of the battleship's primary laser batteries, a weapon designed to fight other capital ships. Compton had been hoping the enemy vessel was down to secondary lasers. They would have been bad enough, but a direct hit from a primary could easily destroy his ship. The hunting expedition had now become a gauntlet Scorpion and Wasp had to run.

Chapter 12

Control Center
AS Wasp
Wolf 424 System

"I want that fire under control." Garret's voice was sharp...
and loud. He was pissed, and it showed. "Now!"

"Yes, sir." Forsten's voice was showing the strain. No one
had wanted to believe the crippled CAC battleship still had any
of its primary armament functioning. The hit Wasp took was
partially dissipated by a well-placed angeldust cloud, and it was
off-center...a glancing blow. But it was enough to rip through
the vessel's engineering deck. The engines were offline, and
there was a fire near the reactor. With the loss of the engines,
the ship lost its evasive maneuvers, making it much easier to
target. Garret was doing what he could to keep up the zigzagging with the positioning thrusters, but they just weren't strong
enough to accomplish much. A second hit, even another glancing blow, would be the end of Wasp.

"Laser interdiction crews, I want maximum fire, best possible dispersion pattern." The angeldust was all Garret's ship had
left to protect itself. They'd be in range to launch torpedoes in
another two minutes, but two minutes could be a very long time.

The com crackled with the angeldust team's acknowledge-
ment, but Garret's attention had already shifted. "Lieutenant,
what is the status on that fire?" Wasp was in rough enough
shape, but if the flames got any closer to the reactor she'd lose
power...and that would be the end.

Forsten took a quick breath. "Sir, Ensign Finch requests
permission to evacuate the affected sector."

Fuck, Garret thought...that was bad on two counts. If Finch was running things, it meant Lieutenant Carson was down. And if he was already looking to smother the fire with vacuum, things were worse down there than Garret had thought. "Ensign Finch is authorized to use whatever means he considers necessary." Garret was angry, not at his crew, but at the situation. At himself. He'd underestimated the enemy, convinced himself it would be an easy kill...not because he had solid evidence, but because he'd wanted to go after the prize. Now they had the fight of their lives on their hands...and the fate of the Burke's crew hung in the balance. If Scorpion and Wasp lost this fight they would die...Charlotte would die.

He pushed that thought out of his mind. He didn't even know for sure she was there. And he didn't have time for self-recriminations now. His ship needed him. If they were going to get through this, it was going to take everything he had.

Wasp shook...Finch depressurizing the engineering deck, Garret immediately realized. It was an extreme measure, but it would work. The vacuum would kill the fire instantly, and the rest of the ship was sealed off from the effects. As long as all the bulkheads held.

"Captain, Ensign Finch reports all fires are out. He is repressurizing now, but he can't assess the damage until they can get back in there." Forsten looked down at the workstation. "Captain, we have a message coming in from the Burke."

"Hold it, lieutenant." Garret's resolve shook a little, but it held. He had to win this fight first before he could do anything for the Burke. He was imagining what the message said, and in his mind it was Charlotte's voice. He knew that was foolishness, and he shoved it hard, deeper into the back of his mind. There was no point in allowing distraction now. They were committed, and winning this fight was the only way anyone was getting out of this system alive. "Arm plasma torpedoes."

Garret had been counting off the time between enemy shots. They were clearly suffering some sort of power loss on the CAC vessel. Normally those lasers would recharge in less than a minute, but the enemy was firing more like every three. If we get through this, Garret thought, that's going to be why.

"Plasma torpedoes ready, sir. Ensign Jinks wants to know if you want to try a long-ranged shot or hold until point blank."

Garret was silent for a few seconds. He'd intended to hold fire until short range, but now he wasn't sure his ships would get that close. Not unless they knocked out that laser battery.

"Sir!" Forsten's voice was loud, almost shouting. "Another laser shot. Scorpion's been hit."

Garret's gut clenched, but his combat instincts stayed in control. "How bad?"

"No data yet, sir." Forsten was frantically working his displays. "Looks like it clipped her port and aft. Captain Compton is still assessing damage."

Garret reached toward his com controls, but he pulled back. The last thing Terrance Compton needs now, Garret thought, was the squadron commander on his ass…he'll report when he can.

"Advise Ensign Jinks to prep his best shot at long range with two torpedoes." Garret swallowed hard…his throat was dry and tight. "But I want two held back for a point blank shot."

"Yes, sir."

Garret sat quietly, staring at the main screen. He wanted to target these shots himself, but he knew Jinks was a top notch gunner…and the ensign had been following the enemy ship in the targeting scope. He and Forsten had proven themselves to be a top notch team so far. Garret knew jumping in now and firing off a shot himself would just be more hubris. You've done enough to get your people killed, he thought…now you have to trust them to do their jobs.

The ship bucked softly, then again. A few seconds later, Forsten turned and spoke softly. "Two shots away, sir."

The bridge was silent. Everyone knew how much was riding on Jinks' targeting. The plasma torpedoes were material weapons, and at this distance it would take almost two minutes to reach the target. Garret was counting down softly. Based on the enemy's rate of fire and the timing of that last shot, he figured it was 50/50 they'd get another laser blast off before Wasp's torpedoes hit. If they hit.

"Enemy ship changing thrust pattern, sir." Forsten was staring into the scope on his console. "It looks like they've detected our launch."

Garret didn't respond. He leaned back in his chair, sliding around as always, unconsciously trying to find the non-existent comfortable spot. There was nothing any of them could do now but wait. The enemy ship would try to evade Wasp's torpedoes, but with its degraded thrust capacity, its options were limited.

"Projected torpedo impact number one in ten seconds." Forsten's tone was edgy, his voice cracking slightly. "Five... four...three...two...one..."

There was silence on the bridge. Not for the first time, Garret envied the ground-pounders, who could usually hear their ordnance and see if they scored a hit. Wasp's target was over a million kilometers away, and its crew would discover quite clinically whether their torpedoes found their way home.

"First torpedo wide." Forsten was narrating the flow of data they all had on their workstations. "Clean miss."

Garret could feel the emotions deflate all around him. The whole crew was watching, waiting. It would take at least five minutes to reload the tubes even if Garret chose to expend his last two torpedoes at long range.

"Torpedo two looks good!" Forsten's voice was high pitched, excited. "Confirmed, captain. Direct hit, amidships!"

Garret let out a long breath. One hit was probably not enough to take out a capital ship, even one that was badly hurt. The damage assessment would give an idea how much Jinks' shot had helped them. He was focused on one thing...knocking out that laser. But had they? At least we're on the scoreboard, Garret thought grimly.

Chapter 13

Control Center
AS Scorpion
Wolf 424 System

"I want that thrust now!" Terrance Compton was usually measured and calm, but he didn't like to repeat himself.

"Working on it, sir." Lieutenant Kiernan was scribbling hard. Scorpion's AI systems had been knocked out, and they were still rebooting. But that was going to take three minutes, and Scorpion didn't have three minutes. She looked up. "This is a little rough, captain." Kiernan was nervous, afraid she'd miscalculated. Plotting courses by hand was difficult to say the least.

"Execute, lieutenant." Compton leaned back, regaining his composure.

"Yes, sir." Kiernan turned, nervously dictating the thrust angles to the navigator in clear, slow tones. This was no time for carelessness. There was enough chance she'd made a mistake in the math.

Scorpion lurched as its thrusters fired at 5g, slamming the bridge crew hard into their seats. A few seconds later there was the relief of freefall, and then another hard burn along a different vector. The ship was zigzagging wildly, trying to shake the enemy targeting. But despite appearances, there was nothing random about the nav plan. Compton was positioning himself for a shot.

"Lieutenant Horton, are you done rerouting fire control yet?" Compton had his finger to his ear, speaking loudly and slowly into his comlink. Scorpion's com was working, but there were overloads throughout the system, and the connection with engineering was staticky. The last hit had taken out Scorpion's gunnery center. Lieutenant Crowel was dead along with his entire team, the primary targeting systems so much torn up junk.

"Not yet, sir." There was a lot of interference, and Compton had to struggle to understand his chief engineer. "I've had to replace two junction boxes and reboot the targeting software." There was a short pause. For an instant, Compton thought the com had failed, but then Horton's voice was back. "I'll have it operational in two minutes…three tops."

"Two, engineer." Compton's reply was sharp and quick. "Two minutes." There was only one person left alive on Scorpion who was going to take this shot…Terrance Compton.

"Yes, sir." The stress was obvious in Horton's voice, even over the damaged connection.

"Sir, Wasp is launching torpedoes!" Kiernan spun around as she spoke, her voice loud with excitement.

Compton's head snapped toward his own screen, watching the plotting trajectory of Garret's two torpedoes. Long range, Compton thought as he stared at the two yellow symbols that represented Wasp's ordnance.

"Project range to target one minute, forty seconds." Kiernan was narrating the progress of Wasp's attack, though everyone on the bridge was frozen, monitoring the torpedoes on their workstations for themselves.

Time passed slowly on Scorpion's bridge. Waiting. Just waiting. Feeling the seconds slowly pass, watching to see if Wasp's attack would succeed. Compton, staring at his screen, impatient for Scorpion's own weapons to come back online. And through it all, the nerve-wracking wait for the enemy to fire its next laser blast…an attack that could come any time or not at all. An attack that could easily destroy Wasp or Scorpion.

"One minute until impact range." Kiernan's eyes were focused on the targeting display.

"Captain…" Horton's voice on the com. "…You'll have fire control in 30 seconds, sir." The distortion in the com line made it hard to understand, but Compton had been waiting for this.

"Very well, engineer." Compton pulled up the targeting scanner, staring intently, waiting for the system to finish booting up. His eyes were narrow, focused. He shut out everything else, even Wasp's two torpedoes. They would hit or not, but his focus was now on Scorpion's shot.

"Missed." It was Kiernan, disappointment replacing the excitement in her voice. "Wasp's first shot missed."

Compton wasn't listening; he barely heard the tactical officer's voice. He was staring, computing the targeting angles, waiting for the system to activate so he could fire. His eyes bored into the scope, his concentration rigid, unshakeable. Good targeting was 99% mathematics and 1% instinct. But it was the 1% that made the difference. And Terrance Compton had been one of the best gunnery officers to set foot on a fast attack ship. He was a little rusty, but with his chief gunner dead, Compton wasn't about to trust anyone else with the shot.

"Hit!" Kiernan almost jumped out of her seat. "Wasp's second torpedo. A direct hit!"

There was a murmur on Scorpion's bridge, but Compton ignored it. His eyes were locked on the targeting computer, watching it come online as Kiernan's shout echoed across the bridge. He had his targeting solution already, but he checked it again. His fingers tightened slowly, pressing down on the firing pad. Scorpion lurched as one of its torpedo tubes blasted its ordnance into space. Two seconds later, Compton's fingers squeezed again, the second torpedo accelerated from the attack ship, streaking toward the enemy vessel.

"Torpedoes away, sir." It took Kiernan a second to realize Compton had fired, but then she was tracking the weapons, plotting their course. "Trajectory looks good." A pause. "One minute, thirty seconds to impact." Another pause. "One minute fiftee…captain, energy spike on the enemy vessel!"

Compton's head swung around. "Angeldust battery…fire! Evasive maneuvers." The energy pulse wouldn't give Scorpion much warning, maybe two seconds. Then the destructive power of the laser shot would lance out from the enemy ship at lightspeed.

"Enemy laser hit on Wasp, sir." Kiernan was a brave officer, and one who would never push off danger on her comrades. But she couldn't keep all the relief out of her voice. Scorpion was in no condition to endure another hit.

Compton leaned back in his chair, outwardly calm, but inside struggling to keep his cool. "Damage report, lieutenant."

"Unclear, sir." Kiernan was frantically working the scanner controls, trying to get an idea how badly Wasp was hurt. "It looks like they managed to partially interdict with their angel-dust launchers, but it still looks bad, captain."

Compton's screen was split, half displaying the meager information they were getting from Wasp, the other side tracking the telemetry of his torpedoes. His eyes darted back and forth, but finally he focused on his shot. There was nothing he could do for Wasp in the next minute anyway…and if Augustus Garret couldn't save her, not a thing Compton did would matter.

"Forty seconds to torpedo impact." Lieutenant Kiernan had come to the same conclusion. It was looking very much like the fate of the squadron rested on those two torpedoes working their way to the target.

Well, Compton thought grimly, if you were ever going to score a hit, now is the time. The seconds peeled away slowly, each instant stretching agonizingly before it finally gave way to the next. Thirty seconds, an eternity…then twenty.

"Ten seconds." Kiernan's voice was edgy. They all knew what was riding on this. Another laser hit and Wasp would be done for. Scorpion might survive a hit, but she'd be a mangled wreck. No…it was now or never. This was the battle. And everyone on Scorpion knew it.

Compton stared at his screen. He'd get the data as quickly as Kiernan, but the tactical officer stayed focused on her duties, relaying battle data to the captain. Scorpion's life support systems were still functioning, and the bridge was a comfortable room temperature. But Compton could feel the sweat dripping down his back, first a single drop, then heavier, the inside of his suit becoming slick and uncomfortable.

"Five seconds." Kiernan sat completely still, reading off the countdown. It was only an estimation, of course. Both the target ship and the torpedoes would be making vector changes. A hit could come 3 or 4 seconds early or as many late. "Two, one…"

There was silence on the bridge, all five officers present simultaneously staring at their workstations and listening for Kiernan's report. The first outburst came 2, maybe 3 seconds after the initially projected detonation point. "Hit!" she exclaimed wildly. Then, a few seconds later, "Another hit!"

A murmur of excitement rippled across the bridge, but Compton's people were too professional to let it get beyond that. Kiernan was reviewing the incoming data, preparing the damage assessment, and she'd report as soon as she knew anything.

Compton was relieved…there were no guarantees, but he knew two hits probably gave Wasp and Scorpion the edge at least, even if they didn't take out the enemy vessel completely. But his thoughts were drifting elsewhere…to Wasp…and to the Burke, which was still careening off into space, its shattered engines unable to decelerate or alter its vector.

"Let's get that damage assessment, Lieutenant Kiernan." Compton's voice was firm, but also distracted. He was thinking about the Burke…and he had a bad feeling. "We need to finish up with this battleship. We've got someplace we need to be."

Chapter 14

Control Center
AS Wasp
Wolf 424 System

"I said increase thrust 25%. Am I going to have to repeat myself again?" Garret's voice was caustic, his eyes glittering with rage. Wasp was hurt...badly hurt. She was finished as a warship, he knew that much. Her main structural spine was fractured, her primary power conduits hanging on by a thread. A battleship might have gone to the shipyard for a total rebuild, but Garret knew his brave little attack ship was on her last mission.

"But, sir...yes, captain." Forsten had started to argue again, but then the resignation flowed over him. "Increasing engine output 25%." His hand paused on the control. He knew the engine wouldn't take it. Garret knew it too, of course, but the captain was determined to take any chance...any chance at all.

The combat against the enemy battleship had been a fight to the finish. Compton's hits had nearly crippled the thing, but they hadn't knocked it out completely. In the end, Wasp and Scorpion had been forced to close to point blank range and finished it off with their cruise missiles.

Now Wasp and Scorpion were chasing Burke. The civilian ship was dying, its life support all but exhausted. It would be a close race between freezing and suffocating, but unless one of Garret's ships could catch the runaway research vessel, everyone on board would die. And everyone included Charlotte Evers. Garret had confirmed it...she was the chief of the ship's xenobiology team.

The battle had lasted hours longer than Garret expected, and both ships had taken heavy damage. Now they were pushing battered systems to their limits, straining to accelerate and match velocity with Burke in time. Garret's responsibility was to every Alliance citizen on that ship, but his mind was focused on only one. He had to save her. He was determined to do it with nothing but pure will if need be, but the limits of his ship's savaged systems were unaffected by his stubbornness.

Wasp lurched forward, her single remaining engine straining, thrusting at almost 5g. But there was just too much damage. The burn lasted ten minutes, almost eleven. Then the engine failed. Garret's crew worked wonders and got it back online. Then it failed again. Wasp was moving at 0.01c, unable to accelerate...or to decelerate and change vector. Unless they could get the tortured engine back online, she would follow Burke into deep space, becoming a ghost ship herself.

"I need that engine back online now!" Garret's voice was cracking, the stress in it obvious, though no one onboard truly understood the true extent of his desperation.

"Negative, captain." Ensign Finch's voice was hoarse, the crushing fatigue coming through loud and clear. "The main power conduit is ruptured."

"We need that thrust, ensign." Garret was still insisting, but the energy drained from his voice. A ruptured conduit meant the engine was junk.

"I think I can patch something together from parts of both engines, at least enough to maneuver..." Finch's voice was guarded...Garret could feel the "but" coming. "But, we're talking about hours...ten or twelve."

Garret sighed hard. There was no point beating up on Finch. Replacing a power conduit with a brand new one in ten hours would be impressive...rebuilding one from scrap in that time would be a miracle. But it might as well take a month. Ten hours was too long for Charlotte. Too long for everyone on Burke.

Garret flipped on the command com. "Terry, our engine is out again. We're looking at ten hours, at least, before it's back online." His voice was a plea for help. Scorpion was her only chance now.

"We're blasting full, Augustus." Compton's words almost choked in his throat. He wanted to promise his friend Scorpion would get there, that he would reach Burke in time to save her crew. To save Charlotte. But he knew he wasn't going to get there in time.

There was silence on the line...Garret slowly realizing that everyone on Burke was going to die. They were going to die because he had decided to attack the enemy battleship. Compton opened his mouth silently and shut it again, not willing to worsen his friend's pain with empty promises.

*   *   *   *   *

Garret sat bolt upright in his chair, oblivious for once to the hard plastic ridge poking his spine. His eyes stung from the air as he stared straight forward, almost without blinking. He felt as though he had jumped over a great chasm...still moving outward, not yet falling, but realizing the ground wasn't there. He knew what was happening, but it was unreal too...like a bad dream from which he was trying to wake.

The line was open, and Garret could hear Scorpion's boarding party. Compton was leading it himself...a gesture Garret would always remember and appreciate. Compton knew his friend would be listening, and he warned his crew not to say anything. He knew what he'd have to report to Garret, and no one but him was going to do it.

Garret listened as Compton and his people searched the silent landing bay, and he knew right away. They found three bodies lying next to workstations, suffocated and almost frozen solid. Scorpion had been hours too late. Everyone on Burke was dead. He could hear Compton's breath, heavy in the helmet of his survival suit. Garret knew his friend would have rather faced an enemy battlefleet than to tell him what he had to.

"Augustus..." It was obvious from his voice...if Garret hadn't been sure before, he was now. "We're too late. They're gone." A short pause, then: "I'm so sorry, Augustus."

*   *   *   *   *

Garret sat silently, lost in dark thoughts. Whatever doubts he might have had were gone. Compton had searched every compartment of Burke. His people found Charlotte in her quarters, slumped over her workstation. It still didn't seem real. He'd only seen her a few times since he'd left for the Academy, and he'd ceased to be a meaningful part of her life long ago. But now, confronting the reality of her death, he felt as if they'd never been apart. The pain was sharp and raw, not the muted grief felt for an old friend, long since parted. His mind went back to that rainy day on the landing pad, remembering his empty promises, regretting the callous ambition that had ruled him.

Wasp's engine was back online, miraculously repaired in less than eight hours. Finch had worked wonders, taking over when Carson was killed and patching the shattered vessel back together. The ship was basically a wreck, but it would get back to base now. Garret was lost in his own misery, but he'd remember to see that Finch's heroism was recognized.

He owed it to her...to go see her one last time. But he couldn't do it. Augustus Garret didn't flinch at marching into hell itself to face the enemy, but the thought of staring into Charlotte's frozen, dead face was more than he could bear. She'd known he was in the system...of that he was sure. He'd sent the original communication to the Burke, and he'd clearly identified himself. What went through her mind, he wondered, in those final hours? Did she even realize he'd known she was there? That was a solace he'd grasped for hopelessly...that she didn't know he'd abandoned her again. But the comfort was fleeting. She'd known he was there...there was no doubt. She'd left him a message.

Compton had found the data chip clasped tightly in her hand. He'd almost kept it, thinking to spare his friend the heartbreak. But he couldn't...Garret had a right to see it, no matter how much pain it caused. He'd delivered it to Wasp himself, unwilling to allow anyone else to do the deed.

Garret rolled the small chip between his fingers. He hadn't watched it...he couldn't. Not yet. One day he would, but now he knew he'd lose the last of his composure if he did. His ship still needed him, his crew looked to him to lead them home. They'd performed magnificently, and they deserved the best their captain could give them. Garret had failed Charlotte again. He wasn't going to fail his crew as well.

Chapter 15

Sector Base Omicron
Alpha 9 System

The two surviving ships of Third Squadron limped into base. Scorpion was shot up badly, her streamlined hull pock-marked with a series of nasty gashes and quick patches. Half her internal systems were shut down by leaks and broken conduits. It was a miracle she was even operating under her own power. If there had been such a thing as a decoration for damage control bots, Garret would have awarded one to Compton's automated repair workers.

As bad as Scorpion was, Wasp was in even worse shape. Garret had burned out her one good engine in the desperate attempt to catch Charlotte's ship in time. Wasp had almost become a ghost ship herself, zooming off into deep space at 0.01c, unable to decelerate or change vector. Finch's people had managed to repair the engine, barely, and bring her back around. The ship could just about put out 4g of thrust, not much, but enough to slowly decelerate and revector for the trip through the Ross 614 warp gate. Garret hadn't know what he'd find there, and he fully expected to emerge in the midst of an enemy task force. Instead, Third Squadron transited into the middle of a full-fledged battle.

The Alliance forces had counter-attacked into the system, seeking to drive the CAC invaders back. The fighting had been raging for days. The two forces had approached at high velocity, engaging in a short, sharp exchange of fire before passing each other. Both fleets decelerated and turned about for another round. They were just about to engage again when Wasp and

Scorpion emerged into Ross 614, behind the Alliance task force.

Neither ship had any functioning weapons systems, so they identified themselves to the Alliance commander and matched course and velocity with the fleet...at least as well as their battered vessels could manage. They would run the gauntlet past the enemy with the entire task force. It was the only option.

The engagement at Ross 614 turned out to be a major battle, and a bloody one too. Tactically inconclusive, it was an Alliance strategic victory, halting the enemy invasion and driving the CAC and Caliphate forces back into their own space. Losses were fairly even, but Third Squadron's destruction of the enemy battleship swung the overall calculation to the Alliance. There were capital ships damaged on both sides, but Wasp and Scorpion had scored the only outright kill.

Combat tactics were transitioning, and the opportunity to catch a battleship alone would turn out to be a rare and fleeting one. The First Frontier War had been fought by small squadrons of ships, vessels that would barely qualify as light cruisers by the standards of later conflicts. Capital ships were something new in interstellar war, and the Second Frontier War saw the rapid development of tactics built around the battlewagons.

Early battlegroup tactics were rough, and the support vessels and their crews were still learning how to protect and screen a battleship. Operations would become very sophisticated by the Third Frontier War, with well-placed escorts providing multiple layers of protection to capital ships...even damaged ones retreating from the combat zone. But in the early years of the Second Frontier War, it was still possible to sneak up and launch an attack on an isolated battleship, especially one limping away from the fight.

With the loss of their damaged dreadnought, the enemy fleet couldn't sustain the offensive, and they withdrew. Garret and Compton and their two small ships had arguably won the campaign for the Alliance, though that victory had not, as they both knew all too well, come without its cost.

*   *   *   *   *

Garret walked slowly across the perfectly manicured grounds, glancing up at the massive hyper-polycarbonate dome and the vast blackness of space beyond. The Alliance Naval Academy was one of the greatest structures ever built by man, a massive series of interlocked modules orbiting a gas giant in the Wolf 1061 system. Under the nearly indestructible material of the domes, the Academy, many sections of it at least, resembled a university. There were fields and buildings that could have been part of any past navy's campus, but instead of clouds and sky they sat beneath the inky blackness and pinprick stars of space.

During the Academy's night, when the artificial lighting of its simulated day receded, the midshipmen could look up at the magnificent vastness of the universe…the battlefield they would fight their wars upon. Garret had always loved that view, clearer and more perfect than any terrestrial panorama, than any visage obscured by atmosphere and pollution. But now it was changed…or he was. Or both. He saw the beauty still, but now it was marred, imperfect. Now he also saw the death, the destruction…men and women struggling to keep their savaged and dying ships in the fight…the horrible, transfixed look on their frozen, dead faces when that beautiful black vacuum took them.

Garret was silent as he walked, deep in his own thoughts, his private struggle with himself. All his life he'd longed to taste glory, and now he had. But it wasn't what he'd imagined, sweet and invigorating. Instead, it was bitter, gut-wrenching. He choked on it. Had he traded Charlotte's life for it? For the fleeting rush of victory? The acclaim he'd ached for so longingly that now tore at his soul? He couldn't imagine any accolades worth Charlotte…sweet, beloved Charlotte. Charlotte, whose love he never truly appreciated until it was lost.

He'd been away from the Academy for twelve years, but he remembered the way perfectly. The little knoll - another construct designed for effect – and the small cluster of stone buildings perched upon it. Stokely Hall, room 311, he remembered. He walked down the corridor, past the bank of lifts to the stairs.

My God, he thought, it hasn't changed at all. He could feel himself drifting back in time, remembering an 18 year-old version of himself, fresh from Terra Nova and cocky as hell.

He turned at the top of the stairs and walked slowly until he stood in front of a small sign that read, "Room 311." He reached out and pressed the intercom button. "Admiral Horn? It's Augustus Garret, sir."

The door slid open, revealing an office that hadn't changed either. Seated at an antique oak desk – the same desk, Garret remembered well – was his professor, older now, but somehow also unchanged. Except for the admiral's stars on his collar.

Horn had long been out of the real line of command in the navy, and his eventual promotion to flag rank was a purely honorary gesture. He'd committed the cardinal sin, the one thing a serving combat leader could never do...he'd lost his nerve. It had slipped away, the ability to go back, to forget the consequences of his command decisions and face the same conflicts again.

Augustus Garret was there to talk to his old professor, to finally ask him after all these years what terrible event had driven him from the combat ranks and banished him to the classrooms of the Academy. He was there to decide if he, too, had lost the driving force a combat commander needed.

The older officer stood up and leaned across the desk toward his visitor, extending his hand. Garret could see it was shaking as he grasped it firmly. Garret had always liked Horn, though he'd pitied the man for what he had always seen as cowardice. Now he knew he'd been a fool. Stupid, obstinate bravery was easy, simpler at least than learning to deal with the consequences of command action. Facing your own death was one thing, but dealing with the phantoms, the faces of those who paid the price of those decisions...that was altogether a different thing.

"Augustus, it is good to see you." Garret snapped to attention and gave Horn a crisp salute, but the older man was already waving him off. "No salutes today, Augustus." Horn could see the anguish in his old pupil's face. "Today it is just two friends talking...catching up. No officers, no chain of command." Horn walked around the desk, extending his arms to embrace Garret.

Garret walked forward and put his arms around his old teacher. "Thank you, sir." He took half a step back from the hug and looked into Horn's eyes. "I was hoping we could talk about a few things."

Epilogue

Garret closed the door behind him and walked through the silent corridors of Stokely Hall and out into the main quad. He'd lost all track of time, and now he realized he'd been with Horn almost four hours. They had spoken of many things, and Horn had told him what he'd come to hear. One thing Augustus Garret knew for certain…he would never again think of Jackson Horn as a coward. There were simply things from which no man could ever recover.

Now he had to decide if he could move past all that had happened to him, to put it behind him…to fight the navy's wars and climb through its ranks…and put the guilt and grief in its place. Charlotte's face was there in front of him as he thought, one moment smiling, an image from their past – and the next, terrified, begging him for help, tears streaming down her raw, red cheeks. She was dead now, and nothing he did would ever change that. Worse, she'd died knowing he hadn't come to her aid, that he'd abandoned her once again.

The grief alone was enough to consume him. He hadn't seen her in twelve years, not since she'd come to his graduation. He'd never intended for so long to go by, but time has a way of slipping past, draining away in small bits until the days and weeks become years gone by. Now he realized, though he'd long thought that part of his life was far behind him, he'd never stopped loving her. Memories kept flooding into his consciousness, the two of them together, always together. All those years he'd longed to leave Terra Nova, to win glory fighting among the stars. Now he wished he could go back; he ached for a single day with Charlotte, a chance to appreciate what he never truly had before, when it had been his. He wondered what life with her would have been, a life with love, but without war, without glory. But he knew that had never been his destiny.

His mind drifted to the tragic days in the Wolf 424 system. He'd been sure he could take out the CAC battleship and get back in time to save Charlotte...at least he'd convinced himself he could. His ambition had made him leave her all those years ago, and now his arrogance had gotten her killed. He would carry the guilt with him the rest of his days...and the images of the life he might have had with her, the one he'd walked away from.

He understood now, at least he thought he did, the pain she must have felt when he left her on Terra Nova, when he walked away from her again after graduation. He imagined what she must have thought, how she reconciled with the one person she trusted more than anyone leaving her behind, alone and abandoned. Garret's own emotions had been masked by his ambition, but now the coverings were stripped away, and he felt the grief, all of it. Charlotte was gone forever...how could that be? How could he deal with that, and with his own failure?

But for all the pain, Garret knew in his heart he wasn't finished, that he wouldn't succumb to Horn's fate. To let the heartbreak and guilt defeat him would be to render Charlotte's sacrifices even more meaningless. The war was still going on, and there would be new conflicts after this one, of that he was sure. He would be there, fighting those battles, making the enemy pay the price for his pain and remorse.

The youthful cockiness that had clouded his judgment, that allowed him to turn his back on Charlotte...that was gone, as was the hunger for glory. In their place was duty, obligation, grim resolution. He could feel the chill, the emotion draining from his eyes, leaving in their place only the cold-blooded stare of a predator. Garret would heed his calling - he would carry the standard wherever his navy went to battle. He would become its sharpened blade, and he would never falter. He would destroy his enemies, the Alliance's enemies, without pity, without mercy. That much he owed to his lost love.

AS Wasp

Barracuda-class Fast Attack Ship
(2nd ship in class)

Complement:
18 officers, 61 crew

Primary Armament:
Dual plasma torpedo tubes
8 – 3 gigawatt plasma torpedoes

Secondary Armament:
2 – dual light laser (500 megawatt) turrets
8 – light cruise missiles, thermonuclear-armed

Defensive Array:
4 – anti-missile lasers (50 megawatts)
2 – laser-diffusion systems ("angeldust" launchers)
1 – wide-dispersal magnetic cannon ("shotguns")

Mark V advanced ECM system

Primary Power Plant:
1 – 16 gigawatt laser-primed fusion reactor

Propulsion:
2 – GDL Model 6 Engines (max thrust – 24g)
6 – gas-ejection repositioning jets

Western Alliance Navy

The Alliance Navy traces its existence to the Frontier Patrol, an early organization tasked with defending the Alliance's first interstellar colonies. With the outbreak of the First Frontier War, Alliance Gov combined the Frontier Patrol with several smaller paramilitary forces into a unified command structure.

The Frontier Patrol had been recruited mostly on Earth, with enlisted personnel drawn from the Cog populations and officers from the lowest levels of the political class. But the privileged classes were reluctant to serve in space, and the Cogs generally lacked the basic education to facilitate the training required by a modern space fleet. As the war continued and expanded, the newly-formed navy began to look to the colonies themselves for recruits. By the time the Peace of Titan ended the First Frontier War, most of the active duty personnel were colonists. In the years immediately following, most administrative and support functions were also moved from Earth to more strategic locations among the colonies.

As the Superpowers continued to raid each other in space while adhering to the Treaty of Paris' prohibition against warfare on Earth, the navy became more and more a frontier-oriented force, with little or no connection to Earth save a chain of command that eventually led to Alliance Gov in Washbalt.

Although an entirely different organization, the Alliance navy considered itself the successor to the British and American forces that had dominated Earth's oceans for several centuries. Prickly about its short history, the young organization quickly developed a significant body of tradition, mostly borrowed from the older, predecessor forces.

The growing colonies embraced the fleet that protected them and safeguarded their trade lifelines back to Earth. Service in the navy became highly respected and, eventually, extremely competitive. As fleets became larger and space combat tactics more developed, the Alliance navy grew into the largest and most effective of all the Power's space forces.

Despite its ultimate skill and power, the geo-political situation generally worked against the Alliance navy, and it was frequently compelled to face the combined forces of the Caliphate and CAC, often alone and outnumbered. As a result, it developed an aggressive officer corps that encouraged boldness and risk-taking. A cult of glory grew up around the senior command-ers, and subsequent generations aspired to equal and exceed the exploits of those who had come before.

Augustus Garret and Terrance Compton came of age dur-ing a period of rapid growth in the size and scale of the navy. Human-occupied space was expanding rapidly and, with explor-ers and colonists, man also exported his wars. The senior officers of the day had cut their teeth commanding the ragtag squadrons of the First Frontier War, and they struggled to keep up with changes in tactics and ordnance. Garret and his breth-ren were the first class brought up from the start within the "big fleet" navy...the first ones comfortable thinking in terms of battlegroups and fleet maneuvers. He and his compatriots would set the standard for naval tactics through the Third Fron-tier War and beyond.

The Gates of Hell

Society in every state is a blessing, but government, even in its best stage, is but a necessary evil; in its worst state an intolerable one.   - Thomas Paine

Excerpt from the memoirs of General Elias Holm, Commandant, Alliance Marine Corps:

Persis. It was...it still is...a major Caliphate sector capital and one of their most important colonies. The system is a choke point, a nexus of half a dozen warp gates leading to almost everywhere worthwhile in Caliphate space. It is a massively valuable piece of interstellar real estate, utterly crucial to the Caliphate, and that's why we were there. The Second Frontier War had been raging for more than a decade, and the scars of battle were everywhere. Tens of thousands of soldiers – and an uncounted number of civilians – were dead, buried in the sands they'd fought to conquer or defend. Dozens of worlds lay in ruins, the battlefields where the Superpowers fought their seemingly never-ending struggle.

The scale of operations, like the colonial holdings of the Powers, had grown enormously in the years since the previous war, and ten years of all-out effort had driven the combatants to the brink of economic collapse. The fleets were worn down, damaged vessels backed up at the shipyards and new construction unable to keep pace with combat losses. The ground forces had savaged each other in a hundred battles, the few surviving veterans pushed to the breaking point. There was growing starvation in the slums of Earth and hordes of refugees in the colonies, as more and more resources were poured into keeping exhausted armies and navies in the fight. Something had to give...the war had degenerated into a stalemate, one that was strangling all the participants. The invasion of Persis was designed to break that deadlock.

The operation was General Worthington's brainchild. It was an audacious undertaking, by far the most ambitious planetary assault ever attempted up to that time. Persis had been considered one of the "untouchables," a world sufficiently developed to fight off any mobile assault one of the Powers could launch. But no one had ever called "Viper" Worthington timid. His perfectly planned and executed lightning strikes had brought the Alliance back from the brink of defeat early in the war. At Persis, he would launch the most daring assault of his career, and it would win the war for the Alliance. But that brilliant victory would not be without cost... in blood and treasure, of course...but also in disillusionment and despair.

As a Marine you plan for anything...anything but being abandoned by your own government, left to die at the hands of your enemy, written off as the price of an advantageous peace. The fighting on Persis was brutal, hard on everyone who served there. But it became a nightmare for the Marines of the 3rd Battalion...the men and women it was my privilege to lead during those fateful days.

Marines stare into the gates of hell every day; it's what we do. But on Persis, we went through those gates...and we came out on the other side. At least some of us did...

Chapter 1

Serapis Ridge
HQ – Force Hammer
Planet Persis – Iota Persi II
Day One

"Alright, 3rd Battalion, let's get moving." Captain Elias Holm turned slowly, looking out over the deep valleys on both sides of the position. The ridge was ideal terrain, a long stretch of upland with a narrow depression running right down the center. Perfect cover. If the enemy wanted to move his people off this high ground they were going to have to throw one hell of a lot of force in to do it...that much was certain. Holm knew they didn't have that much to spare, not without dangerously weakening their main line. His people had landed at a weak point, kilometers behind the enemy's primary defensive axis.

"You all know what to do." Holm snapped out his orders over the unitwide com. "Nothing's changed, so get to work. I want everybody in position *now*." There were landers scattered all around the ridge, and some of his platoons were still unloading and shaking out into formation. He had to get the rest of the battalion up onto the high ground and in position. If the enemy hit them while they were still forming up, he'd throw away every advantage gained by the surprise landing.

You're running the battalion now, he thought, scolding himself, not your company. You should have gone through the company commanders, not direct on the open com. The other captains had almost certainly already ordered their platoons into position – he could only confuse things by micromanaging. You've got good people under you, he reminded himself forcefully…let them do their damned jobs.

The battalion had dropped behind enemy lines and seized the high ground south of the capital city of Tamiar, a high risk operation, but one with a huge potential payoff. Persis was a must-hold for the Caliphate…and the planet's capital was the logistical center of the entire defensive effort. By threatening Tamiar and cutting its supply lines to the Caliphate field forces, the Marines disrupted the planetwide defense network and seized the initiative. But it was a dangerous move, a knife's edge maneuver that could easily end in disaster. The battalion was deep in enemy territory, cut off far from any support. Holm knew his people were on their own.

The rest of 2nd Brigade was going to drive toward the battalion from the main Alliance positions to the north, hopefully taking advantage of the enemy's disorder to slice deeply into the defensive lines. If the plan held, the two forces would link up on day fifteen, cutting the enemy army in two and opening the way for a combined advance on the capital.

Nothing had gone according to plan yet, though. The landing had been a surprise, and the enemy response was late and largely ineffective. Only three landers were hit coming in, but one of them was Major Wheeler's. The battalion lost its CO before the first Marine hit ground.

Captain Jones was next. His company landed first, and they immediately ran into a small enemy strongpoint. They took it out, but not before they suffered half a dozen casualties…including Jones. That put Holm in overall command before his boat even landed, and no Marine considered it a good omen when a mission lost two commanders in less than twenty minutes.

Holm was a veteran captain, but running a battalion was a big jump up in complexity from commanding a company. Especially when that battalion was on its own, the centerpiece of a difficult and dangerous operation deep in enemy territory.

Holm could hear the sound of his heavy breathing echoing loudly in his helmet. The pounding of his heart was forceful too, and it rattled in his ears. He'd known, theoretically at least, that he was third in command. Certainly, the possibility of inheriting the battalion was something he'd considered. Marines took losses, after all, sometimes very heavy ones. But he wasn't prepared for it to happen less than 15 minutes in. Now he had 700 Marines, an entire reinforced assault battalion, shaken by the command losses they'd suffered and looking to him for leadership.

"Captain Clinton, I want your autocannons up and ready to fire in six-zero seconds." Holm was trying to focus on his new role, shoving the doubts and uncertainty into the back of his mind. He had no time for them now, no time to wonder if he could handle the job that had landed on his back. He was in command now, and that was all that mattered.

He was getting there…slowly the training, the experience started to take over. His first priority was setting up a strong defense. When the enemy high command realized they had an entire reinforced battalion less than five klicks from Tamiar they were going to throw everything they could scrape up at Holm's people, even if only to pin them down, prevent them from attacking the capital. "Get your mortar teams and rocket launchers situated in good spots within your coverage area. We had some landers come down in the valley, and we need to cover those teams while they move into position." Clinton's company had come down closest to the top of the ridge, and Holm wanted them ready for action ASAP. "You know we need to be careful with supplies, so I want those guns where every shot will count."

"Yes sir." Clinton's commission was just ten days younger than Holms', but there wasn't a trace of resentment or doubt in his voice. Tom Clinton had known and respected Elias Holm for years, and he didn't have the slightest resentment about following the barely-senior captain's orders. Part of him was even grateful the crushing burden had fallen on Holm and not him. "I'm on it."

Holm looked up at his visor display. He was about to toggle the small control near his left thumb when he remembered the newest suit upgrade. "Nate, display local tactical map. Radius, 10 klicks from current position." The suit AIs were something new, installed right before the invasion was launched. Battle-group Persis was the first major formation to be equipped with the new computer assistants, though only the officers and senior non-coms had them. Like most Marines, Holm tended to be a little reactionary, and he had a modest resistance to change. He hadn't decided exactly what he thought of the thing yet. He was still uncomfortable with it, but he had to grudgingly admit it was a big convenience.

The officers were encouraged to give the new units names. Holm had always been a history buff, and he tagged his AI after an ancient general, Nathaniel Greene…though he'd almost immediately taken to abbreviating it to Nate. Nathaniel was more of a mouthful than he wanted to deal with in the heat of combat.

The historical Greene had commanded a largely outmatched force that lost every battle it fought…but won the campaign anyway. Holm, never a traditional thinker, always found that to be a particularly compelling example of "out of the box" thinking and true generalship. His admiration only grew after he went to the Academy and replaced the partial and heavily fictionalized official histories with the actual ones.

The tech who installed the device had told Holm it was a "quasi-sentient artificial intelligence." Holm wasn't sure exactly what that meant, either in practical or philosophical terms. He supposed it depended on how "quasi" they meant. So far the thing seemed almost human to Holm, not much different than speaking with another person. Except, of course, Nathaniel had access to petabytes of data and could do a lot more things at once than Holm or any of his Marines could.

"Displaying tactical map, captain." Nathaniel had an unremarkable voice, calm and professional. "I have highlighted enemy force concentrations in red and 3rd Battalion's positions in blue. There is activity consistent with imminent movement in the two locations flashing red."

Holm had only asked for the map, but Nate's analysis was spot on, and the added notations were highly intuitive. Maybe this contraption is a good thing after all, he thought.

"Nate, I want you to store all available tactical data from the satcom transmissions while they're active. The Alliance navy had launched a surprise attack, seizing total control over the planet's orbital space, a necessary prerequisite to executing the landing. While Holm's forces were on their way down, the ships of the fleet deployed a network of intel satellites around the planet and destroyed the enemy's own surveillance assets. The invasion force would have its eyes, and the enemy would be partially blinded and restricted in long range com...but only as long as the Alliance controlled orbital space.

"Yes, Captain Holm." The AI's voice was changing slightly, almost imperceptibly. Holm had heard that the units were designed to develop personalities specifically attuned to the officers they served. Supposedly that had caused some unpredictable results during the test phase, though none of that data had been officially released yet. Persis was the first real deployment of the devices, so there was no feedback from actual field use yet.

Holm wondered if the fleet units could hold until the end of the operation. The entire campaign had been a seesaw affair in space, with the arrival of each fresh squadron tipping the balance one way or another. If the Caliphate navy did return in force and drive the Alliance ships away from the planet, Holm would lose those satellites...and it would be the enemy who had the better intel. He intended to get the most he could out of his com advantage...as long as he had it.

"Captain Holm..." – Clinton again, sounding a little more serious – "...we've got bogeys heading our way, sir."

Holm's eyes were angled up, watching on his own tactical display. "I see that, captain." Nate was already filling in details in the readout alongside the display. It was some kind of militia, probably from the Tamiar garrison...third line troops that had no place assaulting an elite Marine battalion. "Looks like militia, captain. I think these people need a quick reminder about who they are facing."

"Yes, sir." Clinton's voice took on a vaguely feral tone. "I agree."

"You may open fire when ready, captain." Holm grinned. These part-timers would run as soon as Clinton's autocannons opened up, he was sure of that. His smile didn't hold, though. Chasing away militia is one thing, he thought, but there are Janissaries out there too. The Caliphate's elite slave-soldiers were trained from childhood, raised in a dedicated warrior culture. They had no families, no life outside their corps. They were feared across human space, just as the Alliance Marines were. The two forces were bitter rivals, and a bloodbath was almost inevitable whenever they met...and they were certain to meet on Persis.

Holm stared out across the valley below. He'd faced the Janissaries before, many times, and his Marines had paid a huge price in blood in each encounter. He wouldn't admit the Janissaries were as good as the Corps; no Marine would. But he knew they were close, very close. And they were out there somewhere, waiting to face his forces.

Chapter 2

Battlegroup Persis HQ
Northern Continent
Planet Persis – Iota Persi II
Day One

"The landings appear to have been successful, sir. Force Hammer is on the ground, and losses are well within the most optimistic range of estimates." Captain Kell stood at attention in front of the general, but there was something in his voice...a hitch, a hesitancy to continue.

"Viper" Worthington sat quietly. He stared out from behind a makeshift desk, nothing more than an old sheet of plasti-steel held up by two plastic shipping crates. He wore a snarled frown on his face, an expression his officers had come to know well. "What is it, captain? Let's not waste each other's time, shall we?" Worthington's tone was sharp, impatient. The general was legendary for going through aides, but Kell had weathered the storm far longer than anyone who'd come before. He was started to get his own reputation...as the aide Viper Worthington couldn't break.

"Well, general..." - Kell cleared his throat - "...Major Wheeler was killed when his ship was destroyed during the landing." No aide liked to report that the commander of a vital mission had been killed five minutes into the operation. But Kell wasn't done. "And Captain Jones was wounded assaulting an enemy strong point." Kell paused, eyes cast down as he did. "They tried to get evac down to him, but there wasn't time. He lived for a few minutes, but the wounds were too severe. We just got the report of his death."

Worthington let out a long breath. Losing two commanders so quickly was damned bad luck. He hoped it wasn't a sign of things to come. "OK," he finally muttered. He paused again for a few long seconds. "That puts Captain Holm in command." He nodded slowly. "Elias is a good man. He can do the job." Though it's a lot for a young officer to handle, he thought, especially in a situation like this.

"Status report on Anvil?" He abruptly changed the subject. Worthington wasn't a man to dwell on things he couldn't change. The landings were done and Elias Holm was in command, and that was that. There was nothing he could do to help Holm now, so he'd just have to proceed on the assumption that the young captain could handle the burden fate had handed him. In the end, Worthington knew he had to have faith in his people. Besides, there was other work to do...things he could do something about.

"Colonel Samuels reports the first wave is ready to go." Kell didn't like Rafael Samuels, and his voice changed as he spoke, a hint of disdain working its way in despite his efforts to hold it back.

"What is it, Jon?" Worthington caught the change. He looked up at Kell, staring at the young aide.

"It's nothing, sir." Kell stood at rigid attention, clearly uncomfortable.

"Don't waste my time, Tom." Worthington didn't use first names often, but he was asking his aide to speak freely about a superior officer, always a difficult position for a young captain. Anything that made Kell feel less formal would make that easier. "Do you have doubts about General Samuels?"

Kell felt like his body was melting under Worthington's withering gaze. "Sir, it is not my place to offer..."

"I'm making it your place," Worthington snapped, and his tone made it clear he expected an answer. "I want honesty, captain. Speak freely."

It was nothing Kell could easily put into words. He just didn't trust Samuels, something he rarely felt about another Marine. It wasn't his place to criticize Worthington's command choices, but the sour tone in his voice had given him up, and now the general wanted to know. "Sir…" - Kell was still uncomfortable with the conversation – "…I have nothing specific to report. I just don't like Colonel Samuels." He hesitated again. "I don't trust him, sir. He seems more concerned about his image and reputation than the men and women under his command."

Worthington sighed quietly, resisting the urge to nod in agreement. He concurred completely with his aide's assessment, but it wasn't going to help anyone for him to admit that. Samuels wasn't his choice for a second-in-command, not by a long shot. Worthington wouldn't have assigned him to the campaign at all if he'd had the choice. But he'd barely gotten the approval for Hammer and Anvil as it was, and he'd had to make concessions. Rafael Samuels might not be his choice as one of the best and brightest officers in the Corps, but he was a first rate kiss ass when it came to massaging the brass and the political bosses on Earth. There's more politician than Marine in that one, Worthington thought. Samuels had come along with the approval for the operation, and there was nothing he could do about that. Charles Worthington was generally considered to be the foulest-tempered human being in all of mankind's domains, but he was a Marine above all. When the Commandant gave him an order he might argue once or twice, but then he followed it…or died trying.

"Well, Captain Kell, the colonel is commanding the Anvil forces, so let's all make the best of it, shall we?" His tone softened considerably.

"Yes, sir." Kell cleared his throat. "Of course, sir."

"Now, would you kindly contact the good colonel and ask him when the rest of Anvil will be ready to move?" Worthington's started at a normal volume, but it built up with each word until it became a small force of nature blasting its way through headquarters. "And if that answer isn't less than one hour from now, you tell him I will come up there myself and rip the backside of his armor off…'cause his ass will be mine."

"Yes, sir." Kell imagined the turmoil in Worthington's med unit when his temper went off the rails like that. Heart rate, blood pressure…it all had to zoom off the charts. He wondered how the general's new AI was handling it…and what world-class profanities had already been hurled its way.

Worthington sat and watched Kell walk swiftly through the portable structure's narrow doorway. No, he thought, I don't trust Samuels either, captain…but he should be able to handle Anvil. He shook his head. "It's Holm who's got the hard road," he whispered softly to himself. "He's the one I'm worried about." Worthington had extensively briefed Major Wheeler the day before the operation, but it hadn't been Wheeler's fate to command on the ground. Now Elias Holm shouldered that burden. Success or failure, the survival of 700 combat Marines… and possibly victory or defeat on Persis, even in the entire war. All on the shoulders of a 27-year old Marine captain.

The op was designed to end the war, but it was nothing more than a well-devised gamble. Maybe Holm's people would break through and hook up with the Anvil forces in time…or maybe they'd be overwhelmed and destroyed before they got close to Samuel's relief columns. War was all calculation and planning… until it wasn't. Then it was guts and determination. And luck.

He stared at the large 'pad on his desk, full of maps and troop dispositions. In the end, he thought, it all comes down to hoping for the best. Once, he'd been full of cockiness, inside and out, sure he could do anything. That was gone now, lost with the other vestiges of his youth, though the image of Viper Worthington remained the same. The invincible warrior, the Marines' relentless combat leader. It was theatrics now, mostly, an iron image he portrayed, while inside he was thinking about the men and women living and dying on his decisions. That's a responsibility men were never intended to endure for so long, he thought grimly. In the end it is caustic, corrosive…it eats a man up from the inside until all he can see are the pale, dead faces staring back at him.

The invincible Viper Worthington. It was an image he'd worked hard to create, one that spread confidence in his Marines…and fear in his enemies. But Charles Everett Worthington didn't feel invincible. He felt old.

Chapter 3

Yellow Sand Valley
Northern Continent
Planet Persis – Iota Persi II
Day Three

"What a shithole this place is." Sergeant Rancik was looking down at his boots, caked with the bilious mustard-colored mud they'd been trudging through for a second straight day. "This fucking dirt is like paste or something."

"It's sand, sergeant."

"What?" Rancik hadn't really expected a response, especially not from the newest snot-nosed puppy recruit in the platoon.

Danny Burke was marching just behind Rancik, exactly where the veteran squad leader had told his brand new cherry private to stay. "It's sand, sergeant." Burke's voice was irritatingly cheerful, as usual. "Sand is finely ground rock, but dirt also..."

"Private Burke, why would you think I'd give a fuck about any of this babbling bullshit?" Rancik stopped and turned abruptly.

Burke had been following too close...he almost walked into Rancik before he caught himself. "Sorry, sergeant." Most rookie privates would have practically lost their voices under the intense attention of their squad leader, their vocabularies reduced to barely audible versions of "yes sergeant" and "no sergeant." But not Danny Burke. The eager private had a strange sort of confidence the rawest of the raw occasionally possessed, a wide-eyed eagerness that overrode the human instinct to flinch from something as imposing as a Marine sergeant. "It's just that this stuff has some impurities that make it almost like concr..."

"Private Burke!" The sound of Rancik's voice hit like a tidal wave, rattling the speakers in Burke's armor. "What are you, a fucking geologist? You will shut the fuck up now and take five steps back. It's bad enough on this miserable fucking shithole of a planet without you humping my fucking armor." Burke couldn't see the withering glare through Rancik's visor, but he could almost feel it. "Do we understand each other, private?"

"Yes, sergeant." Even Burke's nearly unquenchable enthusiasm met its match in one of the Corps veteran squad leaders.

"Now follow me and keep your piehole shut. Maybe you'll even learn to be useful someday."

"Yes, sergeant."

Rancik turned and started forward again. The squad was on point, checking out an intermittent scanner contact about 5 klicks ahead of the main force. They were behind schedule – mostly thanks to having to trudge through the gluey mud – and Rancik was in a foul mood. They'd gone about another half klick when all hell broke loose.

Rancik heard it immediately. "Everybody down!" He flopped to the ground, but too late. The first slug hit him in the leg, just below the knee. His body twisted, the force of the impact pushing the stricken leg out behind his body. Then more pain, his shoulder this time. He crashed to the ground, feeling the air forced from his lungs by the impact.

"Motherfucker," he screamed, his volume impressive despite his wounds. He flipped up his tactical display. It was staticky, hard to read. It looked like the whole squad was pinned down. It was difficult to get a read, but Rancik figured they had two KIA and another two wounded besides himself. That was half the squad down.

He could feel the suit's trauma control system working. The pain was already gone, at least most of it. He knew juicing him with painkillers was the easy part of his suit's medical efforts, but he was still grateful. He needed his mind clear now…he had to get his squad out of this mess. And he had to report back to HQ. Now.

"Goddammit," he muttered, poking at the com controls, trying to contact HQ. Nothing. He tried the unitwide com, but all he got was static. Fuck, he thought...they're jamming us hard. He angled his head as far as he could without getting it blown off, taking as good a look across the valley as he could. The fire was still coming in heavy. He had fallen down behind a small berm, and he was mostly protected where he lay. The tactical display was still a jumbled mess. He wasn't sure where the jamming was coming from, but there was a hell of a lot of power behind it to shut them down cold like this.

"Hammer HQ, this is recon force Beta." He screamed into the com, hoping some portion of his message would get through. "We are under heavy attack. There are hidden strongpoints all over this valley. Request immediate combat support." He slammed his fist down in frustration, the vibrations sending a wave of pain up his arm that momentarily overwhelmed the narcotics the suit had given him. "Fuck," he screamed angrily.

What am I going to do, he thought...how am I going to get this report back to HQ? The suit was still working, trying to stabilize his wounds. He felt a cold, mushy feeling, first on his shoulder and, a few seconds later, on his knee. He winced in pain, despite the heavy dose of drugs in his system. The trauma control system was forcing sterile foam into his wounds, stopping the bleeding and protecting the injured areas. It was a surprisingly effective stopgap measure, but it hurt like hell going in, even with the drugs. The stuff was formed on the spot from a chemical reaction, and it expanded as it was being injected, squeezing and working its way into every corner of the wound.

His mind was racing, trying to figure a way out. They had no com, and they were pinned hard. He felt a shove...then a harder one. What the fuck? Then he realized. Burke!

"Danny..." He instinctively tried the com, but it was completely blocked. He fumbled around, fishing for his visor control. He winced...the switch was controlled by the injured arm, and it hurt like hell fishing around for the lever. Finally, he got his finger in place and pulled. There was a clicking sound and then a small hiss. His visor snapped up, and he was looking at the dark gray image of Burke's armored form hovering above in the corner of his vision.

Burke was leaning over, looking at the med readouts on the sergeant's armor. "Burke," Rancik yelled as loud as his stricken body could manage. "Danny! C'mon, Danny, pop your fucking visor kid." He swung around, trying to lift his good arm, slapping Burke's armor with his gloved hand.

Burke turned and looked down at Rancik. He paused, just staring for a few seconds. Great, Rancik thought...I must look just great.

Burke's visor snapped and retracted with the same hiss. "Sergeant, how bad are you hit?"

"Never mind that, Burke." Rancik was having trouble getting out the words. "Forget about me, kid. I need to you to go find headquarters and report to Captain Holm."

"I can't leave you like this, serg..."

"Do what I tell you, kid. Are you gonna argue with me every time I give you an order?"

"No sergeant." Burke still sounded uncertain.

"Just do what I tell you and stop thinking, OK?"

Burke nodded silently.

"Get your ass outta here and go find Captain Holm. Tell him the enemy has hidden positions all through this valley." He shifted uncomfortably, gritting his teeth. "Tell him they have some kind of heavy jammer around here. They've got all our com completely blocked."

Burke was looking down at Rancik, his face a mask of concern. "Sergeant..."

"Just go, private." Rancik looked up at the young Marine. "Go now. I'll be fine."

"Yes, sergeant." Burke looked around, trying to figure a way out of the depression that didn't expose him to enemy fire. There was a small gully extending back, down the slight slope behind the position. He crawled a step and stopped, turning back toward Rancik.

"Go private! Now!" Rancik waved his good arm.

Burke paused for another few seconds then turned and crawled down the ditch, quickly disappearing from Rancik's view. The veteran sergeant lay back, exhausted. He coughed, a fluid, loose sound in his chest, and he could feel the metallic taste of blood in his mouth. "I'm fucked up worse than I thought," he muttered, laying his head back and letting out a long, painful breath. Then: "C'mon kid…keep your head down and make it back there in one piece."

Chapter 4

Caliphate Outer System Command Station
Orbiting Iota Persi IX
Day Three

"Mr. Dutton, I appreciate your meeting with me on such short notice." Ali Hassan was a tall man, over two meters. He was wearing a tailored silk outfit typical of formal attire in the Caliphate. His beard was neatly trimmed, and he wore jeweled rings on several of his fingers. He was the picture of a Caliphate lord of the highest rank. "I realize that we have been longtime adversaries, but on this occasion, I believe we may be able to work together to end this costly and destructive war."

"It is my honor, Lord Hassan." Jack Dutton bowed slightly to his companion, his eyes remaining fixed on the taller man's. There was wary respect between the two, but no trust. In the Alliance, Dutton would have extended a hand, but Hassan had made the invitation, so he adopted the customs of his host. Dutton was a ruthless spy who had put more men in their graves than the Marines' best sniper, but no one ever said his manners were less than impeccable. "I must confess to a bit of curiosity as to the purpose of this meeting." Dutton was initially concerned Hassan was planning to assassinate him, but then he decided that didn't make sense. They were enemies, yes, but there was nothing to be gained by a pointless killing. Alliance Intelligence would just retaliate in kind. No, there was no advantage in random murder, not for either side. Ali Hassan was ruthless, but he was also capable and coldly rational. Dutton didn't see how a war of assassination between the agencies would help either Power's war effort, and the Caliphate's top spy was only too aware that Alliance Intelligence had the best covert killers of all the Superpowers. Any treachery by Hassan would only seal the Caliphate lord's own fate.

"I will do us both the courtesy of skipping over pointless niceties and, as your people say, get right to the point." Hassan spoke in perfect English, with only the slightest accent. Though not relevant to the matter at hand, he also spoke Mandarin, Russian, and French. "I am authorized to offer peace terms to your government."

Dutton was a master at masking his emotions, but it took all he had to hide his surprise. The war had been trending in the Alliance's favor, but the matter on Persis was far from decided. A peace overture was the last thing he'd expected. "Are you referring to a cessation of hostilities on Persis or a termination of the overall conflict?"

"I am proposing a comprehensive settlement to end this long and destructive war." Hassan paused and sucked in a deep breath. "Again, I will spare us both pointless posturing that can do nothing to benefit either of our nations' interests. The Caliphate's economy is nearing total collapse." He looked up and stared directly into Dutton's eyes. "And the Alliance's as well."

Dutton felt an urge to deny the allegation about the status of the Alliance, but he caught himself. It would be a pointless gesture. There was no way to hide the strain the war had placed on his government and little to be gained in light of his adversary's surprising honesty. The Alliance needed peace, as much as their enemies did. If the offer was sincere – and good enough – it could be a great opportunity. "If I return the favor and withhold my own pointless lies and posturing, perhaps we can expedite our business. What are the details of your proposal?" He knew he had the upper hand. It was weakness that compelled Hassan to call for the meeting. The Caliphate was on the defensive, and if they lost the battle for Persis, their position would be downright dire.

Hassan looked down at the floor for an instant before catching himself and darting his eyes back toward Dutton. He was well aware he had the weaker hand, and he hated being in that position. But he knew what he had to do. "Your General Worthington is a capable adversary. He has brought your nation back from the brink of defeat." He paused again, as if not wanting to say what he knew he had to. "The invasion of Persis was a masterstroke, and his insertion of forces behind our lines to threaten Tamiar was utterly brilliant. He caught Lord Atta entirely unawares." Atta was the commander of the Caliphate defenses on Persis. "Indeed, the fool has already been sent to make his petition to a higher authority. He was executed this morning."

Dutton didn't react. He wasn't at all surprised that a scapegoat had been selected after Worthington's daring operation. And, knowing the Caliphate, he wasn't shocked it had happened swiftly. The landing had been only three days before, and Earth was nearly a full day's transmission from Persis along the Caliphate's Hypernet system. So the Caliph hadn't thought long before handing out the death sentence. If he'd even been told of the situation. Unlike his brilliant father, the current Caliph was dangerously unstable and prone to fits of extreme rage. It was just as likely Atta had been condemned by the Caliphate high command, desperate to retrieve the situation before they were compelled to come clean with their unpredictable ruler. Indeed, after considering the facts briefly, Dutton would have ventured a guess that Hassan himself had ordered the deed done.

Dutton remained silent, looking expectantly at Hassan. The Caliphate spymaster had promised a peace offer, and he was anxious to hear it. "Perhaps, Lord Hassan, we should discuss the specifics of your proposal." Dutton's tone was coolly polite. He wasn't about to show any surprise at the news of Atta's execution.

"Certainly, Mr. Dutton." Hassan walked over to a small table, picking up a 'pad. "We propose that hostilities on Persis cease at once...and on all other contested worlds as soon as orders can be transmitted to our respective forces." He was looking right at Dutton as he spoke. "And we would like your forces to withdraw from Persis immediately."

"Yes, Lord Hassan, I am certain those actions would be most agreeable to the Caliphate." He allowed a trace of impatience to creep into his voice. "May I ask what you are willing to offer in return?"

"If the Alliance accepts this peace agreement without delay, I am authorized to offer the terms set forth in this document." He handed the 'pad to Dutton. "You may read it in its entirety, but allow me to summarize for our immediate purposes." His voice was firm, but Dutton could tell this was difficult for the Caliphate lord. He was accustomed to almost unlimited power, and asking for peace on unfavorable terms was a bitter pill. "The Caliphate will cede the planets Giza, Membara, and Zanzibar to the Alliance."

Dutton had been glancing at the 'pad, but his head snapped up as his host spoke. The Caliphate was offering three prime resource worlds, far better terms than he'd expected. Admittedly, they were on the periphery of the Caliphate. Their loss would hurt in material terms, but ceding them would simplify the Caliphate's defensive obligations in any future conflict. Nevertheless, it was still a strong offer, one Dutton couldn't imagine Alliance Gov rejecting, especially considering how strained the economy and military had become.

"What of the Central Asian Combine?" Dutton was coy, trying to get a feel for the status of the CAC-Caliphate alliance. "Are you negotiating for them as well, or would this peace agreement terminate hostilities only between our two respective powers?"

"I am authorized to make peace on behalf of the Combine as well as the Caliphate. The CAC is prepared to cede the Epsilon Tau system and pay an indemnity of 1.5 trillion credits over a 20 year period."

Dutton felt a small letdown. It wasn't the details of the proposal; the terms were highly attractive. But he'd allowed himself to hope the alliance between the Caliphate and Combine was fractured, that the Alliance could make a favorable peace with the Caliphate and continue the fight against an isolated CAC. Now it appeared the two Superpowers remained allies.

They were offering peace, but they were doing it together. Still, he thought, the offer is a very good one...far too attractive to refuse. The Alliance economy was on the verge of collapse and, despite a few recent victories, it wasn't going to be able to prosecute the war much longer.

Dutton sat silently, looking down at the 'pad but not really reading. Finally, he looked over at Hassan and nodded. "I think we may have the makings of peace here, Lord Hassan." His eyes dropped back to the small screen in his hands.

"There is one more thing, Mr. Dutton." There was concern in Hassan's voice.

Dutton's head snapped back to face his host. "Yes, Lord Hassan?"

"I must have a concession that allows the Caliph to save face."

Dutton's expression twisted into a concerned frown. "And what would that be?" He'd figured the agreement was made. Now he wondered if Hassan was going to spring a dealbreaker on him."

"The forces that have dropped behind our battle lines..." - Hassan took a deep breath - "...you must leave them to us."

Dutton's expression was quizzical. "Leave them to you?"

"You must withdraw the balance of your forces from the planet and leave them behind." Hassan's eyes gazed right into Dutton's. "You must cease all communications with them and withdraw all logistical support."

The Alliance spy took a deep breath, exhaling as realization slowly dawned. "You wish to attack and destroy them? To parade their shattered equipment before the cameras of your media?" His tone was calm, calculating, but without a trace of moral outrage at the suggestion.

"Yes." Hassan didn't even try to offer an alternate explanation. "Mr. Dutton, you know enough about reality in the Caliphate to understand that we — the lords and commanders who are supporting this peace proposal — must have something face-saving, a part of this settlement we can present to the Caliph as a victory." He stared silently at his guest, finally adding, "We must have those Marines. There can be no peace without this concession."

Dutton was surprised at Hassan's straightforward honesty. He must be desperate, he thought. But the peace proposal was a great offer…far better than the prospects offered by continued hostilities. Dutton didn't know if Hassan was bluffing about the Marines, but he quickly decided he didn't care. Seven hundred leathernecks was a small price to pay, he figured, for the worlds to be gained.

"Very well, Lord Hassan." Dutton extended his hand. "Subject to my complete review of the terms set forth in this document…and, of course, the approval of Alliance Gov…" – he held up the 'pad – "…we have a deal."

Hassan clasped Dutton's hand. "And the Marines?"

"They are yours, Lord Hassan." Dutton smiled broadly. "You may do with them as you please."

"Thank you for your understanding, Mr. Dutton." Hassan smiled, the decrease in tension obvious in his expression. May I offer you a drink?" Alcohol was banned in the Caliphate, but the prohibition was widely ignored, at least among the high command and the nobility. "I have an excellent Scotch. I get it through a source in the CAC."

And your source gets it from someone in the Alliance, Dutton thought. He was amused at how those in positions of political power always managed to get their luxuries…even when they came from nations they were fighting desperately. For all the death and destruction, sometimes it all felt like a game to him. "Yes, Lord Hassan. That would be most enjoyable." He followed Hassan toward the small table. "And Lord Hassan, I must ask one more thing from you."

Hassan turned and looked expectantly at the Alliance spy. "Yes, Mr. Dutton? What is it?"

"You may have those Marines you feel you need." Dutton's voice was calm, unemotional. "But you must promise me that none of them will survive. No prisoners, nothing. I don't want to deal with the blowback of live Marines screaming they were abandoned."

Hassan picked up a small decanter and filled two crystal glasses, handing one to his companion. "That will not be a problem, Mr. Dutton." He smiled, and clinked his glass against Dutton's. "You have my word."

Chapter 5

Anvil Force HQ
The Lines of Medillina
Northern Continent
Planet Persis – Iota Persi II
Day Four

"Colonel Samuels, 2nd Battalion has broken through in two places. Major Zander is requesting reserves to push through the valley." Lieutenant Grasso's voice was higher pitched than normal. The young officer couldn't hide his excitement. The entire Hammer-Anvil operation was a high-risk proposition, and everyone involved had been on edge for days. Grasso had been edgy when the Anvil force marched out, but now it was obvious the battle was going well, much better than expected. At least it was for the Anvil units; it was still too early to judge the success of the Hammer force. The fight wasn't over, not by a long shot. But the news was all good so far.

The fighting had been heavy for a while, but it was becoming apparent the enemy forces didn't have the strength to counter the heavy assault units under Samuels' command. Their reserves appeared well below projected levels, and most of their strength consisted of second line units. The Marines had expected to run into Janissaries by now, but there hadn't been a sign of the elite enemy infantry...at least not yet. If things were as success-ful with Force Hammer, Grasso thought, the operation might end way ahead of plan. The two forces were scheduled to link up on day 15, but the Anvil units were running well in advance of that timetable.

"By all means, lieutenant, let us further our advantage." Rafael Samuels towered over Grasso by a good 15 centimeters, his bulk so enormous it almost filled the lieutenant's field of vision. Samuels was a giant of a man, a huge mass of solid muscle who towered over most of those around him. There were rumors the armorers had to construct a custom fighting suit for him because none of the standard sizes could be adjusted enough. No one seemed to know if that was true or just another one of those shadowy legends in the Corps, but it just took one look at Samuels to realize it was a possibility. He'd been called "the bull" as an enlisted man and a young officer, but his pride had grown with his rank, and he eventually cracked down hard on what he'd come to consider a disrespectful practice. He managed to fairly effectively banish the use of the old nickname, at least in his presence...and, in the process, create a whole series of new ones muttered behind his back in private conversations, far more disrespectful ones. The Marines honored Samuels' rank – discipline, after all, ran through the very heart of the Corps. But they didn't really respect the man. He was too arrogant; there were too many stories of him disregarding the well-being of the forces under his command. The Marines assigned to him would obey his commands, but he would never draw the kind of unquestioning loyalty a Viper Worthington could. He was too petty, too greedy and self-centered.

"Order 6ᵗʰ Battalion forward and through the breaches." There was smug satisfaction in his deep voice. Samuels was extremely ambitious, and a notable success with Force Anvil would probably earn him his stars. Finally...they should have been mine already, he thought bitterly, but it's hard to get noticed with the great Viper Worthington stealing the spotlight.

"Yes sir." Grasso snapped back a sharp response and turned to execute the order personally.

Samuels stood and looked out in the direction of the fighting. The front line was about 3 klicks to the north. The enemy had been dug in on a nasty-looking ridge. It was a strong defensive position, and Samuels had expected to have a much harder time pushing through. If the enemy had their front line troops there, it would have been a bloodbath assaulting up that hillside. But there had only been a smattering of veteran regulars among the defenders…and no Janissaries at all.

He walked a few meters, glancing down at the large 'pad set up in the middle of the HQ quad. It displayed a map of the area. His forces were marked by small blue icons, the enemy by red. The positions were updating, and all along the ridgeline, red marks were being replaced by blue ones.

They're giving up the ridge without a real fight, he thought. It didn't make a lot of sense…this was the best defensive position between his forces and Hammer. He'd expected the enemy to make a major stand, but they'd mounted a weak effort and then quickly bailed. Why?

Samuels wasn't half the tactician he thought he was, but he wasn't a fool either. Something was wrong, or at least not going as expected. Could the intel be incomplete, he wondered…was it possible the enemy was weaker on Persis than the scouting reports indicated? Or was there another answer? Had the invincible Viper Worthington missed something?

He reached down and touched the 'pad gently, sliding his gloved finger across, zooming in on a section of the map. Where, he thought…where could they be hiding the Janissaries? Samuels wasn't timid, but he had no intention of running into a shitstorm of enemy elite troops where he didn't expect it. He intended to come out of this operation as a hero and a general…he had no intention of letting Worthington steal all the credit again. And even less of ending up the goat when the great general's plans went to hell.

He hit his com button, reopening the line to his aide. "Grasso, I want scouting parties pushed out from the main line. Platoon-sized." He was thinking as he spoke. "I want them five klicks out. The main force is to hold position until the scouts are at the designated distance." Five kilometers was pretty far out for an unsupported reconnaissance…but Samuels didn't really care if a platoon got caught out too far and wiped out, as long as he got the intel he needed. He damned sure wasn't going to take any chances with his main force. He wasn't going to end up facing the music if Worthington's intel was for shit.

"Yes, colonel." Grasso's voice was tentative. Clearly, he was thinking 5 klicks was far out too, but he was more concerned about the Marines who'd be sticking their necks out.

"Now, lieutenant." Samuel's tone was sharp, demanding. "Now."

Chapter 6

Hammer Force HQ
Painted Hills
Northern Continent
Planet Persis – Iota Persi II
Day Four

"Still no contact with Recon Beta, sir." Lieutenant Masur had been at the com board for two hours, but he hadn't been able to penetrate the interference and reach the lost patrol. "Whoever's jamming them is putting out a hell of a lot of wattage."

Shit, Holm thought bitterly. He didn't like any of this. If they were jamming, they were doing it for a reason. And that reason was a hell of a lot more than just picking off a patrol. Was it a trap? Or were they planning to hit the Anvil Force hard and this was just an attempt to distract him? It could be anything, but one thing he was sure of…it was *something*. They weren't wasting a whole fusion plant's worth of power generation just to inconvenience his people or to take out ten of his Marines.

One thing was certain. They'd stopped his forces cold. He couldn't lead his troops through that valley, not without knowing what was waiting for them there. The approach might be heavily fortified, and the risk of moving forward blind was just too high. But every hour they stayed put, the timetable fell further behind. His forces couldn't move forward, but they couldn't stand where they were either. The enemy had hit them hard late on day one, and again throughout day two, but they'd been quiet ever since. Still, it was only a matter of time until the next attack came…and his people were still vulnerable, deep in enemy territory and surrounded by enemies.

Holm's mind raced, trying to consider every fact at his disposal. He'd had an aching pit in his stomach for days now, ever since he'd gotten the word that Captain Jones had been hit and the attack force was his to command. His…the meaning of that had quickly become apparent. He was responsible for the success of the op, for the lives of 700 Marines, every one of them looking to him to get them home. One of the most crucial ops of the war was under his command, and he was cut off…from the fleet, from HQ. He was totally on his own. I'm not ready for this, he thought when he'd first been told…but he realized it didn't matter. Ready or not, the obligation was his. He was scared to death, but Elias Holm didn't shrink from his duty, not while there was still breath in his body. If these Marines could look to him for leadership, he owed them nothing less than every shred of strength and wits he had to give them.

They needed his caution too, he thought…his careful analysis. It was much easier to wave the sword and charge forward gloriously into the fight, far tougher to exercise care, to truly think about each step. The mission was a difficult one to start, fraught with risk. But the enemy wasn't behaving the way he expected…or the way the mission planning had projected. And that scared the hell out of him.

There was an explosion in the distance, followed by two more. They could hear the muffled sounds of combat from the patrol's position but, with their scanners and com blocked in that direction, they had no idea what was going on up there.

Holm turned toward Masur. "I want another patrol pushed out there." He'd been hesitating. He didn't like sending more of this Marines into the unknown, but he realized he didn't have any choice. Staying put wasn't an option. Plunging forward blind with the whole battalion wasn't either. "Send a whole section…and I want them to leave a chain of pickets every 500 meters. They are to report at once when they lose contact with the lead sentry." At least, that way we'll be able to keep track of the patrol.

"Yes, sir." Masur snapped his response as he leaned over to work his com, relaying the order.

"And I want another flight of drones sent out." The last two had been shot down by enemy fire before they'd gotten a good look at things in the target zone. There was definitely heavy resistance there - that much was certain - but he needed a lot more intel, and he needed it fast. "Send them 1 klick north and south of the prior flight. Let's see if we can sneak around their main defenses and get a look in from the sides."

"Yes, captain." Masur turned then snapped his head back toward Holm. "Sir!" His voice was shrill, excited. "I'm getting a report, captain. We've got one of the privates from Recon Beta, sir. He's on the com. Says he's a little over one klick from here. His signal's weak, but we're definitely getting it."

Holm's head whipped around. "I want an escort sent down there to get him." He leapt up to his feet. "Immediately."

"Relax, private. I know you've been through an ordeal." Holm was speaking through the com, but then he popped his visor. "Open your helmet, son. Let's talk face to face." The kid was almost hysterical, and Holm wanted to try to calm him down.

Private Burke stood in front of Holm. "Yes sir," he replied nervously. A few seconds went by and then there was a soft cracking sound. The opaque visor slipped up and over the helmet, revealing the private's pale, wide-eyed faced. Burke didn't say anything else. He just tried to keep his eyes focused on Holm's.

"I know you've been through a lot, private…Danny." My God, Holm thought, how old is this kid? He tried to keep his voice steady, reassuring. He'd always had a gift for comforting less experienced Marines, especially in times of distress. It was a combination of factors – patience, calm, quiet courage. General Worthington could rally a force of Marines, and get them excited to charge into hell itself. Holm's command style was only starting to develop, but it was clearly different. He had an empathy, a connection with the troops he led…a calmness he could impart to Marines facing the worst kind of danger. Even now, when he was under enormous strain himself, his mind stayed focused, steady…his tone calm, soothing. "You've done your duty well, private. Now I just need you to stay calm, and tell me what is going on up there."

"Yes sir." Burke was trying to control his nerves, but his voice was still shaky.

"OK, son, give me a status report. Take your time…just tell me everything." Holm looked into the young private's wild eyes, feeling old by comparison. Though he can't be more than five or six years younger than me, he thought, even if he got to camp at 15. Holm had spent those extra years on the front lines, however, surrounded by blood and fire and death. He hadn't become what he was overnight, certainly…but had he ever been so green, such a raw cherry thrown into the firestorm of war?

"Yes sir." Burke was struggling, slowly getting a grip on himself. "We were pushing forward…" – he gestured toward the 'pad, pointing to an area on the tactical map – "…here. We'd just moved out into the desert…the yellow sand…"

Holm was staring at the 'pad as he listened. "Continue, private." His voice was soft, encouraging.

"Yes sir." Burke cleared his throat. He was still nervous, but he was getting steadier, more sure of himself. He reached out and pointed at a spot on the map. "Here, sir." His eyes bored into the 'pad. "This is where we were attacked."

"Lieutenant Masur." Holm barked out the command. "I want a patrol to head to this location." He pointed to the spot Burke had identified. "Coordinates 089-7416." He glanced back at the 'pad for another second. "Send a full platoon." A pause, just a second or two. "And position another in support." He wasn't about to send his people in there to get picked apart piecemeal.

"Yes, captain." A few seconds later: "Sergeant Farner acknowledges, sir." A short pause. "They should be there in a few minutes, sir."

"Very well." Holm started to turn back toward Burke, but he paused and stared at Masur again. "Farner is to exercise extreme caution, lieutenant. Is that understood? I want information, not dead scouts." Mack Farner was a blood and guts type, and Holm knew that well. But right now he wanted careful Marines…not dead ones.

"Yes sir. I will instruct the sergeant to exert all possible caution."

"Very well, lieutenant." Holm moved his head back toward Burke. "Continue, private."

"Yes sir." Burke's voice was firmer, more focused. There was help on the way to his comrades, and he felt a wave of relief. He pointed to the map again. "That's where we ran into the jamming. At first, it was heavy, but we could still get some readings….but then it blanketed out everything. No com, no scanners, no sat relays. Nothing."

Holm nodded slowly. "Go on, private."

"Then the fire started. It came out of nowhere…from directly ahead. From the flanks too." Burke's voice was getting shakier as he recounted the firefight. "We had people down right away, but that's when the jamming really amped up, and the sergeant couldn't even get readings from the medical transponders."

"How were you able to communicate with Sergeant Rancik?" Holm's voice was even, steady…a lifeline for Burke to grab onto while he recounted the battle that had savaged his squad.

"I was right behind him, sir. A meter, maybe two." Burke was struggling to maintain Holm's gaze as he spoke. "He got hit, captain." He paused, taking a deep breath. "He was hit twice, sir." He just stopped and looked back at Holm, his eyes wide and glistening.

"Then what happened?" Holm gave the young Marine a few seconds. "Was Sergeant Rancik killed, private?"

"No sir." Burke's eyes flashed back to Holm's. "He was hurt bad, though. I was trying to check his med scanners, but he popped his visor and started yelling and waving for me to do the same." Burke cleared his throat and paused.

"What did he say, private?"

"He told me to get back to HQ and report." Burke's voice

was quivering. "He told me to leave them there, sir...and to run." Burke was getting upset again; the memory of leaving his squadmates behind was tearing him apart.

"You did the right thing, private....Danny." Holm nodded slowly. He was beginning to like Danny Burke. The young private was raw, but the kid's heart was strong. He must have been terrified, but his biggest concern was leaving his squad behind. "It's the hardest thing we have to do, son...leave friends in trouble. But the mission is always first. There's more than one Marine on the line, more than a squad. You need to remember that. Always. Sergeant Rancik was right sending you here to report. He did his duty. And so did you."

Burke looked back at Holm, clearly struggling to maintain his composure. "Thank you, sir." He paused then added, "I had to do what the sergeant said, sir. I didn't want to leave..."

"Captain, we have a report back from Sergeant Farner's patrol." It was Masur, speaking on Holm's com even though he was standing only five meters away.

Holm waved off Burke and turned away from the private. "Go ahead, lieutenant," he said, keeping his back turned so Burke wouldn't hear Masur through the open visor. Holm listened impassively as the lieutenant relayed the update. "Very well, lieutenant. Advise Sergeant Farner to find a strong position and dig in. Lieutenant Clinton is to advance and support Farner's people."

"Yes sir." Masur nodded and turned to trot to the com tent.

"Sir?" It was Burke. "I need to get back, sir." The private's eyes wandered, darting from Holm to the rear...roughly the way back toward his squad. "They're pinned down, captain...in big trouble. They need every gun. I have to get back and help them. I can't leave them."

Holm sighed gently. "I'm sorry, son." He reached out and put his arm on Burke's shoulder, a gesture more symbolic than anything else while wearing armor. He paused, looking sadly into the young Marine's eyes. "I'm afraid your squadmates are all dead."

Chapter 7

AS Courier Vessel
Near Battlestation "Henry"
Orbiting Iota Persi V
Day Six

"The terms are agreed, Lord Hassan. I have just received word from Alliance Gov." Dutton's face wore a broad smile, a change from his usual unreadable expression.

"All of the terms, Mr. Dutton?" Hassan was looking right into his counterpart's eyes. "As set forth in our proposal?"

Dutton nodded and walked toward a small credenza. "Yes, Lord Hassan. All of your terms." He turned and glanced back at his guest. "You may have your Marine battalion…your face-saving victory." His tone was businesslike, emotionless…to a random listener, he could have been trading away an outpost or 100 shipments of heavy elements instead of the lives of 700 Marines.

Hassan's eyes darted to the wall behind Dutton. A tall man stood there, silently watching.

"You may speak freely." Dutton had caught Hassan's hesitation. "Please allow me to introduce my associate, Gavin Stark." He paused while Stark stepped forward and extended a hand to the Caliphate lord. It was a presumptuous gesture for an underling, especially by the standards of highly structured Caliphate society. But Hassan held his anger. The deal was made, and he wasn't going to risk it over a minor affront. "It is a pleasure to meet you, Mr. Stark." He simply nodded, ignoring Stark's hand but excusing the insult as ignorance. He'd have been rather more offended if he'd known that Gavin Stark was an expert in

Caliphate customs and culture. Stark had played a role in most
of Alliance Intelligence's recent ops, but he'd managed – at great
effort - to maintain a low profile.

"The pleasure is mine Lord Hassan." Stark offered his
response in perfect Arabic.

Hassan nodded again, a bit deeper this time. "Your associate
is to be commended, Mr. Dutton. His Arabic is flawless." One
wonders where he acquired such an accentless dialect. I suspect
I would find his exploits...how shall I say, enlightening?

"No doubt you would," Dutton said pleasantly, filling two
crystal glasses with amber liquid as he did. "But surely, today is
a day to celebrate peace, not seek to dig up old grievances? We
have been adversaries for many years, my Lord, but today we
are friends."

Hassan glanced at Stark uncomfortably for a few more seconds, but then he turned to Dutton and smiled. "Of course you
are right, Mr. Dutton."

"Shall we drink to peace?" Dutton walked toward Hassan,
holding out one of the glasses. "I know it is normally forbidden..." - He smiled at the nearly toothless nature of the Caliphate's prohibition against alcohol, especially among the elite – "...
but this is a very special drink for a momentous occasion." He
held his glass up to the light. "A pre-blight brandy."

Hassan nodded as he took the glass. "Impressive." He
smiled at Dutton. "One hesitates to even guess at its value."
He swirled the snifter, holding it to his nose and inhaling. "So...
to peace?"

"Indeed, Lord Hassan." Dutton nodded as he held his glass
aloft. "To peace."

Dutton took a large swallow and gestured toward a small
table with two chairs. "Please, Lord Hassan. Sit. Let us discuss
a few minor details."

Hassan looked back suspiciously. "What details? I thought
the terms were agreed."

"Indeed, they are." Dutton gestured again and smiled as
Hassan lowered himself into the proffered chair. It was buttery
leather, overstuffed and extremely comfortable. "We just have

some minor requests in how you deal with the Marines…and some assistance we'd like to offer." He sat down softly.

"I must have those Marines, Mr. Dutton." Hassan's voice was guarded, a touch of concern creeping into his otherwise cheerful tone. "We must have something to satisfy the Caliph's honor." Or he is liable to start lopping off noble heads like mine, he thought but didn't say.

"Indeed, Lord Hassan, you shall have them, as we agreed. It is a small price for the joys of peace."

"Then what are these…details?"

Dutton exhaled softly. "We would like to help you."

"Help us? How?" Hassan stared back, confused.

"We would like to assist you in defeating…in destroying… that force of Marines."

Hassan just sat silently, a shocked look on his face and his eyes focused on Dutton's.

"You must understand, Lord Hassan. We are willing to sacrifice these men and women to you, but such a course is not without…ah…difficulties on our end, as I am sure you can understand." He paused, seeing comprehension begin to spark in Hassan's eyes. "Our Marines tend to be somewhat more of a…hmmm, how shall I put it…discipline problem than your Janissaries. Unfortunately, it is frequently necessary to do more than simply give them orders. They often expect explanations as well." There was distaste in Dutton's voice, resentment from past adventures with the Marines. "And General Worthington is even more difficult to handle. If he knew we were sacrificing 700 of his Marines to you…"

"Yes, Mr. Dutton." Hassan nodded. "I begin to understand."

"Good." Dutton turned toward Stark. "Gavin, perhaps you could provide Lord Hassan with the materials we prepared."

"Certainly, Number Three." Stark referred to Dutton by his Directorate designation, the closest thing to a rank system in the upper levels of Alliance Intelligence. He turned toward the Caliphate lord. "This data chip contains a complete order of battle, equipment manifest, and real time status reports as of two hours ago." He slid the small, flat crystal across the table. "It also includes all of the tactical maps and plans we were able to obtain from General Worthington's headquarters as well as the most recent intel from our satcom network around the planet." Stark's voice was emotionless, his expression utterly non-committal. "Those satcom assets will be deactivated in…" – he glanced at the chronometer on his wrist – "…exactly one hour and forty-seven minutes."

"Well, Mr. Dutton…" – Hassan glanced over toward the frozen figure standing next to him – "…and Mr. Stark, I am impressed to say the least." He reached out and took the chip in his hand. "This will all prove very useful, I am sure. Thank you, gentlemen." He suppressed a small shiver. The data that Dutton's protégé had provided would be extremely useful…but something about the man troubled him. There was a coldness there, almost a lack of humanity. Hassan had spent a lifetime plying his trade ruthlessly, but something about Gavin Stark was unsettling, even to his hardened sensibilities. Don't be a fool, he thought, pushing back the strange thoughts…he's just one of Dutton's goons. But he still felt a coldness in his gut.

"No thanks are required." Dutton responded. "Just use the information and rid us both of these troublesome Marines. I fear if the matter drags on too long, we all risk unpleasant blowback." He raised his glass to his lips, draining the last of the precious liquid.

"I assure you, Mr. Dutton, we shall complete the operation as quickly as possible." Hassan drank the last of his brandy and rose to leave.

"And, Lord Hassan?"

"Yes, Mr. Dutton?"

"As we discussed previously…" – Dutton's face wore the same satisfied smile – "…no survivors please."

Chapter 8

Battlegroup Persis HQ
Northern Continent
Planet Persis – Iota Persi II
Day Seven

"General Worthington, we're getting a Priority One transmission notification from fleet command." Captain Kell couldn't hide the surprise in his voice. The fleet used Priority One communiques with great care. Whatever it was about, something big was up.

Worthington had been staring at the tactical map, his face contorted into a concerned frown. The Anvil units were well ahead of target, but contact with the Hammer force had been intermittent. The enemy was jamming them hard, and it looked like they were stopped in place by heavy enemy resistance, unable to move forward. They weren't very far behind schedule – at least not yet - but Worthington was still worried. It took a lot of power to jam so effectively. Why would the enemy waste so many resources blocking routine communications? Especially when they were putting up such a weak fight against the Anvil forces. Colonel Samuels was trying to portray Anvil's rapid advance as a brilliant assault by his troops, but Worthington could recognize a token defense when he saw it.

His head snapped around at Kell's words. "Pipe it through as soon as it comes in, captain."

What the hell, he thought…what could this be? Maybe fleet command had some intel on Hammer. Something had been eating at Worthington ever since Samuels reported his rapid advance. The Janissaries. Where were the Janissaries? He knew

the elite Caliphate troops were somewhere on the planet, but he
had no idea where. They were dodging the satellite surveillance,
hidden in some wood or underground bunkers...somewhere
they couldn't be seen. Anvil hadn't reported any contact with
the enemy's front line troops, and Worthington was sure they
hadn't encountered any. If they'd been up against Janissaries
Samuels' people would be fighting for every centimeter right
now, not advancing 3 klicks a day. So where the hell were they?

Kell sat quietly, staring at the screen, waiting for the transmission to commence. A minute passed, maybe 90 seconds,
then the board lit up. He hit a switch and nodded to Worthington. "On your line, sir."

"Worthington here."

"General Worthington, Admiral Clement here. I have news."
Clement was the fleet commander...and marginally Worthington's superior. "Let me get right to the point. The war is over."

Worthington rarely allowed himself to be surprised, but this
time he sat silently, struggling for words.

"Yes, you heard me, Charles." Clement had a reputation for
being nearly as irascible as Worthington, but now he couldn't
keep the cheer from his voice. "It's over, my friend. It's over."

"I can't believe it." Not a very military thing to say, he
thought, but it was all he had. The news was so overwhelming,
so sudden...it just didn't seem right. He couldn't get his mind
wrapped around the idea. "I didn't know there were even nego-
tiations going on." It was all he could think to add.

"Neither did I. Not until this morning. Apparently, the
whole thing was very hush hush. They just signed the treaty
yesterday. We got word from Commnet a few minutes ago. But
it's over."

Worthington just stared out across the HQ quad. "My
God..." He just sat silently for another few seconds, his mouth
wide open, trying to think of something to say. Finally: "So, do
you have orders for me?"

"I do. The communique had directives for both of us."
The cheerfulness in Clement's tone continued, but Worthington thought he heard something else...a passing doubt of some

kind, perhaps. He'd known Clement for decades, and he was sure there was something uncomfortable in his friend's voice. "All forces are to stand down immediately and hold position pending further instructions."

Worthington smiled. "That's an order I will carry out with great pleasure." He paused, feeling a sudden wave of discomfort, despite his joy. It all seemed too sudden…too good to be true. "Assuming, of course, our adversaries have received their corresponding orders," he added. He damned well wasn't going to order his people to stop shooting until the enemy did. Worthington had a reputation for aggression, but in truth, he was thrilled at the prospect of peace. As long as everything was on the up and up.

"They have." Clement's voice was back to its cheerful tone, whatever doubts that had momentarily surfaced re-submerged. "I have confirmed it with Admiral Sulieman."

Worthington let out a long sigh. Ten years of war. A decade of non-stop fighting that saw the Alliance driven to the brink of total defeat only to claw its way back, one bloody campaign at a time, to victory. At least he assumed it was a victory. He hadn't seen the documents yet. For all he knew, the politicians had bargained away the advantage his men and women had fought and died to attain. But that wasn't likely. The politicians cared less for the suffering of their soldiers than they should, but they were greedy for the gains their warriors could obtain for them. He was sure Alliance Gov had wrung every advantage to be gotten from the enemy.

"There's more, Charles." There was a hitch in Clement's voice, the discomfort returning to his tone again despite his best efforts to suppress it. "We'll be commencing the evac of all ground forces on the planet within 24 hours…and that means you need to get your people ready ASAP." Another uncomfortable pause then: "We are to be completely off-world in 72 hours."

Worthington felt a renewed jolt of concern. "Complete evac in three days? What the hell is the rush?" There was a flash of inquisitive anger in his tone, though it wasn't directed at

Clement. The admiral was a good man, one who had Worthington's complete respect. Clement was just a messenger, one who sounded like he had his own concerns about the whole thing. But Worthington was still getting angry. He and Clement were in joint command of the whole operation, and it was starting to sound like they were getting incomplete information. He paused, running his mind over his entire OB. Three days was a very short period to withdraw a force the size of Battlegroup Persis. It was almost unprecedented. He was as excited as anyone at the prospect of peace, but the urgency of the withdrawal worried him. It didn't make sense. There had to be something he didn't know.

"I know it's fast, Charles." Clement ignored Worthington's angry tone...he knew it hadn't been intended for him. "But those are our orders, and they are explicit." He paused then added, "There's no point in us second-guessing. Both of us have full plates getting your people offworld in three days."

Worthington snorted loudly. "Full plate doesn't describe it. I'm not even sure it can be done." The anger slipped away as his mind focused on the practical concerns of moving almost 8,000 fully armored Marines and their equipment off planet in less than three days. Even in the best case scenario, he'd be destroying most of his equipment so he could focus on just embarking his people. "How soon can you get a wave of boats down here?"

It was Clement's turn to let out a long sigh. "Can you be ready in three hours?" he blurted out suddenly. "I think I can get a partial wave down by then."

"Sure, three hours is good." A tiny smile crossed Worthington's lips. Three hours was a damned short time to have anything ready, but he wasn't about to let the navy show him up. If Clement could get boats down in five minutes, he'd have Marines ready to embark in four. "I'll send up the wounded first."

"Then let's get to it." Clement's tone was businesslike, but the concern was there too, creeping back in. The admiral was as uneasy as Worthington. "Let's do this right, Charles. Meticulous. By the book. And let's keep our eyes open."

"I'm with you, Tom. All the way. Worthington out."

He turned to face Kell. "Start working on an evac plan, lieutenant, beginning with the field hospitals. I want the wounded ready to evac in 2 hours 45 minutes." He hesitated for a few seconds. "But first, get me a line to Lord Samash." Samash was the enemy ground forces commander, Worthington's Caliphate counterpart. "We have a ceasefire to declare, and it's going to take two of us to make it work." He wanted to be happy when he said it, but the worry was still there, eating away at him.

Chapter 9

AS Belleau Wood
Mid-Level Orbit
Planet Persis – Iota Persi II
Day Nine

"All ground troops are off the surface now, sir." Kell was reading reports on his 'pad as he followed Worthington through the hatch of the shuttle and onto the gray plasti-steel of Belleau Wood's landing deck. "That is with the exception of Force Hammer, of course." He glanced down and read for a few seconds before continuing. "The first wave of transports is scheduled to depart in 30 minutes to begin their evac, sir."

Worthington stepped through the hatch and walked across the landing bay toward the armory, his heavy steel boots clanging loudly on the deck. His initial euphoria at the prospect of peace had faded, overwhelmed first by unfocused concern...and later by a growing anger. "This is the most fucked up evacuation plan I've ever seen." He'd been stonewalled ever since he heard about the peace treaty, and he was fed up with it. "Who the hell planned this clusterfuck, anyway? Force Hammer should have been the first troops evac'd...not the last. Why the hell is Alliance Gov telling me how I can withdraw my Marines?" He turned and looked back toward Kell, the aide instinctively backing away from Worthington's withering glare.

Kell took a deep breath. He knew Worthington was close to one of his rages. The general was a virtual force of nature, especially when his almost uncontrollable temper kicked in. Kell had won the respect of the entire Corps by lasting so long as Worthington's aide, and he'd done it largely by knowing when to stand aside and let a storm blow itself out. The Marines loved their fiery general, but preferably from a safe distance. Charles Worthington could tear down a veteran sergeant in half a minute, without taking his attention away from whatever other tasks occupied him. He'd done it many times, though fewer than the stories would suggest. It was the legend as much as the reality that inspired his warriors and intimidated his enemies. It served his purposes, and he did what he could to feed the legend. His men and women would follow him into places they wouldn't dare tread if they'd known he was a mere mortal.

"Well, sir, I can't speak to the prioritizations, but at least most of the force has been evac'd." Kell agreed with Worthington to an extent…he didn't see why the embarkation was such a rush job, and he couldn't understand the high command's interference in routine details. But they had successfully pulled most of their forces off the planet, and they'd done it in just over two days. In a few more hours, when the Hammer troops were back aboard their transports, it would be finished. The fight for Persis would be done…the war would be over. "The Hammer forces are much closer to the Caliphate capital. Perhaps that has something to do with the specified embarkation plan." He realized it didn't make much sense as he listened to it come out of his mouth, but it was all he had to offer. He really had no idea why Alliance Gov had provided such detailed orders for the withdrawal, but then it wasn't the first time he'd been at a loss to explain the dictates of the Alliance's political masters.

The heavy steel doors of the armory slid open as they approached, revealing long rows of harnesses. Most of them held suits of armor, blackened and pitted from recent action. Worthington had come up in the last wave, and most of the Marines from the Anvil and HQ forces had already embarked. The armorers would face weeks of work repairing and re-arming the fighting suits, though with the declaration of peace, it didn't seem likely they would be needed any time soon.

"I'll feel better when everyone is off-planet." Worthington backed into one of the harnesses, expertly guiding his suit into the locking bolts. "This whole thing still stinks to me, and I don't like leaving any of my people behind." Worthington had wanted to shuttle over to Hammer's location and come up with Holm and his people, but he'd been expressly ordered to remain with the HQ group. "There's another shoe to drop...I can feel it." There was a loud cracking sound as Worthington popped his suit and stepped out, buck naked and covered in almost two weeks of sweat and grime. A fighting suit kept you fed, medicated, and tended to your normal bodily functions...but they hadn't developed armor yet that offered a hot shower. "Something's wrong." He was shaking his head in disgust as he opened a small locker and pulled out a gray jumpsuit.

Kell popped his suit and jumped out next to Worthington. He leaned down, reaching into one of the lockers and grabbing his own set of the zip-up fatigues. "It was sudden, sir, but we can't know everything involved. There must be a reason the evac was so rushed." He climbed into the suit and zipped it. Then he pulled out a pair of soft rubber-soled shoes and slipped them on.

"I hope you're right, captain." Worthington slid on his second shoe and stood up. He turned and looked over toward Kell. There was a long, hot shower in his future, but it was going to wait until all his people were back on their ships. "Let's get to the command center. I want to monitor Hammer's evac." He took a small comlink from the locker and slipped it into his ear before turning and walking across the armory and opening the hatch to the main corridor. Kell followed right on his heels, still jamming his foot into one of his shoes.

"General Worthington." His com crackled to life a few seconds later. "This is Captain Craig in the combat command center."

"Yes captain..." – Worthington's response was instantaneous – "...what is it?"

"Sir, there have been several nuclear explosions in orbit. It doesn't appear any attacks were targeted against the fleet, but we just lost contact with Force Hammer, sir."

Worthington stopped in place. "All contact?"

"Yes, general." Worthington knew what the captain was

going to say before it came through on the com. "The detonations appear to have generated considerable EMP, and the after-effects are jamming our orbit-to-surface communications. Admiral Clement initially placed the fleet on alert, but it was canceled a few minutes later without explanation. I've been unable to reach the flagship since. We have a clear line, but they are not responding."

"Captain, I want all units on immediate alert. First and Second Battalions are to report…" He could hear a strange hollowness on the com. "Captain? Captain Craig?"

"I'm afraid I have had to temporarily disable your communications, General Worthington." The voice came from behind, and the general snapped around just in time to see half a dozen armed men walk around the corner.

"What is the meaning of this?" Worthington's roar seemed to rattle the walls.

"I intend you no harm, general, I assure you."

Worthington's eyes focused on the man speaking, the apparent leader of the group. He recognized him, though it took a few seconds for it to gel. He was an Alliance Intelligence operative, a very high ranking one if he remembered correctly. "Look, Mr…Dutton, isn't it?" Worthington walked down the hall, glaring angrily. He completely ignored the armed men and the assault rifles pointed at his chest. "I don't have time for whatever bullshit this is, so if you just…"

"I am sorry, general, but I am afraid I have orders from the highest authority to temporarily detain you and your aide." He stepped toward Worthington and handed him a small 'pad. "I must ask you to come along voluntarily, or we will be forced to restrain you and arrest you for insubordination."

Kell felt a chill work through his body as he watched in astonishment. The senior field commander of the Marine Corps was being arrested. He knew Viper Worthington…far better than these Alliance Intelligence hacks did, and he didn't see the general going along peacefully.

He was sure the Marines on board would intervene…if they knew what was happening. These operatives may have cut the comlinks, Kell thought, but he still had a portable field link in his pocket. It was a backup unit designed for use in case of an armor failure on the battlefield. Normally, he'd have left it in his locker, but it had been a little staticky when he'd last used it, and he wanted to take it to the lab and get it checked out. There was no way to pull it out and contact anyone, not before the agents grabbed it…or just shot him. But he managed to put his hand in his pocket and flip it on without anyone noticing. The unit would be on the Marine emergency frequency, which the thugs standing in the corridor were hopefully not monitoring. He couldn't call for help, but he might be able to let other Marines know what was happening. That just might be enough.

"Why is Alliance Intelligence arresting General Worthington?" Kell almost shouted the question, speaking for the benefit of anyone listening to his com unit, but trying to sound like he was losing just his temper.

"Silence, captain." Dutton's tone was sharp, icy. "Do not make the matter worse by resisting. You will both be released after a short confinement if you cooperate. If not, I'm afraid things could be far less pleasant."

"Mr. Dutton…" – Worthington's voice bellowed from his throat with all the subtlety of an erupting volcano – "…I am quite finished with this nonsense." He turned and started back down the corridor, away from the cluster of guards.

"I am warning you for the last time, general." Dutton did not raise his voice, but the threat was unmistakable in his tone. "Surrender at once." He gestured with his arm, and the guards raised their rifles.

Worthington stopped. His anger was surging, but he clamped down hard on it, grimly controlling himself. He'd play for time. It was the smart play. Getting shot here wasn't going to help anything, and he'd probably get poor Kell killed too if he made a stand. They may have him captive, but they were on a ship full of Marines, and Dutton was going to have a hard time keeping him a prisoner here or sneaking him off with no one knowing.

"This is far from over, Dutton." His voice was like solid ice. He stood stone still, staring into the spymaster's eyes with a blazing hatred. "Far from over," he repeated, as the guards ran up and put shackles on his wrists.

Chapter 10

Anvil Force HQ
Yellow Sand Valley
Northern Continent
Planet Persis – Iota Persi II
Day Nine

Holm was nervous. It didn't make sense. None of it. He wanted to give himself up to joy, to rejoice and celebrate the peace like everyone else seemed to be doing. But something was wrong. He didn't know what it was, but he was convinced, and he just couldn't put the nagging feeling aside. He was tense, unsettled. He'd come down hard on anyone who started celebrating, reminding them they were still on active duty in a combat zone. There would be time enough for that nonsense aboard ship. He wasn't going to tolerate it on the surface of an enemy planet. Let them think he was a first class, titanium hardass if they wanted to…he was only concerned with getting them off this rock alive. If he was wrong, he'd be the first one to admit it…and the drinks would be on him. But he wasn't wrong. He was sure of it.

"The first wave of landers should be launching shortly, sir." Masur stood just behind Holm, looking out over the valley filled with Marines. There was activity everywhere, the men and women of Force Hammer rushing around across the hillsides like a swarm of ants, preparing to ship out. Masur knew they wanted to celebrate the coming of peace, but they were following Holm's orders to the letter. Every work party was accompanied by a squad fully prepped for battle. Masur knew Holm well enough to be sure that would continue…until the last squad to board was covering the second to last. "That would put them on the ground in about 35 minutes, captain."

"I want all defenses manned until the last wave embarks." The orders were redundant…Holm had given several versions of the same command already. He turned to look back at his aide. "And God himself won't be able to help the first sentry I find who lets his guard down."

"Yes sir." Masur was beginning to feel unsettled himself. He couldn't understand at first why Holm was so edgy, but now it was starting to get to him, and he began to have his own doubts. He was beginning to question the suddenness of the peace… and to wonder why their isolated force was the last to embark. "I will make sure all defensive protocols are rigidly observed."

Holm walked slowly across the flat, sandy area just outside the HQ tent, staring out across the open plain. It was an ugly piece of ground, he thought, flat and covered with bilious yellow sand. The water table was high and, with the constant moisture, the sand felt more like a viscous clay that clung to boots, armor, equipment. It'd be a bitch, he imagined, fighting in this shit without armor.

His people had fought hard for it, taking out the hidden strongpoints Rancik's patrol had found…and a whole series of additional ones they hadn't discovered. It was a sharp, nasty fight, one that cost Holm 33 dead and 40 wounded. He'd had no intention of staying here after the battle…indeed, he'd planned on moving forward as soon as the wounded were collected. Without the prepared fortifications the enemy had possessed, it was a wide open position…not very defensible at all. He'd been surprised the enemy had chosen the spot to make a stand. There was better ground along his line of advance both before and after the sandy plain. Those questions were still there, and they were feeding his unease. It just didn't make sense. Elias Holm wasn't afraid of the enemy, but he was damned scared of anything he didn't understand.

At least it was good ground to bring down landers, he thought, trying to improve his mood but not drawing much comfort from the effort. It was all he could do, though. His doubts were irrelevant. Word of the armistice had come in just after the battle, and his orders were clear – cease hostilities and remain in position. He'd have preferred someplace a little more protected, but his requests to reposition had been denied. Orders were orders, and Elias Holm knew how to follow them, whether he agreed or not. Besides, the ground was ideal for an LZ. He had to acknowledge that much, at least.

"I want constant patrols on duty, lieutenant." He didn't have a choice about the position, but no one had said anything about not keeping an eye on the enemy. The battalion's dispositions were his call. He was exactly where he'd been ordered to be, and if he decided to postpone the celebration and keep his people on their toes for a while longer, it was no one's business but his and theirs. He suspected the Marines digging trenches were less than happy with their commander, but they didn't get a vote.

"Yes, sir." Masur was reading a feed on his helmet's tactical display. "We have four squads out on patrol now, sir, and four fresh ones set to relieve them in an hour." He paused then added, "And all other units are on alert, sir."

"Very well, lieutenant." Holm was still staring out across the ugly yellow sand to the low mountains five klicks to the south. "I want to know the instant the landers disembark from the…"

"Sir, we've lost contact with orbital command." Masur interrupted, his voice thick with concern. The comlink connection was suddenly noisy, staticky. "It's almost like…" He paused, staring at his tactical projection.

"Like what, lieutenant?" Holm's tone was impatient, demanding. He raised his voice, compensating for the interference. "Lieutenant," he repeated when he didn't get a response.

Masur's voice went cold, numb sounding. "Sorry, sir." He hesitated for an instant, checking for the third time even though he knew what had happened. "It's some sort of atmospheric jamming, sir. Not like before…it's different this time." He hesitated a few seconds before continuing, the alarm in his voice increasing substantially. "I've detected several nuclear explosions in the upper atmosphere." Another pause, slightly longer this time. "Sir, they've blocked our fleetcom with enhanced E3 EMP." He was yelling, trying to be heard over the growing noise on the com. "Someone deliberately cut our communications with the fleet." A brief hesitation then: "And I don't see how the landers are going to make it down through that, sir." He stared at Holm. "I think we're stuck down here."

Holm's eyes blazed as he glared back at Masur. He knew immediately. The peace had been a trick, some kind of ruse. The enemy was coming. And his people were stuck down here...cut off, alone. "All units, prepare to repel an attack." His voice was sharp, definitive. "All personnel are to take immediate cover." Maybe they'd cut their paranoid commander a break now, he thought. The trenches weren't done yet, but they were a helluva lot better than nothing out on that flat open plain.

"Yes, sir."

Holm realized his caution was right, but there was no satisfaction in being vindicated. His people were about to be in a world of hurt, and it was going to take all he had to pull them through. If that was even possible. His armored hands balled up into metallic fists, the frustration turning quickly to anger... then rage.

"I want all heavy weapons deployed imm..." Holm stopped when his comlink practically exploded in his ears, dozens of voices fighting through the maddening static. Every scout and sentry in the battalion was calling in at once. The reports were all the same. There were enemy troops approaching from all directions.

Chapter 11

AIS Stryker
Docked inside AS Belleau Wood
Mid-Level Orbit
Planet Persis – Iota Persi II
Day Eleven

Worthington stared down at the untouched tray. Two tur-key sandwiches, some raw vegetables with dip, a small pack of almonds…whatever they're up to, they aren't trying to starve me, he thought. The lunch would certainly have passed muster with the fleet nutritionist, though he doubted anyone in the naval chain of command was a party to his imprisonment. Whatever this was, he thought grimly, it had the filthy stink of Alliance Intelligence all over it.

He wasn't interested in food, however, no more than he'd been when he sent back breakfast…and dinner the evening before. His stomach was twisted into knots. It was anger cer-tainly, but also concern. This abduction was going to have repercussions. There were going to be a lot of questions to answer. Alliance Intelligence didn't have him locked away in some cell for no reason. Something was going on, and he'd have bet his last credit it was bad. Probably worse than anything he could guess.

He considered jumping the guard when he came for the tray, but he discarded the plan for the same reason he had that morn-ing. There was a two-part security system in the detention area, designed just to prevent an escape of that sort. All he could achieve by breaking out of his cell was to be stuck in the anteroom beyond, without any means to open the external door. He longed for the days depicted in the historical novels he enjoyed reading, when all a prisoner had to do was jump a guard and grab a physical key. Unfortunately, the locks on Worthington's prison were all electronic and centrally controlled…and hacking into a top tier security AI was well beyond his abilities. An abortive escape attempt would accomplish nothing except increasing the watchfulness of his jailors. That was the last thing he needed; their carelessness was his only hope of getting out in time to deal with whatever scheme was going on, miniscule chance that it was.

He was on a small ship; he knew that much. He'd been led aboard blindfolded, unable to ID the vessel itself. It couldn't be more than a 200 tonner, or it wouldn't fit inside Belleau Wood's bay. There hadn't been any outside vessels in the bay when his people had launched the invasion, but he'd been down on the surface for weeks now, and he had no idea what ships had docked with the big troop carrier since. He hadn't felt any acceleration, or any movement at all since he'd been imprisoned, which meant his prison ship was still inside Belleau Wood. Hundreds of his Marines were just meters away. But he had no way to reach anyone. The frustration just kept building.

He wondered how Kell was faring. The two had been separated when they were brought aboard, and they were put in different cells. Worthington was a little worried about the aide. Kell was good at his job, the best he'd ever seen. Between his cantankerous personality and his unceasing demands, the faithful captain had taken everything he'd dished out and come back for more. Worthington respected that…and beyond that, he just liked the tenacious officer.

He knew how Alliance Intelligence operated. They wouldn't hesitate to do away with an officer who got in their way, at least not for any moral or ethical reasons. Worthington himself was too high profile to simply disappear or to end up dead, shot by intelligence operatives. There would be too many questions, too much scrutiny. He was famous throughout the Alliance, a war hero of massive proportions. But a miscellaneous captain could easily be written off, a manufactured list of infractions slipped into his record along with the tragic report that he'd resisted arrest and been killed in a firefight with agents. Kell was probably worth more to Dutton alive, as a tool to gain Worthington's cooperation, but he was still worried.

He glanced down at the tray, considering taking one of the sandwiches. He'd refused to give them the satisfaction of eating anything they sent him, but now he started to wonder if he should keep his strength up. If he did manage to get out of the cell, he didn't know what he'd have to do. He had to be ready for anything, including fighting his way out. He was just reaching down to grab the top sandwich when he heard it…a sound he'd know anywhere. Marine assault rifles firing.

He scanned the room quickly, instinctively, searching for anything he could use as a weapon. There was nothing useful on the tray, just a set of soft, pliable plastic utensils. He might poke someone in the eye with them, but that was the extent of their combat potential. Alliance Intelligence had its faults, but the organization had enormous expertise at handling prisoners. It was very unlikely he'd find anything that could be weaponized in a meaningful way. He grabbed the tray itself, knocking the food all over the floor. It was light plastic, not very useful as a club. But it was all he had. He leapt up and stood alongside the door, waiting, ready to spring at whoever came through.

There was more fire, distant at first and then closer…in the anteroom just beyond his door. "General Worthington, sir. Get away from the door. Take cover in there."

The voices were muffled by the heavy door, but he understood every word, and his heart leapt. They were Marines. He was sure of it. His Marines. He moved away from the door, ducking quickly down below the small bunk. He was crouched low, his head tucked down between his arms. The training had been decades before, but he remembered it. At least the important parts. He listened to his heart pounding, each beat reverberating loudly in his ears. The delay seemed like an eternity, though he knew it was only a few seconds. Finally, there was a loud crack, and the door came flying out of its frame, blown inward by the controlled blast. It smashed into the opposite wall with an earsplitting crash. An instant later, armored figures poured inside. One of them looked down at him as he raised his head up and returned the stare. "We're here to get you out, general. Come with us, sir." The armored Marine extended a steel-gloved hand.

Worthington pulled himself up to his feet, grabbing ahold of the proffered arm. He stared at the looming figures, huge and imposing in their dark gray fighting suits, assault rifles extended, smelling faintly of ozone from recent use. He could see through the door at an angle. His field of view was poor and incomplete, but he could make out at least two bodies, both wearing the dark brown uniforms of Alliance Intelligence guards. Whatever was going on, he knew his Marines had acted on their own. There was going to be hell to pay, he was certain of that. But none of that made a bit of difference now…they had more important things to do.

He stared at the leader of the group, the Marine who had helped him to his feet. He'd thought the voice was familiar through the heavy door, but he hadn't been able to make it out. Now it was crystal clear. He'd know it anywhere.

"Colonel Thomas, I've never been so glad to see your ugly face before."

Chapter 12

Anvil Force Perimeter
Yellow Sand Valley
Northern Continent
Planet Persis – Iota Persi II
Day Thirteen – Morning

The fire was thick all along the line. They'd been fighting nonstop for three days, and there was no sign of a letup. The enemy had been throwing fresh assaults at them every few hours. Holm's forces had over 200 casualties, and the toll kept growing. But they were holding everywhere. All along the perimeter, Elias Holm had been wherever the fighting was heaviest, anyplace his Marines were wavering. He'd shifted his scant reserves wherever they were most needed, and he'd stood in the line with a battered platoon, firing his assault rifle along with theirs.

Everywhere Holm went, Danny Burke followed. Lieutenant Masur had been hit two days before. He was alive, but the shell took one of his legs clean off and only left part of the second one. He was in the field hospital, stabilized but still in critical condition. He'd be a candidate for the new regeneration process…a medical miracle that would allow him to grow two new limbs from his own DNA. Regeneration would give him the chance to return to the colors as good as new, but the Marine hospital on Armstrong was the only place off Earth equipped to do regens. Armstrong was lightyears away, and Masur was stuck on Persis, half-conscious on painkillers and sedatives, waiting to see if his brethren won the battle…or if he'd die in a POW camp.

Burke had convinced Holm to let him fill in for Masur. Holm had doubted the idea at first. His impression of Burke was positive, but he wasn't sure any rookie could be up to the job. He considered other options, but he finally decided he couldn't afford to pull even a single veteran officer from the line. He needed his people where they were, all of them. So the cherry private, last survivor of his squad, became a makeshift aide, carrying out Holm's orders, moving from one beleaguered section of the line to another. Burke found courage and resourcefulness he'd never imagined he possessed, and he stood firm wherever Holm's orders took him, running without hesitation from one meatgrinder to another. Not a doubt, not a shred of fear interfered with his executing Holm's orders. He was afraid, certainly, as every Marine on Persis was, but it didn't affect his duty, not one iota.

The fighting along the front lines was brutal. The open plain had seemed to be a death trap, devoid of natural cover. But the Marines quickly adapted, benefiting from Holm's earlier paranoia. Instead of celebrating peace, they had been digging makeshift foxholes, later expanding those scratchings into a legitimate network of trenches. If the enemy had expected to overwhelm Holm's Marines in the open country, they had gotten a nasty surprise. The attackers faced one strongpoint after another, hastily built but powerful nevertheless. Their attacks broke on the Marine defenses, and they lost hundreds to the defenders' withering fire. There were mounds of enemy dead lying in front of the trenchlines, the detritus of a dozen failed assaults. The Marines had taken heavy casualties too, but they had inflicted vastly greater losses on the enemy. The Caliphate line troops and the Persis levies were no match for the Alliance's Marines, and it showed. Mathematics would ultimately have its say - Holm knew that - but so far the skill and tenacity of the Alliance's elite shock troops had been enough to hold back the overwhelming numbers of the enemy.

"Captain, we're getting reports from all along the line." The comlink was still staticky, and Burke's voice was hoarse from shouting. The enemy had continued with the atmospheric detonations every few hours. Line of sight ground to ground communications were only marginally affected, but all contact between Force Hammer and the Alliance fleet had been interdicted without a break. The enemy clearly had no intention of allowing Holm to reach the ships in orbit...or the fleet to contact the Marines on the ground. "It's very strange, sir." He paused, only for an instant. "The attack forces are withdrawing."

Holm's head snapped around, a natural gesture, but a relatively pointless one when buttoned up in armor and communicating by comlink. "They're pulling back?" There was an edge to his voice. This was unexpected.

"Yes sir." Burke's voice was high-pitched. He was just as surprised as Holm. "I've confirmed it with all commanders, sir. They are withdrawing everywhere. All along the perimeter."

Holm was silent. He felt a tightness in his chest, a constriction in his stomach. Something was wrong, very wrong. The enemy had been attacking relentlessly for more than two days. His people couldn't take much more...they'd been pushed to the brink. Why pull back now? It didn't make any sense. Or did it?

"Sir, we're getting reports of smoke shells landing in front of our positions." Burke sounded confused. The rookie had never encountered the ordnance the Marines called smoke. But Holm had.

Fuck, he thought angrily. I should have known; I should have been ready for this. Smoke was an interdiction system...a radioactive chemical steam seeded with tiny metallic particles. It blocked line of sight and interfered with virtually all scanning technology...providing perfect cover for an attacker. It was used by one corps of shock troops, one of the best and most feared in human space.

"Prepare to receive Janissaries." Holm's voice was like ice. The Caliphate's Janissaries were the Marines' most hated enemy, the only troops in space who laid claim to being their equals. No Marine would admit the Janissaries could beat them in a straight up fight. But this was far from an even matchup. Holm's people were exhausted and shot to pieces...and they'd be running low on ordnance soon too. The Janissaries were fresh, and Holm expected them to outnumber his people too. He'd known there were Janissaries on Persis, but they hadn't shown themselves. No matter how many losses the Marines inflicted on the defenders, the Janissaries remained inactive, hidden somewhere the Alliance scanners couldn't penetrate. He'd finally begun to hope the reports had been wrong, that there were none of the Caliphate's elite soldiers onplanet. Now he knew…the intel had been right all along. Now they were coming. And his battered Marines had to dig up the strength to hold them off. Somehow.

"Get your Goddamned heads down now!" Sergeant Tremont crouched behind the berm of the hastily-built trench firing his assault rifle into the billowing cloud of steam ahead. He couldn't see anything more than half a meter in – and his scanner was giving him nothing but incomprehensible garbage – but he knew the Janissaries were there. He turned his head left then right, checking to make sure his orders were being followed. The Marines were edgy, even more than they had been. A hopeless fight was one thing, but now the Janissaries were coming. Now it was more than just a fight to the death; it was a matter of honor. They carried the pride of the Corps with them.

He didn't know where the attackers were in that swirling green mass of toxic steam, but he wasn't about to let them get through unscathed. "I want those clouds bracketed with fire." His voice was raw, edgy. "They're in there somewhere, so let's take 'em down."

The steam was a terror weapon as much as a camouflage system. It didn't block projectiles, and the Janissaries inside the clouds could suffer considerable losses from fire, especially since they tended to favor mass attacks. Their tactics were highly effective at intimidating their enemies, filling them with fear as they waited for the attacking masses to emerge from the sickly green clouds. It worked well against many of their adversaries, already half beaten by the legend of the Caliphate's elite slave-soldiers. Against many adversaries, but not the Marines.

Tremont's section consisted of veterans. They'd all faced the

Janissaries before, and they'd be damned if they were going to let a bunch of theatrics get to them. They stood firm, meticulously crisscrossing the clouds with fire, working to maximize the casualties they inflicted. It was frustrating not being able to see what damage you were doing, but the discipline of the Marines was being buttressed by their rivalry. They might get overwhelmed on Persis, but to a man they'd be damned if they were going to shake in their boots because the Janissaries were coming.

Tremont was focused on the forward edge of the nearest cloud. It was barely 80 meters from the line. When they emerged, the Janissaries would cover that distance in less than ten seconds. Then they'd be in the trenches. Hand to hand combat wasn't common on the 22nd century battlefield, but it did happen, especially when elite forces clashed. The Janissaries wouldn't falter...Tremont knew that. And his Marines damned sure weren't going anywhere.

"Incoming!"

Tremont's head snapped around. It was Corporal Connors on the com. An instant later he heard the whoomp sound of mortar rounds exploding. The Caliphate mortars were similar to the Alliance's. They could be highly effective against an unarmored enemy, but troops in modern fighting suits were well protected against anything but a direct hit. The Marines rarely bothered with the weapons except in special situations, but it was all part of the theatrics so central to the Janissary way of war.

"It's just the enemy's popguns, people." Tremont kept his voice slow and calm. "Maintain rifle fire. You can't see it, but we're taking these fuckers down while they're hiding in those clouds throwing water balloons at us." He glanced at the scanner. The mortar rounds had been mostly ineffectual, as he'd expected. Mostly wasn't entirely, though. It looked like two of his people had taken minor hits...nothing their suits couldn't patch up, but a wound didn't do anything to increase a Marine's combat effectiveness.

Tremont was snapping another clip into his assault rifle

when he saw it. The first Janissary, pushing forward, out of the swirling green mist and into the open, less than 100 meters away. "Fuck," he muttered under his breath. Always when I'm reloading, he thought. The enemy soldier was running quickly, heading straight for Tremont, firing away at full auto with his own rifle. Then there was another just behind him…and more to the left and right.

He crouched low, pushing himself forward against the front wall of the trench, his rifle in front of him. He fired at full auto, sweeping the area directly in front of him. The first Janissary went down, struck by at least three projectiles. Then another, stumbling forward, crashing hard into the yellow mud. There were at least a dozen still heading for him, and they'd covered at least half the distance. He aimed at another, letting his guard down for just a second and lifting himself up a few centimeters to get a good shot.

The impact slammed into him hard, knocking him backwards from the edge of the trench. He landed on his back, splashing wet muck all over as he hit the ground. His shoulder was hit. It was a glancing blow, not a serious wound, but it hurt like hell. He struggled to focus, and he held his rifle up with his good arm just as the Janissaries reached the edge of the trench. He was shooting wildly, spraying the whole area with fire. He took out another enemy, maybe two, and then he was hit again. It was worse this time, somewhere in the abdomen. There was pain, then a rush of painkillers and amphetamines. Tremont wasn't done yet, and his suit would do everything possible to keep him in the fight. He flipped the switch in his right glove, activating his blade. The weapon thrust out from his suit's arm, an almost impossibly thin shard of iridium, honed to an edge barely a molecule wide.

He thrust himself upward, slashing hard. His extended blade sliced through the leg of the closest Janissary, sending the enemy soldier crashing to the ground. Doug Tremont wasn't finished…not yet.

Chapter 13

Marine Lander A34-V111
Upper Atmosphere
Planet Persis – Iota Persi II
Day Thirteen – Afternoon

The lander bounced around wildly. Worthington was bolted in firmly, but he still felt like he'd go flying off any second. It had been years since the Marines' celebrated field commander had ridden a first wave landing sled. The first Marines to hit dirt had the roughest ride...the follow up units and headquarters elements came down in larger, more comfortable shuttles. Worthington had never forgotten what a rough ride the front line troops endured, but it was still a shock to re-experience it after so many years.

He was regretting the sandwiches he'd eaten after Thomas' people had freed him. There'd been no time for intravenous feeding periods or most of the other pre-landing protocols. He'd barely allowed a few minutes for the doc to administer the anti-emetics and other standard injections to the attack force. For the guys who'd celebrated the short-lived peace with greasy pizzas and sloppy burgers, it was just so much bad luck. A number of his officers pleaded for more prep time, but Worthington's response was simple, and he repeated it to anyone suggesting delay. "There are Marines dying down there Goddammit." He didn't think any more needed to be said...and neither did anyone else.

The landing wasn't as well planned as most of his ops had been...indeed, it had been the most seat of the pants thing he'd ever done. But he was going to get help to his men and women on the surface, whatever it took. Whatever happened, he was resolved those Marines on the surface would not die alone and abandoned.

The repercussions would be ugly; he knew that much. His career would be over...there wasn't much doubt of that. Alliance Gov had approved the hateful terms of the peace, and Worthington's actions were in direct violation of orders from the highest level. Court-martial was almost certain, and a firing squad wasn't out of the question. He'd escaped from an internment approved by Alliance Gov, left a trail of dead intelligence agents behind, and rallied the Marines on Belleau Wood to follow him on an unauthorized landing, heading right back into the fight on a world they'd just left. His actions, which he considered profoundly justified, threatened the new peace and risked a return to full-scale war. Worthington knew the risks, but he didn't care. He wasn't leaving his people behind, no matter what the cost.

The Marines had behaved exactly as he'd expected. He hated involving them in this, but there was no choice. He'd been straight with them all. They were going into another blast furnace, where their deaths were far likelier than a successful rescue. They could end up alone, with no one coming to their aid as they were coming to Holm's. There was no way to be sure any of the forces on the other ships would follow their lead...or that they'd even be able to now that Alliance Intelligence was alerted. The 300 Marines from Belleau Wood might find themselves trapped and overwhelmed just like the forces they were trying to rescue. And even if they somehow made it back, they'd likely face disciplinary action. Their careers could be destroyed...they might even do time in a penal facility. But none of that mattered. Every one of the 400 Marines on Belleau Wood had volunteered to go. Worthington ended up drawing lots...for the 100 who had to stay behind for lack of landing craft to get them to the surface.

His comlink crackled to life. "Charles, what the hell is going on?" It was Admiral Clement, his voice barely audible over the growing static.

"I'm going to help my people, Tom." Worthington's voice was calm, though he had to yell to be heard over the interference. "Those pigfuckers at Alliance Intelligence bought their peace with the lives of my Marines...and I'm not going to allow that!"

"What are you going to do with 300 Marines?" Clement was pleading with Worthington, his voice thick with concern. "Abort this insanity, and we'll deal with the situation together. You know you'll have my full support. If you do this it won't make any difference. You'll all die...and you'll just be tried for mutiny even if you do somehow manage to make it back." He paused for an instant and added, "Don't throw your life away, my friend."

Worthington smiled. Clement was a good man, a friend. "My people don't have time, Tom." He spoke simply, matter-of-factly. "It's no different than you'd do if one of your ships was in trouble...and you know it."

Clement paused, sighing hard, but not responding.

"If you've got anything else to say, old friend, now is the time." Worthington knew he wouldn't. Clement had to try to convince him, but deep down the admiral felt the same way. He'd led his ships and people from one murderous fight to another, and cutting them loose, abandoning them to the enemy...it wasn't in his DNA and more than it was in Worthington's. "We're taking as wide and approach as we can, but we'll be clipping the EMP area in a minute. The ships will make it through, I think, but we'll probably lose our com channel with the fleet."

Clement sighed again. "I know I'm not going to change your mind, Charles. I've fought alongside your stubborn ass long enough to realize that." There was a long pause, only the growing static on the line. "So, let's cut the crap. How can I help?"

Worthington smiled again. He'd always respected Clement, but the crusty old admiral would never know how much that last sentence meant to him. Still, he wasn't going to drag his friend down with him. "Stay out of it, Tom. You tried to convince me to come back. You did your duty. Now you and your people lay low, stay out of it. I'm not taking you down with me."

"Bullshit," Clement roared loudly enough to rattle the speaker in Worthington's helmet. "We fought a war together, and by God we're going to finish it that way. And if you tell me again to cower on my bridge while good men die, I'm gonna show you just how an admiral can kick the shit out of an uppity Marine general."

Worthington paused for a few seconds. He felt a wave of guilt for dragging Clement into the whole mess. He struggled with it briefly then pushed it aside. Tom Clement was his own man. What he did, he did because he knew it was the right thing to do. And nothing would change that. "You're a good man, Tom. And a good friend." The static was growing louder. Worthington glanced at the positional display. He was going to lose contact any second. "We need more strength down there, Tom." He was shouting as loudly as he could, trying to overcome the almost-total interference. "Get the word to the other ships. Tell the rest of my Marines we need them." There was a loud burst of static and then the line went dead.

Chapter 14

Anvil Force Perimeter
Yellow Sand Valley
Northern Continent
Planet Persis – Iota Persi II
Day Thirteen – Late Afternoon

It was over. He knew that much. Tremont was on his back again, two more slugs in his body. His right arm had been hit, a random shot that shattered the bone. There was more pain, but he ignored it. The suit was still pumping him full of drugs, keeping the agony at least moderately under control. His blade was still extended, but the deadly weapon lay half buried in the yellow mud, the arm that had wielded it sprawled uselessly at his side. Even with the nuclear-powered servo-mechanicals of his suit, there was no way to move the obliterated arm.

There were Janissaries all around him, like angels of death floating over his dying body. He could see at least two bringing their rifles around to finish him off. He knew he was looking at his end. He'd been afraid earlier, waiting for the assault to come. But now, lying in the mud, facing the reality of his own death, the fear was gone. There was something else there in its place, regret possibly? He ached for his Marines, for the rest of Third Battalion, abandoned on an alien world, facing almost certain destruction. He couldn't understand how this had happened… how it had been allowed to happen. How long a fraction of a second can be, he thought, watching his impending death as if it was unfolding in slow motion.

He gritted his teeth, waiting for the pain of the kill shots.

At least they would be mercifully quick. Death now was better than a few more hours of life...watching the battalion slowly destroyed. But those shots didn't come. He saw the shadows looming over him, watched as they moved away...falling, landing in the mud around him. He was groggy, weak. Realization came slowly...figures running down the trench toward him... firing. Marines! His Marines, shooting at his attackers, taking them all down. Saving his life.

"Get that weapon set up, private!" The voice on the com was rough, hoarse. "We've got a second wave coming, and we're gonna need that SAW fire."

Tremont was wavering on the edge of consciousness as he listened. Mueller, he thought. "Corporal Mueller? Is that you?" His voice was weak, throaty.

"Yes, sergeant. We're here for you. Just relax...we've got things under control."

That was a lie...Tremont knew that much. But however bad the situation, Mueller's people had this section of line better defended than he had by himself. Maybe, he thought...maybe they'll hold. At least for a while. He lay back in the mud and took a deep, painful breath.

Mueller fired off another series of orders. Tremont tried to move his head to see, but he couldn't do it. Finally, he looked at his display. Mueller had nine Marines, including himself. Less than half the starting strength of his section, Tremont realized grimly. Still, they could put out one hell of a lot of fire. Nine Marines and two SAWs could hold a section of trench for a long time...even against Janissaries. But what were they holding out for? A single battalion, alone on an enemy world, low on supplies and hopelessly outnumbered...what chance did they have?

Burke was crouched low as he shuffled along the back of the small berm. It was a weak defense, desperately put in place. The Janissaries had hit hard in this sector, and they finally drove the Marines back from their trenches. The defenders had held to the last, and the Caliphate's elite troops paid a heavy blood price to break through. But they had reserves, and the Marines didn't.

No more than a quarter of Captain Clinton's company were still in the line when the fallback order finally came. They retreated, fighting all the way, and hastily erected a fallback position. Clinton had given the order to retreat, but he wasn't with his people when they followed it. He'd been fighting in the ranks with his Marines as wave after wave of Janissaries threw themselves at the trench line. He was one of the last to fall, seconds after ordering the retreat. He lay on the line, under a pile of bodies… a handful of his Marines who'd desperately tried to reach him instead of pulling back, only to discover he was already dead. They'd sacrificed their chance to escape, and run head on into the main enemy attack. They had died to a man, bravely, but in the end, vainly.

"Captain Holm, I'm up at First Company's position." Burke's voice was scratchy, deep. There was an authority in it, a confidence that hadn't been there two days before. The nervous-sounding rookie was gone, replaced by a man who'd seen too much, too quickly. He struggled with the horrors he was facing, but he'd done all Holm had asked of him and come back for more. Baptism by fire…that's what they call it, he thought. Part of him was overwhelmed, longing to give in to the fear, to flee for his life. But there was more inside him than he'd ever imagined. The training appealed to his rational mind. Fleeing would do no good…there was nowhere to go. But in his heart, in the place courage came from, there was a resolve he'd never imagined he'd possessed. "They're in bad shape, sir," he continued. "The enemy was badly disordered taking the trenches, and that's buying us a short break. But as soon as they are able to regroup, I don't see how Clinton's people are going to hold."

"Who's in command up there?" Holm's voice was hard, steady. He already knew Captain Clinton was dead. He and Clinton had been close for years, but he just filed the information and focused on the matter at hand. There would be time to mourn lost friends later…if anyone survived.

Holm was exhausted, but his mind was sharp, and kept firing out orders, micromanaging every part of his shrinking battle line. The worse the situation got, the calmer the young captain in command seemed to become. He was growing into his responsibilities, and even while his beleaguered forces faced overwhelming odds, their confidence in their commander grew. Elias Holm would one day succeed General Worthington as the Corps' fighting commander, and his journey to greatness began in those fateful days on Persis.

"Lieutenant Fargus, sir. But he's wounded. He's still on his feet, but he can't be 100%." Burke paused, looking up toward the front line. "Sir, I'll move forward and get a better look at the defensive positions..."

"No you won't." Holm's tone pre-empted any argument. "I need a live aide, Danny, not a dead hero." He paused. His respect for Burke was growing. He'd had serious doubts about the young private serving as his aide, especially in a desperate fight like this, but Burke had vastly exceeded his expectations. "Stay the hell back, and get your ass over to 2nd Company's position."

Burke was distracted by chatter from Fargus' people on the line. He knew what it was immediately. "Captain Holm, the enemy is moving against the fallback position." The Janissaries were coming in...and they outnumbered the 50 or so Marines manning the hasty works at least 10-1. The defenders would fight...but that was just a formality. The enemy would overrun them all...and burst into the rear of the entire battalion.

James Fargus knelt in the deep yellow mud, staring across the flat, featureless plain. His people had fallen back a little more than a kilometer from their abandoned trenches. They'd fought long and hard to hold the painstakingly built defensive line, but ultimately numbers had prevailed...as they usually did in war. Perhaps, he thought, we could have held indefinitely against the regular line troops...but the Janissaries were elite shock troops. The Marines had made them pay dearly, but in the end, there had simply been too many of them.

The Janissaries were coming again. It looked like a whole orta...at least several times as many as it would take to wipe out Fargus' battered force. Worse, their formations seemed intact...

which meant they were fresh troops, not the battered units that had finally taken the trench line.

He'd been crouched behind the berm his people had hastily erected, ready for what was almost certainly going to be his last fight. The wound in his side ached, but his trauma control system had packed it in sterile foam and flooded his system with painkillers and amphetamines. He felt a little weakness, but nothing he couldn't handle. He didn't think it was going to matter for much longer anyway.

"Lieutenant Fargus, I am receiving intermittent signals from approaching aircraft." Fargus' AI spoke with the same human-sounding tone as the others. "Approximate location 30 kilometers southwest, altitude 9 kilometers."

Fargus sighed. It just kept getting worse. The Alliance and Caliphate air assets had fought each other to mutual annihilation early in the campaign. If the enemy had hidden aircraft during the initial fighting, they would have total air superiority now. Third Battalion was already doomed, but the end would come almost immediately if they had to face coordinated ground attacks and air strikes.

He glanced left and right, looking at the thin, ragged line of Marines waiting for the enemy assault. His instinct was to prepare to receive an air attack, but there was no point. Let them focus on giving the Janissaries one last good fight, he thought. They had almost no AA ordnance left anyway. His mind was dark, resigned to his fate.

"Aircraft positively identified as Reynolds-class landing craft."

Fargus heard the AI's statement, but the reality of it lagged, following a few seconds behind. His mind raced. Reynolds landers? Marines!

"Confirm aircraft identification." He was looking up as he snapped the order to the AI, cranking his magnification and trying to get a glimpse of the incoming landers.

"Identification confirmed. Approximately 60 Reynolds-class ships currently inbound...projected landing zone 1.5 kilometers northeast of our position."

He felt his stomach clench. If those were reinforcements, they were coming down close to the enemy position…too close. He felt his hands ball into fists. His people had to hold the line, at least until those ships came down. If the Janissaries broke through and were waiting in the LZ, the landing would be a bloody fiasco. He couldn't imagine why the landers were coming in so close…landings were usually better planned. But if those were Marines…

"We've got reserves incoming, Marines." He shouted his orders on the com, his renewed energy and determination clear in his voice. "We've gotta hold this line, people…long enough for our brothers and sisters to hit dirt. We don't give a centimeter. Not a motherfucking centimeter!"

He heard a ripple of cheers and acknowledgements…and then a single clear voice shouting. "Here they come!" The entire line opened up, blasting away at the approaching Janissaries with renewed enthusiasm.

Chapter 15

Painted Hills
HQ – Force Hammer
Northern Continent
Planet Persis – Iota Persi II
Day Sixteen

"Sergeant Mulligan's strike force has been overrun, sir...
sirs." Burke snapped out his report, his eyes shifting involun-
tarily between Holm and Worthington. It was a lot of brass
for a rookie private to deal with. He was Holm's aide, but
Worthington was so lofty a figure he thought he'd get a nose-
bleed just being near him. "I can't raise any of his people...I'm
afraid there may be no survivors." Burke put his hand up for a
few seconds as he listened to another incoming report. "Lieutenant Barret is down as well. His company is retreating with
the enemy in pursuit."

Holm turned and looked at Worthington. "I think we're
down to the last stand, general." Holm's voice was raw and
tired...but unbeaten. He would fight to the last, with the final
bit of strength in his body. He was beyond exhausted, but he
took a stim whenever he felt like he was losing effectiveness. He
couldn't imagine the wear and tear on his body, but none of that
was important now. Staying sharp...as sharp as drug-induced
consciousness could be...that was the most important thing.

He was a realist too. Worthington's relief force had bought
them some time...a little at least. Confused and surprised, the
enemy pulled back all along the perimeter as Worthington's
landers hit ground. The new troops deployed immediately and

went right into battle, gaining back a few meters of lost ground and giving Holm's exhausted Marines a little rest…a day's worth. Then the reformed and resupplied Caliphate forces redoubled their efforts, throwing themselves at the Marines' reinforced lines. For the last two days the forces had been locked in a death struggle. The reinforced and resupplied Marines held firm at first, but then numbers began to tell again. The enemy could replace its losses; the Marines couldn't. Slowly, grudgingly, the combined Alliance force was forced back into an ever-shrinking circle. The front lines were less than a kilometer from HQ in all directions now. There was no more room to retreat. They would fight and die where they stood.

"Captain Holm, sir, this is Lieutenant Fargus." The lieutenant's voice was weak. He'd been fighting with two holes in his side for three days. His suit's med systems had stabilized the injuries, and they had stopped the bleeding again every time he tore open the packing and reopened the wounds in combat. But there was a limit to what the human body and spirit could endure, and James Fargus was close to it. "It's Colonel Thomas, sir. He's been hit."

Holm winced. Sam Thomas was one of the most loved and respected officers in the Corps…and the closest thing Viper Worthington had to a protégé. "The general is listening in, lieutenant. How bad is it?"

"Yes, sir…and general, sir." Fargus paused, his tension increasing at the mention of Worthington. "It's pretty bad, sirs. I sent him back to the field hospital." It wasn't so much a field hospital as a small stretch of ground where Force Hammer's two surgeons worked on the most critically wounded, low on equipment, drugs…even shelter. "I think…" He paused, a coughing spasm interrupting his report. "…I think he'll make it."

"I want you off the line too, Fargus." Holm spoke slowly, his hand sliding slowly along the assault rifle clipped to his side. "Get back here and see one of the docs."

"Sir, I can't leave…there's no one else up here to take command." He was struggling to keep his voice firm, but it was obvious he was struggling.

Holm pulled the assault rifle from the harness. "You bet your ass there is. I'll be there in two minutes. Now follow my orders and get to the aid station." Holm turned to face Worthington. "You don't need me here, do you sir?"

Worthington opened his mouth then closed it again. He wanted to order Holm to stay put. Things were bad at the front and getting worse by the minute. But those were Elias Holm's people out there, at least half of them were. The general knew what was going through the heroic captain's mind. It would be over in a few hours anyway. The lines were collapsing everywhere, and there were no reserves left to plug the holes. Why shouldn't Holm die on the lines with his Marines?

Worthington felt a rush of guilt. He'd failed the captain and all his people. His 300 reinforcements were woefully inadequate, and the hope of more help from the fleet had faded steadily as the hours passed. He was sure Clement had tried to help, but Alliance Intelligence probably had everything locked down. He cursed himself for obeying the original evac order, for not seeing through the scheme sooner. He just couldn't order the captain to stay at HQ, not when the end was so close. He owed this to Holm, to let him die fighting alongside his Marines. "Go, Elias," he finally croaked, turning away as he did.

"Keep up that fire." Holm was crouched in a small foxhole, targeting the approaching Janissaries and dropping them with perfectly aimed, three-round bursts. He'd been first in marksmanship in his basic training and officers' Academy classes, and the enemy troops were getting a lesson in precision shooting. The Janissaries were going to win this round by virtue of sheer numbers, but it wasn't going to be a battle that went down in their unit lore. They'd taken horrendous casualties fighting a force they outnumbered at least 5-1. The Marines had fought with a savage determination beyond anything the Caliphate's elite troops had ever seen. Elias Holm had directed his outnumbered forces with enormous skill and determination, and his people had responded to his leadership, giving them all they had.

Holm watched as the advancing Caliphate forces staggered

and fell back to regroup. His people had dodged another bullet...beat back one more charge. He felt a rush of elation, but it didn't last. His people were near the end. The next attack – or maybe the one after that – would be the last. There was no more room to pull back, no fallback position this time. When the enemy broke through and burst into the rear of the Marines' position, Third Battalion would be destroyed.

"Let's use the break, Marines." Holm pushed his dark thoughts aside. They served nothing...and if his people were going to die here, they were going to go down fighting. "Shore up your foxholes, and check your ammo supplies." And stay busy, he thought. He didn't want them to have too much time to think now. It couldn't do anyone any good.

"Sir, Simm's company is down to their last 2 or 3 cartridges per man." Burke trotted up behind Holm. "He's requesting resupply."

Holm sighed, turning to face his erstwhile aide. "Danny, all I've got for Lieutenant Simms is my best wishes." The supplies were gone, even the extra ordnance Worthington's reinforcements had brought down. The Marines on the line had whatever ammunition they carried on their suits...then they'd be down to deploying their blades and hunkering down until the enemy got into close quarters. "Tell Simms' people, burst fire only...no full auto." He paused a few seconds then added, "And tell them to use up their popguns...they may not be that effective, but I want every weapon we've got put to use. Understand?" They were almost out of reloads for their assault rifles, but Holm would have bet his last credit they all had full mortar racks.

"Yes, sir."

Holm could hear the fatigue in Burke's voice. The lack of sleep, endless fighting, constant terror...it was a terrible burden on any man, but an almost unimaginable strain on a young rookie thrust into the responsibilities he had borne over the past ten days. Holm had nothing but admiration and respect for the Marine Burke had become, but he also knew the young private had to be near the end of his endurance. All the Marines on

Persis were.

Holm sat on the edge of his foxhole, taking a few deep breaths. His AI had been adjusting the mix of his suit's atmosphere, feeding him extra oxygen when he was in the heat of battle. A fighting suit not only increased a Marine's strength and protection…it also allowed the human warrior inside to maximize his or her own natural capabilities. Holm knew that none of his people would still be standing, much less fighting, after what they'd been through…not without their suits. They were all strung out on stims, fed a bunch of chemicals and raw nutrients, and kept in the fight…far longer than their natural equipment could have sustained.

"Here they come again!"

Holm's eyes snapped to his tactical display. Sure enough, another wave was advancing, coming across the blood-soaked plain directly at the Marines' fragile line.

"All units…fire on my command." Holm stared out across the yellow sand, his eyes darting up to his tactical display every few seconds. "Fire!" He screamed the command, the word ripping across his parched throat like a knife. He pulled his trigger as he did, firing an unaimed 3-shot burst…a waste of ammunition he did not intent to repeat. He looked out, choosing a target and coolly dropping the soldier with another burst.

All along the line the Marines were firing, using the last of their precious ammunition to meet the Janissaries with a wall of death. The elite enemy soldiers pushed forward into the deadly maelstrom, firing as they did. Then, at 200 meters their line staggered. They didn't run, didn't fall back. They began to go prone, singly at first then in groups. They hugged the ground, taking advantage of the cover offered by any small hills or gullies. The intensity of their fire increased as they opened up at full auto…then again as their autocannons and heavy rocket launchers deployed.

The small patch of ground between the two forces became a nightmare, a horrific demonstration of man's powers of destruction. Holm knew his people would lose this duel in the end. The Marines could match any force of devastation the Janissaries could unleash, but they were almost down to the last of their supplies, and their adversaries could resupply themselves. In the end it would be materiel and not men that determined the outcome of the battle on Persis.

He focused on the enemy in front of him, picking them off one by one. The supply situation was beyond his control, but until they ran out completely he and his Marines had a job to do. There was no command responsibility left…his people knew what to do. For the moment, Elias Holm was just one more Marine in the line, his assault rifle one of many. If he had to die on this miserable enemy rock, he thought, this is how he would go…shoulder to shoulder with the Marines he led.

"Captain Holm, I am tracking a wave of attack ships approaching from orbit." It was Nate, the AI's voice calm, unaffected by the savage fight going on all around.

Holm was startled by the sudden announcement. "Is that confirmed? Whose ships?"

"Scanning report is confirmed. Incoming craft are broadcasting Alliance transponder protocols."

Holm was silent, stunned. He opened his mouth, but before he could ask another question, the forcewide com channel crackled to life.

"Attention all Marines…this is Lieutenant Samson, commanding attack wing 6. Admiral Clement sends his complements."

Holm heard a loud explosion, followed by another…then another. He could see plumes of smoke rising up behind the enemy lines. Samson's attack ships were bombarding the enemy rear areas, targeting supply lines and headquarters and spreading disorder in the enemy's ranks.

The fire from the Janissaries slowed, and they began to gradually pull back. The Marines let out a cheer, and they kept firing all along the line, gunning down their retreating enemies.

"Cease fire." Holm understood the bloodlust taking hold of his Marines, but they weren't off Persis yet, and their ammo was still running low. "I said cease fire!" He roared into the com, angry that he'd been forced to repeat his order.

He watched on his tactical display as a group of Reynolds landers came in after the attack ships. In a few minutes there would be fresh Marines on the ground. He felt a rush of hope, a wave of excitement. Maybe…just maybe his people would make it off of this stinking planet.

"Danny…get back to the LZ. I want a complete report as soon as those ships land."

Silence. Then a response…soft, weak, forced. "I'm… sorry…cap…tain."

Holm felt a chill inside. He spun his head, looking all around for Burke. He found him a few meters to the rear, lying on his back in the mud, at least half a dozen holes in his armor. "Medic!" Holm shouted into the com. "I need a medic here, now!"

He ran over, his eyes running up and down the stricken private's armor. The holes in the suit were large, and blood was pouring from them. He'd been hit by one of the enemy auto-cannons, and the big hypersonic projectiles had cut through his armor like it was paper.

Holm opened his visor and reached for the controls on Burke's armor, pulling the release and opening the private's helmet. He looked down at the young Marine. "It's ok, Danny. I'm here." He tried to keep his voice steady, but he knew immediately there was nothing he could do. Burke's suit would fight to stabilize him, to save his life, but Holm could see that the damage was just too extreme.

Burke looked up at Holm, his face splattered with blood, tears streaming down his cheeks. "Please…help…me. I… don't…want…to…die…sir." His words were slow and tortured, his eyes wide with fear. He tried to move his arm, to reach out for Holm, but he didn't have the strength.

"Just stay still, Danny." Holm was struggling to hide his grief. "The medic's coming."

Burke took a deep, raspy breath. "I'm…scared…captain." His voice was shaky, weak. "I…want…to…go…home." Holm looked down at his mangled body.

"I know you do, son." Holm closed his eyes for an instant.

He watched the blood pouring out of Burke's suit and into the pale yellow sand. He tried to imagine the wounds hidden by the armor, the massive, gaping holes the autocannon rounds had torn into this young boy's flesh. He could see wet pink foam oozing out of the holes. Burke's trauma control system was trying to stop the bleeding, but the wounds were just too large, too deep. Holm knew the system was pumping artificial blood substitute into Burke, but that wouldn't last long. He could already see the change in color, more orange than deep red…the synthetic blood coming out as quickly as it was pumped in. "The medic will be here in a minute, Danny."

"I'm cold, sir." Burke was crying, trying again, unsuccessfully, to reach out for Holm. "I can't feel my arms." He coughed, spraying blood from his mouth as he did.

Holm's steel-gloved hand was resting on Burke's armor. He couldn't imagine a less effective way to succor a dying man. Barely a man, he thought, more a boy. Holm was fighting back his own tears as he tried in vain to comfort his young aide. Burke had shown his true quality over the last ten fateful days. No one's first mission should be in hell itself.

Burke coughed again. He struggled to breathe, choking on blood as he did. Holm watched silently as he took one last throaty breath and then lay still. The struggle was over. Daniel Burke was dead.

"I'll organize a rearguard and hit the enemy. It will buy us some time, hold them back from the LZ." Holm was watching Marines board transports all around as he spoke. The initial wave of ships had included a contingent of Reynolds landers and 200 fresh Marines, but the follow up flights were retrieval craft only. There was no point in sending down too many Marines…anyone who came down only had to be evac'd.

The ships were coming in slowly, a few at a time. Clement only had limited control of the fleet, his deadly dance with Alliance Intelligence and the operatives deployed on his ships still going on. Some of the troopships had rallied to the admiral… others had been neutralized by the agents onboard. There had been fighting and arrests on some ships…even a few assassinations. But Clement kept the ships coming…and one group at a time the Marines were getting off Persis.

Holm had been loading the ships as they arrived and sending them back as quickly as he could…gradually pulling strength from defensive lines. Those defenses had been bolstered by the 200 fresh reserves from the first wave. He tried to get the wounded and most exhausted Marines onboard first, but he took who he could get, taking them from the strongest sections of the line first. He watched himself as Lieutenant Fargus and Sergeant Tremont were loaded onto the first boat. They both had stayed long in the front lines, fighting despite wounds and unimaginable fatigue. Both had almost died there, and they'd only made it back by the slimmest of margins. Now they were going home.

"You can supervise the rest of the loading for me, can't you general?" He was standing next to Worthington, staring across 20 meters of wet yellow sand, watching more wounded being loaded onto an evac boat. The operation was just beginning, and the enemy was throwing everything at the Marines, trying to breach their lines and wipe them out before they could complete their evac. Holm was grateful that at least some of his people would get off the Godforsaken planet, but his thoughts were still grim, the dead face of Danny Burke staring back at him from the dark recesses of his mind.

"No."

It took a few seconds for Worthington's unexpected reply to sink in. Holm turned toward the general, his surprised look hidden by his visor. "Sir, we need to hit them now…or they'll overrun us before we complete the evac. I have to go, sir…or it will be too late."

"No, Elias." Worthington's voice was strangely calm. "You stay here and see that your people get on those boats and get out of here." He paused for an instant, turning to look at the wounded being helped onto the transports. "You owe them that. We owe them." He turned back toward Holm. "I'll lead the rearguard. That's my job."

Holm started to argue, but Worthington put his hand up. "That's an order, captain." He stood still for a few seconds, staring at Holm, and then he turned and began walking toward the perimeter. He stopped about 50 meters away and turned back briefly, facing toward Holm. "Good luck, Elias. Your Marines were lucky to have you here. I can't begin to tell you how I respect and admire the job you've done."

Holm started to speak, but Worthington raised his hand again and turned back, marching off to the front line. Holm just sat in stunned silence and stared...until the general walked up over a hill and out of sight. Then he turned back and focused on getting his people loaded onto the transports.

Holm had listened to the whole thing on the com. He hadn't expected many of the rearguard to make it back, even when he was planning to lead it himself. But he'd never imagined anything like the savage counterattack General Worthington had launched with 50 volunteers. It was insanity...it had no chance to work. But it did. At least for the few moments it had to.

The general had held the line for over an hour, repelling attack after attack as the waves of landing ships swooped down into the LZ, picking up the battered Marines and ferrying them up to the fleet. He kept weakening his line, sending units back to board the waiting shuttles. Finally, he was alone with his 50 hand-picked veterans. There weren't enough of them to hold the line...so Worthington put himself in the front and ordered an attack.

The enemy had been caught by surprise. There were 50 Marines, charging across the shattered landscape, directly into the maw of a force ten times their numbers. Holm listened to them on the com, screaming as they charged at the stunned Janissaries. They had no chance to win, no hope of defeating the enemy. But all they wanted was time...time for the last of their comrades to board the shuttles and get off the ground.

Holm was listening when he heard it. "The general's down!" He never knew which one of Worthington's fifty said it first, but he could hear the horror in the voice. His stomach clenched, waiting, listening. When the words finally came they didn't seem real. "He's dead. General Worthington is dead!"

Holm wanted to drop to his knees and vomit. He couldn't believe it. The general was dead? How could that be? Worthington had been a hero since Holm had been a raw cherry doing garrison duty on a dustbin of a planet out on the rim. Now he was dead. The fighting heart of the Marine Corps was gone.

"Take off...now." Holm snapped the order to the shuttle pilot and jumped back, out of range of the backblast. The Marines were finally off Persis...all except Elias Holm and the survivors of Worthington's force. There was nothing Holm could do for Worthington now...nothing but take care of his people. "All personnel...retreat to the LZ immediately. All other units have successfully evac'd."

He knew they'd have a hard time breaking off. The surprise had worn off, and the enemy was fighting them hard. Half of them were down already, and the survivors had half a klick of open ground to cross.

Holm stood out in the open, ten meters from the last shuttle, watching the Marines running toward the shuttle. "C'mon," he screamed. "Move your asses!" He watched them approach, the enemy in pursuit, firing. He saw one fall...then another. Five in all, but 18 survivors made it into the LZ, running toward the ship.

Holm stood alongside the shuttle. "Let's go...get onboard." He stepped to the side, grabbing his assault rifle and firing at the pursuing enemy, blazing away on full auto. He watched Worthington's survivors climbing onto the shuttle until the last one was aboard.

Elias Holm snapped his last clip in place, firing as he fell back, grabbing onto the handholds on the shuttle. He was the last live Marine on Persis, and he grabbed on and pulled himself aboard. "Let's go," he screamed to the pilot, and a second later he felt the g forces as the ship's engines blasted hard, lifting them off the planet...on the way back to the fleet.

The Battle of Persis was over.

Excerpt from the memoirs of General Elias Holm, Commandant, Alliance Marine Corps:

I survived my journey through hell on Persis, though barely a third of my Marines came through with me. Those men and women were some of the finest I've ever been privileged to lead. It was a tragic, brutal battle that never should have happened, but it has entered into a proud and revered place in the history of the Corps…an example of the tenacity and brotherhood of the Marines.

Third Battalion was destroyed as a fighting force; its survivors would be dispersed to other formations and the unit's colors cased, retired. Some of us who survived would go on to new battles…the God of War was not done with us yet. But most of the men and women who'd fought at my side and bled with me through those fateful days had seen enough of war. Peace had come, however foully achieved, and with it, most of the surviving Marines of the Third Battalion mustered out to seek another kind of life, one where they could share the opportunities their sacrifices had for so long defended.

News from the Caliphate came quickly. The lords and generals who'd been so afraid to present the Caliph with the treaty terms now had to explain how they'd been unable to wipe out a small contingent of Marines, despite suffering over 2,000 casualties in the effort. They chose an alternate route, one less likely to end badly for all of them. Caliph Mehmet was strangled in his bath and succeeded by his six-year old son, a pudgy child who had shown no signs yet of the rabid insanity that had so ravaged his father's judgment. The nobility and military quickly forgot about the disaster on Persis and took solace that they now had a leader who promised to be far easier to control.

The peace held, despite the fact that the Alliance had reneged on the terms Dutton promised. The truth was a stark one. Neither the Caliphate nor the CAC had the capacity to continue the war. The failure of the Janissaries to crush an outnumbered and beleaguered force of Marines sapped the already shaky morale of the Caliphate military. The elite soldiers themselves were unbowed, aching for a rematch, but the colonial nobility and the line troops were demanding peace.

The Alliance was in rough shape too, but not as bad as its enemies. The war would have ended on Persis anyway, even without the twisted bargain that sold my Marines' lives to the enemy. Dutton's devilish deal had done nothing to change the outcome…except to sacrifice 500 veteran Marines…and to fracture the bond between the Corps and the government back home. That suspicion and distrust would grow over the years, and the Marines would slowly shift their loyalty to the colonies they defended and not the Earth government they would come to distrust more and more. That process culminated in the colonial rebellions, when the Corps would side with the insurrectionists, but that was more than 30 years after Persis, and another story entirely.

The joy of peace was bittersweet. We had paid heavily, both in the war itself, and in emotional impact of the disgraceful affair on Persis. We had lost so many friends and comrades, it was difficult to focus on the benefits of war's end, at least initially, when empty chairs and absent voices were so noticeable. The treachery of it all was profoundly disillusioning. To me, it was on Persis we lost our innocence. Until then, the Corps considered itself the space-based ground force of the Alliance. But afterward, the colonies began to think of themselves differently, and so did the men and women of the Marines. We had crossed a Rubicon, one that would be decades in realizing its full effect, but a profound change nonetheless.

General Worthington's death had been a shock. He'd sacrificed himself to save what was left of the battalion. On a spreadsheet of military effectiveness, his life was a bad trade for the tattered remnants of one shattered unit. But as tragic as his loss was, I can't imagine a better way for a Marine to die… saving the lives of hundreds of his men and women. He'd only have faced court martial and disgrace if he'd returned, and I can't imagine a more tragic injustice. Dying a hero was a better end, at least for his legacy…and I think for the man too. Being stripped of his rank and ejected from the Corps – that would have hurt him far more deeply than those hyper-velocity rounds that ended his life. They killed his body on Persis, but the horror of being paraded around as a traitor would have killed his soul.

I have only come to respect Charles Worthington more over the years. We'd all looked to him for strength for so long, we never considered the toll it took on him. I would come to know that strain myself, the constant pressure of command that hollows you out day by day, year by year, until there is nothing left. But that was still years ahead of me, and it would take another war, larger and more terrible even than the one just concluded, before I truly understood. I'll always be grateful to General Worthington and will revere his memory for the rest of my life…as a true hero of the Corps and one of the best men I ever knew.

Colonel Thomas survived his wounds, and he retired to a new colony world settled primarily by Marines mustering out of the service. They'd named the place Tranquility, and I've never been sure if that was supposed to be a hopeful prediction or just an inside joke in the Corps. I never knew exactly what transpired with Thomas after the battle and, even years later, I never asked him. I know the Commandant had intervened with Alliance Intelligence and the government on his behalf. In the end, his part in Worthington's actions cost him his career. But he was discharged honorably and avoided prosecution. And the general's reputation was intact, his insubordination – treason to some –washed away in the sanitized records. Alliance Gov had more to gain from the worship of a dead hero than the memory of a disgraced traitor.

Admiral Clement had rounded up a hundred Alliance Intelligence operatives and held them captive while he launched the rescue operation. I know there was talk of prosecuting him, but nothing ever came from those rumblings. I suspect Dutton would have liked to see Clement punished, but it simply wasn't worth the trouble. The admiral was old, and as disillusioned as we were by what had happened. He served another year, mostly overseeing the mothballing of part of the fleet and the return to a peacetime footing. Then, sure his retiring naval personnel had received the benefits they'd been promised, he also mustered out, immigrating to a beautiful new colony called Atlantia. It was peaceful world that resembled his original home along the Maine coastline...or at least what that had been like centuries ago, before mankind ravaged her natural beauty. Near the end of the Third Frontier War, I got word that he had died, at home and of natural causes. He'd spent the nearly thirty years of his retirement walking the rocky coastlines and exploring the peaceful blue oceans of his adopted homeworld. Clement had been a sailor his whole life, whether he navigated the salty ocean spray of Atlantia's seas or the frozen blackness of space.

But my clearest memory of Persis...the face I will see for the rest of my life, the true image of the brutality and disillusionment of those days in hell, is that of Danny Burke, crying in agony, calling to me in bewildered fear as his lifeblood poured out through the breeches in his suit and into the yellow sands of an enemy world.

He died young, far from home, terrified and in pain. I remember the feeling of futility, the miserable lack of comfort I had to offer that boy. I will have those memories until the day I die. For me, that lost private will be an eternal reminder of the darkest side of what we do...of the horrendous cost of holding the line, so our people back home can live their lives and watch their children grow on a hundred different worlds. If mankind is to have a new beginning among the stars, it will not come cheaply, for we are our own enemy and bring our demons with us as we have done throughout history. The forces of conquest and oppression will always be there, wearing down the resolve of men, creatures so easily led and manipulated. When that line is held; when civilians sit in their homes and enjoy the freedom so dearly bought, I hope they think of Danny Burke and the thousands like him, at least occasionally while they build their lives and families...that they appreciate the sacrifices that other men and women make every day to preserve all they value.

But whether they do or not, we will guard that line, my brothers and sisters and I, and all those who come after us; it is not for gratitude that we do what we do. I came close to retiring myself in those terrible days after Persis. I was disillusioned and angry, despairing of truly making a difference. It was Sam Thomas who convinced me to stay. My work wasn't done, he said simply. I had more to give, and it was my obligation to those Marines who had come before me, who had given their all on Persis and a hundred worlds before that, to stay the course, to follow my destiny.

The Corps Forever.

Crimson Worlds Series

Marines (Crimson Worlds I)

The Cost of Victory (Crimson Worlds II)

A Little Rebellion (Crimson Worlds III)

The First Imperium (Crimson Worlds IV)

The Line Must Hold (Crimson Worlds V)

To Hell's Heart (Crimson Worlds VI)

The Shadow Legions(Crimson Worlds VII)

Even Legends Die (Crimson Worlds VIII)
(April 2014)

Also By Jay Allan

The Dragon's Banner

Gehenna Dawn (Portal Worlds I)

The Ten Thousand (Portal Worlds II)
(June 2014)

www.crimsonworlds.com

CPSIA information can be obtained at www.ICGtesting.com
Printed in the USA
BVOW08s1916150916

462275BV00001B/12/P